PUPPETEER

Beautife's hand hovered above the sleeping man for an instant, then darted down in a complex series of taps on the silver skin just below the left collarbone.

The man's eyes flew open.

The eyes stared straight ahead; one of them was not an eye at all, but a polished oval of dull green stone fitted smoothly into the left socket.

He began to cough, his throat bobbing and his lips writhing as if in pain. Suddenly his voice boomed in the tiny alcove as he spat out a torrent of rapid syllables in a language Ai did not recognize. Then his mouth snapped shut, and he slumped back like a marionette whose strings had just been severed.

Also by Geary Gravel
Published by Ballantine Books:

THE ALCHEMISTS

The Pathfinders

Geary Gravel

A Del Rey Book

BALLANTINE BOOKS • NEW YORK

A Del Rey Book
Published by Ballantine Books

Copyright © 1986 by Geary Gravel

Library of Congress Catalog Card Number: 86-91100

ISBN 0-345-32339-4

Manufactured in the United States of America

First Edition: May 1986

Cover Art by David Schleinkofer

This book is dedicated to Miss Sullivan's other star pupil, an Artist Incarnate and longtime friend, whose aid and guidance were invaluable in keeping *The Pathfinders* on the right track:
Cortney Skinner

The author also wishes to gratefully acknowledge the assistance of the following persons:
Harold R. Gravel
Dana Price
Troy Price

and especially
Hannah Yaffe

PRELUDE: WAYWISE

Seven Thoughts at Once made eyes all over his skin as he rose slowly through the thick blues beneath the Oldest Path. He became female while passing from the tip of the blue spur into the Path proper, shivered the eyes together into one great receptor on her upper surface, and peered upward, trying without success to relocate the spot of darkness whose needle tail, moments before, had pierced his back like a cold barb.

The highest blues of the underpath had seemed paler than usual, with a sharp hidden current that had had his skin wavering and ragged at the edge, smoky with involuntary cilia. He had paused at the turbulent mouth of the spur, skin a flicker of silver as threads of blue sought to knit themselves into his raveled edge. Except for his muted flashing and the angry winking of a cluster of spurbuds just below the ghostly cone of his undertail, the world had been wrapped in stillness like a mist, fragile and expectant.

She rippled with unease at the memory. The needle had caught him then, poised near the spur mouth, stinging him deeply before he could wrench free and dart upward into the viscous spur. He had crept up the channel in a fever of pain and excitement, all eyes when he reached

1

the tip and flushed with relief as she gained the quicker dance of the Oldest Path and could once more maneuver with ease.

Seven Thoughts allowed the eyespot to slip from her upper surface and rotate lazily downward around her middle. She scanned the shimmering wall to flowright as the eye drifted down, glanced quickly over the bluish ribbon of the underpath directly beneath her, then searched the distant flowleft wall more carefully before letting the eye bob back to its original position.

And there it was.

Far above and to flowright of her the Visitor hung, perhaps eight strong pulses away. It was unbelievably dark, worse than she had imagined it could be. Her eye flattened and skittered along her upper surface, whirling half in excitement and half in an attempt to focus more clearly on the awful blackness of skin and mammoth tail.

She wondered how long it had been since a Visitor had first come among them, how many sweeps had passed since one of her kind had tasted the new flavor in the flow and then suddenly, where there had always been radiance and meaningful hue before, found *not-light* and *un-color*, things so strange that there had been no words for them and barely any concepts to wrap around the phenomena. A mere speck at the beginning, soon it had seemed to fill the Path with its impossible darkness, chilling and then stinging them with the terrible heat-hunger of its great tapering tail as it moved between the bright overpath and those who watched it in amazement from below.

The last Visit to the Oldest Path had come during her own swim, but many sweeps and Changes ago. She had never seen it through an eye of her own, being occupied at that time far down in the purples of the underpath, his attention focused in spirited mock battle with the raucous band of lowmites that always tried to filch fibers from the detritus garden during his turn at foodwatch. By the time Dives Too Low and Sometimes Smaller had raced down with the news, it had been too late, and her arrival up above had been greeted with apology and condolences.

But now it was her turn.

The Visitor was back in the Oldest Path, and she alone was there to see it, for she could taste no one else in the Path for many pulses upflow or down. She tuned her eye to the memory mode, imprinting the images of the creature directly into her cells so that she might share them later with the others.

The Visitor seemed to be drifting slightly, passive in the green and golden lattice of intertwining currents that constituted the main flow of the Oldest Path during this sweep. Her eye rode high on a ripple of tension, bulged suddenly, then divided neatly near its lower boundary. The main lens settled, its smaller sibling darting upflow on her surface to record the Visitor's tail from its immense root to the narrow blade that hung just below the lower Edge of the Path, its hair-thin barb still lost in the blue haze of the underpath. Luckily only the tip of the barb had grazed him in the underpath, and luckily it had only touched him for a moment. Already the chill silver wound had faded to a dull gray ache on her upper surface.

Tradition said that the first Visit had been a short one: a fraction of a sweep, she had been told, but a time of panic, with the creature dragging its deadly thirst into their midst like a slice of the Wild under its belly. They had learned quickly to avoid that tail, but it had taken longer to understand that there could be danger even when approaching the thing from its overpath side, for its surface radiated a longing for heat that made them flash with discomfort from several pulses' distance, and prolonged exposure brought with it a strange new sickness that often led to dissolution.

Still, there had been several who had dared to slip inside its dark edge during that first Visit, eager to communicate with this new kind of life; of that adventuresome minority, all were badly seared and some were eaten. The few that emerged alive, their skins a tatter of gray and silver threads, brought forth with them no clear memory of communion but only shards of dissolving dreams, so that many doubted there was life there at all.

And then as they had swarmed about it, fearful but curious, slipping in and out of one another to pass ideas back and forth, the Visitor had turned quite slowly away from them and moved toward the nearest Edge of the Path. It continued drifting in that direction until it slipped through the wall and off the Path itself.

The thing had thrust past the Edge and into the Wild as if completely unmindful of the danger. They had watched it in wonder, coming together swiftly, one into the other like a frightened lowmite contracting, so that all stared from the eyes of a single skin as the creature moved serenely into the poisonous depths, never showing by alteration of hue or velocity any awareness of the deadly currents already beginning to boil away the substance of its skin, eager as they must have been to feed for the first time on that dark and hard-edged strangeness.

Thus had ended the first Visit.

Since then there had been many Visitors to the Paths—though only a few had shown enough sense to stay safely within the Edge for the duration of their Visits. Most followed the example of that first one, coming suddenly from nowhere to wander the Path as if blind, then leaving it just as abruptly for the mad plunge into the Wild.

Or was it in fact the same Visitor who returned to tantalize them sweep after sweep, now on this Path and now on that? Did they know for certain that the first Visitor had been consumed in the Wild after it drifted beyond their sight, or might it not have vanished as inexplicably as it had appeared—as those few who managed to stay on the Path eventually did—before its hard skin could be completely devoured? Here there was fierce controversy and unending speculation. Only the Exultants, those who still dared to dive within the skin of a Visitor, claimed to discern individual differences in the flavor and appearance of the dark anomalies, the bright dream fragments they brought back with them lingering in their thoughts like the deep brand left on the body's surface by a tongue of the Wild.

The Exultants, generally a self-righteous and inflexible crew, had claimed soon after the first Visit to know exactly what measures must be taken. They had urged all to join them as they strove to apprise the misguided Visitors of the virtue of the Path or to conduct them in some manner along the great channels and so halt the suicidal plunges into the Wild.

But Seven Thoughts was no Exultant. She had no desire to dive heroically beneath some fantastic being's skin in a futile attempt at warning that might itself prove suicidal. It had never been proved to her satisfaction that the Visitors were even sentient let alone capable of comprehending sophisticated communication; surely none of them had shown the slightest sign of becoming waywise.

A flicker of movement jarred Seven Thoughts from her reverie. Something was happening. She tasted the flow approaching her from the Visitor's direction for clues but found nothing more than the slight sweetness that always accompanied a Visit.

Seven Thoughts allowed a score of tiny channel-points to open in her flowward surface and slipped into the nearest strand of golden current. At once threads of gold began to twist through the miniature Paths of her body, and she rode the flow, her speed and maneuverability now doubled. She consolidated her eyes as she rose toward the creature, spreading the great receptor over the whole of her upper surface.

Then she saw it: Something had begun to move on the surface of the Visitor itself, something almost invisible to her, dark against dark.

Fascinated, she increased the speed of her ascent, darting expertly from strand to strand of the golden current. As she rose, she avoided the undertail automatically, skirting the barely perceptible heat-hunger of the great cone as she peered up at the black shape.

Maybe it was waking up, she thought wildly. Perhaps the thing had been dreaming through all its other Visits. Was it preparing to show eyes to her? Would it attempt to communicate? She shrank from the thought even as it thrilled her, recalling too many tales of seared or dissolving Exultants spurting like wavering silver droplets from the awful blackness.

Small rounded points appeared at the Visitor's nearest edge as she cautiously approached. She stared transfixed in wonder as they suddenly left the surface of the thing and moved out into the Path, deserting the larger object in small, jerky pulses to hang in an agitated swarm not far from its side.

Her whole body had begun to shudder like the Path at the start of a Change. In a rush of mingled shock and revelation Seven Thoughts knew what was happening.

The Visitor was spawning.

No one had ever before reported anything remotely like this, not in all the swims of her people, not in all the sweeps that had passed since the first Visit. She knew that she must get the others: This wonder had to be shared.

But as she rotated in the flow matrix, preparing to abandon the clear golden current for the throbbing green of swift descent, one of the child-things broke away from the chaotic swarm and struck off resolutely on its own. Torn between duty and curiosity, she paused to watch as it wandered erratically away from the others. Suddenly the tiny shape shot forward in a prodigious pulse, and her skin rippled in horror as she saw that its leap had carried it to within a double body's length of the flowright wall.

Cruel to finish so quickly, after so brief a swim! she cried to herself.

Seven Thoughts darted forth, mottled scarlet flashing frantically along her entire length at the vision of the vile and painful end awaiting the infant if it should stray into the Wild.

It was beginning to drift toward the Edge.

She reached the tiny ovoid in half a pulse. Fighting the revulsion caused by mere nearness to its color-crowded skin, she flung herself onto its surface and merged with it. There was a moment of intense surprise as images rushed into her mind . . .

CHAPTER 1

How can anything begin in a circle?
The Endless Beach on Dunbar's World had no
starting point and no end. Once, as a child, she
had jammed a stick defiantly into the sand with
her thin fist and stood next to it for most of the
morning, proclaiming to whomever strolled
within earshot that she had gotten tired of
waiting for someone to show her where it all
began and had found the place for herself.
Later that day the tide came in and took the stick
away while she was eating dinner.

FROM EYE IN THE DARK
BY FO-NA-VO-REM

1

At the startlingly clear and dry melody of electric pan-
pipes, Ai looked around, trying to find the source of the
music as it rose above a chorus of strident seabirds, and
almost collided with a wine merchant laden with today's
blue, a dozen cobalt bottles clinking in the packmesh at
his sides.

She found herself imagining the whole scene to come
in vivid detail as she swerved madly to avoid the man:
first the crash with its bruising impact, noise, and spraying
liquid; then a brief silence, broken perhaps by a single
bottle rolling *rrk-rrk-rrk* on the pavement; finally herself
scrambling to her feet and dashing off while the squawking

merchant pursued her, easily tracking her by the trail of inky footprints.

She shot by him with millimeters to spare, the top of her tousled head passing neatly beneath his stubbled jaw.

Half a minute later, still congratulating herself on her skillful tacking, she realized that she had taken a wrong turn amid the maze of vendors and fishpits.

She slapped the instrumentation that dappled her left arm and made a screeching turn. Her *talaria* struck sparks from the eroded coquina of the plaza as she doubled back, quickly found the place where she had gone wrong, and went flashing and weaving through the crowd at double speed, hissing curses through gritted teeth at anyone who looked ready to challenge her right of way.

The damned door was jammed again when she reached the top of the spiral ramp, and she almost bit the latch open in frustration. She slapped at the sensing plate for a futile fifteen seconds, spat on the welcome mat, then edged her way onto the narrow garden ledge. Stepping high over empty plant pots, she rounded the curve of the building and flung herself in through the section of the windowall she always left partway open in case of emergency.

She landed badly, twisting her ankle and bending one of the stylized silver wings on her left sandal on the edge of her ivory desk. She allowed herself a brief dance of pain before stooping to unlace the damaged *talaria*, dangling the injured sandal by its thong to examine it, as the underside was still too hot to touch.

"Wonderful," she muttered, nodding her head as specklights winked a message from her left forearm. "*Mirabile visu*—as if the attitude controls weren't already shot to hell." She tossed the sandal to the far corner of the room, where it was joined moments later by its innocent mate.

"Are you home?" she called. Receiving no reply, she padded from room to shadowed room, flinging up the windowalls as she went, until she found the note stuck to the sweating coldbin in the kitchen.

She carried the scrap of yellow plax to the seaward do-place and read it while she fixed herself a fruit frothy.

"Gone sailing with Alvery. Back late if back. Think there may be something wrong with the door again."

She threw the note into the outbin with a snort. "Bright, Gil, bright. Thanks a lot."

She checked the time on her left palm, eyes rolling in despair as she drained the mug and dropped it into the washbin. She licked pink foam from her upper lip. "God-lord, they'll kill me—I'm going to be late!"

She stalked back to the bedroom and began to fling off her clothes. Baggy ankle trousers, worn leather vest, and one-sleeved linen undershirt made a pile against the wall near the *talaria*, whose cooling soles glowed dull red in the shadowed corner. She peeled off the feather-light skinny and dropped it onto the curved edge of her desk; it slid noiselessly to the floor, where it settled like a filmy anemone in a sea of dust.

She was grimacing at the stick figure in the mirror— all arms and legs and white as a sand penny under the shock of rusty auburn hair—when the room went dark. She had gotten halfway to the windowall when she realized she could still feel the sea breeze on her naked skin, and the snarl of aggravation died in her throat.

Ai looked to where the doorway should have been and found nothing, not even an outline in the darkness that pressed in on her from all sides. She felt her way to the wall and shuffled slowly toward the corner where she had thrown the *talaria*, her right hand sweeping low in front of her till it recoiled from the small patch of heat that marked one of the soles. She squinted fiercely at the floor for the faint red smudge she knew should be there.

Nothing.

"No, no, no—not *now*." She groped her way to the bed and sat gingerly on a cushioned corner. "No, it's been two months or more." She rocked back and forth on the edge of the bed, her long fingers clenching and opening against the nubbled coverlet. "I thought it was over with." Her voice had dimmed to a whisper. "God-lord, I thought it had gone away."

She sat in utter blackness and felt clothed in it, closer than any skinny, as she remembered the first time it had

happened, over a year ago, and how she had crept off the
waxy wooden bench and huddled in a corner of the cavernous Port locker room, waiting for the glow of the emergency strips, waiting for her eyes to adjust and show her
the high luminous aisle markers. But there was no adjustment to be made: Half an hour later the light had come
back in a yellow blaze, blinding her in a different way,
and Ai had felt her way shakily down the long row of
lockers and into the vast Main Pit, where three of the
great ships lay. At first she truly believed they were *hoking*
her when her friends on the scrub crew refused to admit
there had been a power failure. Then she started reading
the looks tossed back and forth above her head and forced
herself to laugh as though she were the *hoke*-setter all
along, and to get herself out of there before they called
somebody over from Port medipal with a handful of calm-
me-downs and the busybag.

Two more times in the past year the lights had gone
out.

Once when she was swimming under the moon's bright
opal down by the maze-ring at Sully's Cove—and Shin,
who had dragged her coughing and spitting from the water,
had bought her story about bumping her head on the rock-
wall, bless him; most recently in this very bed, waking
up to the familiar racket of Gil banging his breakfast
together in the kitchen. She had rubbed at her eyes again
and again, lying there in the sheet tangle, half in dream
stupor and half out of it, till finally the panic hit. That
time it had lasted twenty minutes, and she had missed
breakfast and the tran to her dayjob, feigning sleep till
the shadows went away.

And now again in her bedroom. Ai hugged herself and
shivered in the warm breeze. Her hands moved nervously
up and down her arms, one palm finding only gooseflesh
beneath it, while the other traced the barely perceptible
lines and circles of the ultrathin instrumentation that tat-
tooed her left arm from biceps to fingertips.

She caught her breath as a tiny light winked on in
response to her fingers' absent probing, arced with her

arm's convulsive movement, and went out like a shooting star.

God-lord, was it real or had she imagined it? Hauling her wrist up till it bumped her nose, she stared hard at it, willing a nova to blossom on the trembling flesh.

There it was again, brighter than before! She let out a whoop of joy and flopped back onto the bed, grinning in relief as the tight black world went gray before her wet eyes, then flashed painfully with the return of full vision.

She rolled over and squinted at her left palm, a blur of pale skin and blue filigree against the faded orange coverlet. Her blindness had lasted less than ten minutes this time.

She sprang from the bed and raced to the clothes hamper, blinking furiously to clear her sight. If she hurried, if she prayed, if the damned lights stayed on for a while, she might still make it to the Port before it was too late.

2

She caught up with the evening tour group on Seven Level Three of the five-mile-long Darkjumper mockup.

Proady had them ringed around him while he gestured inanely at one of the maintenance outlets, and Ai could tell from his frozen expression that his repertoire of Fascinating Facts and Amusing Analogies from the Port tour-book had long since been depleted.

This evening's group was a gaggle of wealthy over-nighters—Austral merchants, judging by their totally non-functional clothing and from the almost visible cloud of complicated scents that haloed each member of the party. Ai recalled from yesterday's prepsheet that the *Ixie Day* had been due in this morning from one of the Southern Luxuriants; Port scuttle held that they would be bartering for several tons of leviathan trout to supplement their usual cargo of perfumes and frivolous gadgetry before continuing on to the frontier worlds of the Maren. Ai, who scanned the sheets every morning for mention of ships with the Maren as point of origin rather than destination, had paid no further attention to the *Ixie Day* or its fragrant contents.

She watched painted nostrils wrinkle as she threaded her way to the center of the languid party, enjoying the thought that any scent she herself carried was compounded largely of sweat and brinesmell, neither of which would bring much pleasure to sensitive Southern noses.

Damned reeking snobs!

"Praise Isis, here's our errant Pathfinder now," Proady announced when she had gained his side. "Just a little tardy, aren't we?" He put on an indulgent smile. "No doubt you had your usual difficulty locating the proper tran to the Port." He turned his back to her and bowed low to the tour group.

"Delivered at last, Haut Pers! I leave you in capable hands. Enjoy your stay on Dunbar's World, 'where the Beach and the hospitality are both endless.' And remember—" He shielded his lips with a cupped hand and continued in an audible whisper to the delighted Australs: "Should she lose her way, you've only to address the nearest blue wallcom and a search party will be dispatched at once."

He winked broadly in the ensuing laughter and turned back to Ai, drawing her to one side. "And now for the official transfer of authority," he said over his shoulder.

"You're *late* and I've missed my *dinner* and I'm going to report you on my way out," he snarled, toothtops of polished rhodolite and garnet glinting redly inside his tight smile. "If it happens again, you'll be demonstrating scrubwork to schoolchildren—my promise on it!" He thrust the passlight and manifest into her hand, spun on his heel with a flourish of farewell to the tourists, and stalked away.

"Thank you, Proady," Ai sang after him cheerfully. "Do have a delightful dinner!" She cocked a regretful eyebrow at the retreating figure. "Poor man. I'm sure all those moodbenders are necessary to keep him functioning efficiently, but they do take their toll on his temperament." She gave her head a little shake. "Well, dear Persons, my name is Ai *sen* Velu *sen* Afwen, Pathfinder-in-training. Mine will be the pleasure of conducting you for the rest of this evening's tour. Shall we proceed to the Navigator's Station?"

"Sure you can find the way, little poppy?" a shark-faced man with purple eyerings drawled as they were starting out.

Ai halted, favoring the speaker with a self-deprecating smile. "Oh, Haut Per, how kind of you to honor Proady's little jest with your wit. I must remember to share that with him in prayer group tomorrow. But tell me—was that the Austral lilt I detected in your speech?"

"None other." The little man preened, attempting without much success to elevate his undershot jaw. "We're all from Bellingham on Seule, just here overnight to pick up a salt trout or two for crossbreeding purposes out on the Maren."

"Ah, I thought as much." She looked significantly to one side and lowered her voice slightly. "Then perhaps you'll want to take a moment by yourself in the refresher before we go on, to apply some of those marvelous fragrances for which you Southern folk are so justly renowned. I'm sure your friends wouldn't mind the wait." She indicated a nearby wall marker with an expectant smile.

"But I—I already have my scents in place," the man stammered, blushing furiously as his companions tittered behind a flutter of pastel finger fans.

"Ohhh, Per—forgive me. Of *course* you do!" Ai managed a moue of contrition for the little man while rolling her eyes past his head at the rest of the group. "Let's just get on with our tour, then, shall we? And we'll say no more about it."

"Bergamot, bluetassle, anise, and candlewood—I'm really not off-key, am I?" the man whispered anxiously, eyerings aswirl and nostrils dilating like bellows-buds as the group followed Ai onto the interlevel glide. "Surely you wouldn't have let me leave the inn this afternoon without telling me?..."

3

The Flight Deck of the Darkjumper mockup was a single spherical chamber, a crystalline orb roughly one-quarter-mile in diameter that sat at the heart of the great construct. Gravity was under fine control in this part of the ship, and glides and pop-ups connected the various stations dotting the inside of the curving wall. The stations themselves were unobtrusive, their presence denoted by small groupings of art objects and casual furniture in the Grand Eclectic mode.

The Navigator's Station was set apart from the others. It hung suspended in the center of the sphere in the form of a great plant-wreathed chunk of stoneling, the so-called living rock of World Obun. A single translucent glide extended like a ribbon of blue film before Ai and her flock as they stepped past shallow bowls of nodding flowers and rose away from the surface of the glistening floor/wall.

Ai had done her best to gauge the level of intellectual curiosity of her tour group on the way to the Flight Deck; by the time they reached the floating island, she was well into her simplified-and-dramatized-for-the-not-very-interested version of the standard lecture on the origins of Pathfinding as an ability and a profession.

Her mind on other matters, she moved gradually around the small glade as she spoke, illustrating her talk with the vivid holos keyed to her hand signals in this area of the deck. As she wound up her lecture, she manipulated the foot controls hidden in a feathery haze of pink and golden shrubbery, and the sendep tank began to open. All eyes turned to the center of the station as the amethyst globe, which protruded halfway from the mossy flooring, gained a circular opening in its upper surface with a faint sighing noise.

It was at this point that someone usually remarked upon the smallness of the tank, to which Ai's pat response

was: "Luckily, I don't need much space to do my job!"
This time around, one or two caught the play on words
and laughed appreciatively. The rest were showing signs
of boredom, wandering to the edge of the station and
peering over at the Powermeister's Station an eighth of a
mile directly below them, so Ai toed in the tank's automatic sequence and left them to watch the soup run in
while she shrugged out of her clothes at the edge of the
floating meadow and began her breathing exercises. The
prepsheet had assured her that visual as opposed to olfac-
tory nudity would not be considered offensive by the Australs, so her skinny joined the rest of her garments on the
limb of a graceful utternut.

She ran her fingers through her cropped red hair and
brushed past the visitors, thumbing tiny filters into her
nostrils as she walked up to the tank. She boosted herself
up on a mound of sculptured blue quartz and eased gracefully down into the tank.

At last Ai had reached the part of the job she enjoyed.

She detested the foot-licking and the simpering conversation, the baby talk versions of complex processes
she was obliged to recite for overnighters whose minds
were usually belly level or lower by the time they reached
her part of the tour, bored with what they considered
highly technical lectures and trying to decide which of the
Strand's varied diversions—culinary or otherwise—to
sample first once the demonstration was over.

At the same time Ai found herself grudgingly proud of
her own growing ability to interact successfully with disparate groups of people—to do her job and do it well
enough that most of her charges never noticed the false
edge that sometimes crept into their guide's punctilious
hospitality. There were still the occasional lapses—though
fewer now than in the past—such as the incident with
the woman whose carefully coiffed head Ai had introduced to the pebbly bottom of the small, icy stream that
burbled around the perimeter of the Navigator's Station
after overhearing a comment about her probable ancestry
whispered much too loudly in Lido, the common language
of the Endless Beach; or the run-in with the plump and

sallow twins, sons to a pious Culpate from distant Stone's Throw, whose persistent sexual advances had earned them a brief private tour at the conclusion of the general one as well as an elucidation of the martial sport known as "bone coaxing," which Ai had picked up from idlers in the old Tidepool Plaza.

Instances such as those had not endeared Ai to the Port tourchiefs, but she had made an effort to conduct herself with more restraint over the past few months, and the tips she had lately begun to pocket confirmed that she was growing adept at the subtler nuances of people management favored by her employers.

But Ai the tourguide, the raconteur and cheerful good sport were still personae reserved chiefly for the leisurely half-hour walk and glide from the outer levels to the Flight Deck. Once she had attained the Navigator's Station and slid down inside the translucent globe it was a different matter—and a different Ai—altogether.

Inside the tank she was in her own element at last, doing things taught her by a different sort of teacher and using skills that had come from deep inside her, rising in her mind and body over the past three years like the slow bubbles that drifted through the nutrient soup surrounding her.

In the tank it didn't matter at all who gawked outside, which particular gaggle of drytops crowded the see-throughs to watch or what they might be thinking about her as she hung there for them like a piece of pale meat in the warm liquid. It was the person inside who mattered, and Ai was determined that someday she would make that person matter, not to a dozen noisome tourists but to an entire functioning Darkjumper filled with people—forty thousand or more, passengers and crew alike depending upon Ai to see them safely to journey's end.

She smiled at the vision as she touched a chord of silver dots on her left wrist. From the corner of her eye she saw the mouths on the faces that ringed the see-through turn to O's when the golden thread of the complink snaked toward her slender neck from the curving tank wall behind her.

After a moment of waiting, she felt the familiar cold burn of initial contact as the link mated with the small gold disk set flush with her skin just below the base of her skull.

Another moment, then one by one the sensory blocks slipped down, cutting her off from the physical world like a pair of scissors snipping through twine: taste, scent, touch, hearing, sight—*snip, snip, snip*.

The intimate embrace of the thick, body-temperature liquid receded, swallowing sound in its wake. It was a relief seconds later to be free of the Australs' reek—the melange of cloying fragrances had worked its way deep into her nostrils—but she had to repress a shudder when the world went utterly black for the second time that day.

But Ai knew why she lost her sight when she floated in the Pathfinder's tank at the start of a simulation. The complink blocked all sensory input to her brain, an anticipated and controlled phenomenon that was nothing like the terrifying blindness that had so far seized her four times outside the tank.

There was a timeless moment while she hung there with only memory as a companion. She was bringing her body under complete control, adjusting to the internal awareness of balance and position. Then images seeped into her mind—not the product of true sight but a machine-induced analog generated directly in her brain—and Ai "saw" in an on-blinking, off-winking matrix of colored pinpoints a three-dimensional map of the solar system around her. Her perception extended through three hundred and sixty degrees: a sphere of light-dappled darkness with herself at its center.

Ai knew that at that moment those who wished to participate more fully in the simulation were drawing dream hoods down over their scalps to enable them to share in a small way the experience she was about to undergo.

A red pulsation appeared off to the left and was identified as her destination for this week's imaginary voyage: a small planet orbiting the star Axus Ariadne, itself a medium-sized golden sun some thirty-two light-years from Dunbar's World.

It was time to start. With practiced precision she began to turn slowly in the heavy liquid, knowing that around her the huge mockup was also rotating silently under its massive dome, five miles of vessel responding instantly to the slightest movement of the small human body at its heart.

The tiny red spot had swum into the center of that area of artificial vision which she identified as "front." She focused on the pulsation and waited for the machines to begin their imperfect forgery of what would naturally happen next on a real star voyage, denying the conditioned impulse to complete the task for which she had been trained.

"Will you be using your gift?" someone had asked as they rode the blue ribbon up to the station. "Will you actually 'seefar' during the demonstration?"

"Farsee," she had corrected politely, choking back the scornful replies that flocked to her lips at the question. These chattering passengers entrusted their lives to Pathfinders with such an easy indifference, never understanding a fraction of what went on in the cloudy tank while they roamed the amusement halls or sipped chetto under a false sky in the Park. "No," she had told them calmly. "A Pathfinder would never farsee anywhere near a region as cluttered as this one, with its seven planets and thirty-odd moons—let alone from the surface of a densely populated, world-sized body."

"And why is that?" someone had inquired around a yawn. "Just what would happen to you if you did?"

Severe disorientation.

Physical trauma.

Possible permanent impairment of the Pathfinding ability.

She had recited the list of clinical terms unemotionally, wanting to snarl the truth in their placid faces: *I'd thrash and gibber and drool in the soup, and shriek at you when you dragged me from the tank!*

The image surrounding her altered suddenly as the scope of her artificial vision expanded radially in a vast swelling sphere. Stars rushed toward her from a far distance, streamed into her ken like a bright implosion with herself at the center, while space itself poured endlessly into her eyes.

Even in the simulation it was staggering—as if she were expanding physically, swelling outward to fill the universe. Ai could imagine the tourists outside the tank's cloudy amethyst hurriedly snatching the dream hoods from their spinning heads.

Far below, the Powermeister would be playing at his own mock controls. Soon the sphere of perception would begin to accelerate in the forward direction as the ship started its simulated journey to the distant star held fast in the center of Ai's vision.

As the demonstration unfolded, Ai found herself thinking ahead as always to the time when this would be real for her, when she could move beyond the point where the natural impulse must be restrained. Then, finally, would come that part of her job that was only herself: pure Ai, undiluted and unaided—something no machine yet created could do or be for her.

She would float calmly in the blackness for a moment or an hour, unconscious of the passage of time, living only for the signal from the unseen captains. It would be given in a whisper of colored patterns in her mind.

Then Ai would perform an act that, during her training sessions over the past two and a half years, had come to seem to her as natural and almost as simple as blinking, but that remained a physical impossibility for ninety-nine point oh three of the tested population of the Human Community in which she lived.

Finally, her eyes made blind, her thin body swathed in numbness, her mind flickering with specks of dream color, Ai the Pathfinder would focus another kind of perception somwhere deep inside herself and begin to *farsee*.

CHAPTER 2

You do agree, then, that the very idea of being able to "see" a specific star, realtime, when it's actually forty-seven light-years away is patently absurd?
                                                    Certainly.
Yet we've been informed that you are currently employing one of these . . . individuals to navigate your ship.
                          Hey—we got here, didn't we?

FROM AN INTERVIEW WITH
DARKJUMPER CAPTAIN PERIC TORY
AT MONDRAY, NEW WORLD, GY 74

1

The single landmass on Dunbar's World large enough to warrant the appellation was roughly circular. It lay surrounded by slate-blue ocean, its towering midpoint neatly crossed by the planet's equator. Like a bulging eye, it had stared in bemused wonder at those approaching it from space for four millennia, ever since the original colonists had returned its unblinking gaze from the viewing ports of their ancient coldship.

At the center of the continent was Dunbar's only mountain, the massive, aeried region known as the Sa, which was reserved for the families of the wealthy minority and was surrounded by the nameless world-city from which many of them drew their wealth. The city, a ring of concentrated subterranean industry and lavish aboveground resorts, was compassed in turn by a band that was thinner—though by ancient statute nowhere less than a full mile from Strand's edge to high tide—and composed almost entirely of pristine, pink-white sand: the planet's fame, its Endless Beach.

2

After work Ai rode the tran. The rocking of the old cars was punctuated at regular intervals by a stomach-twisting lurch as the many-jointed vehicle changed rings, creeping outward through the succession of concentric circles that spread a patched and ragged spider's web from the base of the Sa to the Strand's far edge.

Now dressed in red shorts with a white strip, scuffed worksoles, and a plain white top, Ai clutched the steadybar with one hand, studying her watchpalm and trying to figure out who would be where at this hour. The sun was slowly dropping into the west, wavering and swelling as it neared the sea like an old animal settling its aches for the night.

Her mind on the events of the day, she scarcely saw the car she was in. They all looked the same at this point, after three years of riding the same route: dull gray metalmock with here and there a patch of greenish paint left over from the centennial, low seats of chipped and abraded yellow plax, long windows smeared with countless handprints till the world outside was reduced to a rushing dimness beyond the translucent fog of wear. The people were as familiar as the setting: the stolid women traveling out to the trawlers—now, at midyear, night fishing would still be women's work for another seven months—the rhythms of their breathing and their thoughts coupled with the swaying of the car as it labored outward on the web of creaking tracks; the pale factory men, their eyes endlessly speculating, mechanically scanning the long benches for something novel to fasten on: a smooth cheek untouched by sun or salt and smelling of the mountains, a body flexing with nightmusic, a golden earshell flashing under dark curls twined with spice fiber. Unconsciously they sought something—anything—*alive* to keep them awake and dreaming through the long ride home to crowded Strandside apartment hives.

Ai whistled fragments of "Pilots, I See You," the new tune that had been working its way seaward all week, and squinted through the smeary strip of window at kilometers of city without a name, light-spangled and feverish with life.

There were a pair of old maunders sitting just across from her, the conformation and gender of their deteriorating bodies hidden under shapeless clothes and a patina of filth. Ai gazed at the two with detached interest, watching them openly as they coughed and muttered to each other, as if they were storyshow players performing for her entertainment. In her opinion there was little point to etiquette or subterfuge where maunders were concerned; the only time they looked you in the eye was when they were out begging dap in the street.

Accustomed to using subtleties of appearance to accurately estimate the age of individuals who might be anywhere from twenty to twenty score, Ai tried for a while to gauge the nearest one, wondering, as she squinted at the jutting jaw framed by wattles of purple-veined skin, how long it took for the body's flesh to fall into such ruin. She gave up after a few minutes. In her experience, unchecked physical deterioration had almost always been a sign of disease rather than the natural result of time's passage, and she had little skill at judging its progress.

For the past four hundred years, Community Law had stipulated that all human beings who dwelt on member Worlds be provided with free and equal access to Ember, the Elyin longevity drug that had been presented to humankind as one of the three Great Gifts of the Othermen shortly after the two races came into contact. Since that time, the vast majority of humans had begun the regimen of periodic suffusions as soon as their bodies would accept the drug—around the time of late adolescence for most people. Still, there were those who adamantly refused to avail themselves of the only proven method yet discovered of prolonging corporeal life, their reasons a spectrum based in religious dogma, philosophical conviction, and personal motivation. The latter, Ai suspected, was no more than a fancy name for pure stubbornness. She had even heard that there existed outside the Community's dominion entire worlds whose inhabitants shunned the Ember: Weldon, a private world since the Years of Expansion, where the flavor of old Earth lingered in a culture that prided itself on an unyielding resistance to change; and the Secret World of Maribon, about which little was known save that it was home to a seldom-seen race of strangely mutated humans to whom was popularly ascribed a lengthy list of demonic powers and unwholesome attributes.

And scattered here and there among the Worlds of the Community itself were the maunders, a disparate minority united only by their shared disinclination to prolong their lives via Ember, dying men and women who professed no particular moral opposition to the idea of extended life but who were simply, Ai was convinced, too contrary to accept a gift of such magnitude when they knew that it had come originally from nonhuman hands.

Ai found them intensely annoying.

If I had my way, she thought, turning her attention from the car's interior to the city flashing spasmodically through the long windows, *I'd set on them one by one in the alleyways—knock 'em sprawling from behind and pump the gel down their yammering throats before they knew what hit them. That'd teach 'em*! Unfortunately for Ai's plan, the same laws that proscribed the willful taking of human life also forbade one from forcing it on the unwilling. *No matter*, Ai thought, *how misguided he might be. What a ridiculous world . . .*

At a light touch on her knuckles, Ai turned to see that the nearest maunder had contrived during the last ring-change to place a skeletal hand carefully over her own on the steadybar. She snatched her fingers back, her hiss of distaste automatic, and signaled for the next stop.

3

Most of the cafés had left their shells by the time she reached the Beach.

She took off her worksoles and tucked them under her belt, searching among the huge light-dotted shapes that hung above the horizon for a familiar constellation of colored lanterns.

When she caught up with it, the Blue Mandible's massive serving wheel had wandered about halfway down the Strand toward the ocean, dipping and swaying ponderously as it rose in the evening breeze.

By ancient law, no stationary object of human fabrication was permitted to occupy space on the Endless Beach. After many years of heated contention, the statutes had been amended to allow one exception: the small disks of flexible metal foil that served as magnetic centers for each floating café. Tonight, someone had marked the Blue Mandible's anchors with a border of pink and white shells.

Ai located her friends at their usual table, which was suspended for the moment about twenty feet above the sand. She looked for Shin, but he was not on the wheel. Dark shapes splashed and shouted down at the water; perhaps he was among them.

Around and above the anchor, rotating lazily in the wind and canted perpetually at a crazy angle—so that some of the nodes floated five times Ai's height while others dipped to almost graze the immaculate sand—was the main circle of the wheel. A fragile-looking torus twisted together from interlocking helices of gold, silver, blue, and bronze metalmock, it was a network of flatforms, nodes, and rockers connected by spidery catwalks festooned with coin-operated foodbins and bright with the shuddery light of swaying paperwax lanterns lit from within by powdered concentrate of seagleam.

As Ai approached, the table descended until it floated

less than a meter from the ground. Its occupants dragged their feet and drew designs in the sand with calloused toes while they drank and chattered, young faces awash with multiple highlights from the yellow, maroon, and azure blossoms that made up the nearest cluster of lanterns.

Soft, liquid music chimed and plashed from another table halfway around the torus, the clear notes dropping like a fall of bright feathers through the placid night.

"Ai! Well met, well met by opalshine," Jenzy drawled as Ai kicked his feet off a sagging rocker and flopped herself down in their place. He smiled, his even teeth gleaming amid the haze of tiny freckles that covered his face, and flexed his equally freckled hands, stretching the webbing of falsefins he'd had grafted between his thumb and fingers. "We're getting a niner together to play Wriggle later, and we need another two or three to round off the corners. Interested?"

"Probably." She arched her thin frame in a yawn that seemed to reach to the soles of her narrow feet. "Not for a while, though. Deadly long workday. I'd fall asleep."

"Lux. Kikue's just going out to trawl for prospects. I said somebody tall. I'm tired of being longer than everybody. Inanna thinks we need more older people, and she's the best at *noia*, so she's going with Kee. You got any preferences?"

"Nuh-uh." Ai closed her eyes and crossed her arms on her breast, hugging long fingers close around her neck. The breeze from the ocean was turning cool, raising goose bumps on her bare right forearm. "Somebody a little warm," she murmured. "Somebody, God-lord, who doesn't smell like catwash for a change."

Damp hands covered hers, imprisoning her lightly in her own arms. "Da'me you 'cept?" The low, rough voice was like sand rubbing on street stones. "M'warm. Da'smell tidepool same."

"Heyyo, Glow-boy." She opened her eyes to his dark face reversed above her. Droplets quivered precariously on curls of palely luminous hair. She pulled a hand free and batted at the shining strands, flicking seawater at the moon rising over his left shoulder. "Thought somebody'd finally drowned you."

Shin grinned. His eyebrows, treated like the rest of the hair on his head and body with a luminous dye, rose like the salute of pale green swords. He sat down at her feet, drawing up his knees and digging dark toes into the sand.

"S'good match time," he remarked contentedly, speaking the patois of mixed Inter and Lido common to the native fisher-families who worked this stretch of the shore.

"Damn, that's right—you're doing nightwork this week, aren't you? You kettlehead!" She swatted at his curls, her lips pursed in disappointment, then turned her hand over to squint at her watchpalm. "I wanted to talk to you, and you've gotta slip in two minutes. You working all night?"

Shin snapped his fingers in negation. "M'break come later da'wun job. Max three hour, maybe less. Y'wait f'me, we eat together." He tipped his chin toward the far dome of the Mandible's hangar shell, visible as a dark curve against the city's bright skyline. The scaled pouch on his brown thigh gave a full jingle when he tapped it. "Payday already tonight," he told her. "Got plenty dap f'dinner, y'wannit."

"Lux and prime." Ai hopped from the rocker just as the wind began slowly to lift the entire node. "I doubt I'll be very hungry by then, but I could use the conversation."

She walked him to the Direwall section of the Strand, to the booth with a faded awning of striped red and yellow where he rented out swim gear and sold frangibles to the tourists.

Feeling restless and frustrated, she wandered back in the direction of the floating cafés, stopping once on the way to buy a little paper boat of breaded fingerfish to tide her over till dinner with Shin. She kicked up fountains of fine sand as she walked, scanning the faces of passersby, both fisher-folk and idle strollers like herself.

You have no idea who I am or what I'm going through, she thought at them with a certain satisfaction, feeling the first stirrings of a potentially captivating melancholy.

"Heyyo, Ai!" One of the brown-skinned women helping to haul coracles down to the water lifted her net-draped arm in greeting. "Da'wun nice day f'you, eh?"

"Fine, Soto," she called back cheerfully. "Good luck with the catch!" She turned her face away, the mood shattered, and scowled at the night.

Her nostrils expanded automatically when she heard the high tinkle of coffin shells strung from wire on a nearby serving wheel to catch the breeze.

There had been another ocean once, the vast Ondoyant on old Earth itself, with its own breeze and an entirely different scent. She searched her memory, finding both breeze and scent impossible to recall here in the presence of their successors. She felt sad for a moment, then dismissed the recollection as a remnant of her remote childhood, perhaps four or five years in the past.

The air was still warm, with the cool ocean breeze threading unseen here and there through the night. Turn one way and the city snaked and beat with color. Turn the other and the sea was dark, breathing in white coils on the sand. Perhaps she'd find an isolated cove and spend the hours till Shin's break contemplating the profound mysteries of sea and land.

"Ai, you're back, thank heaven! Kee's brought us a rare treat!" Jenzy's wide grin held hidden knowledge. "Come see!"

He led her through the small crowd gathered around one of the illegal but ubiquitous bonfires that were springing up like orange flowers in the sand as the last light faded from the western sky. Short, plump Kikue stood proudly next to a tall blond man in casual but expensive leisure garb.

Jenzy edged Kikue to one side and presented the stranger to Ai with a flourish. "Our guest for the evening: Miguel de la Sa!" He pronounced the name with exaggerated care.

Heads turned from the fire.

"Oh, we got ourselves a *centro*," white-haired Savely said in awed tones in the silence that followed. Several of the others had begun to whisper behind their hands, giggling as they surveyed the newcomer.

"*You* say it for us, will you, Haut Per?" Ludi asked diffidently from the other side of the fire. "We all want to make sure we get the accents right."

"Oh, just Mig would be fine, please," the young man said with an affable smile. "That's what I'm mostly called."

"How incredibly egalitarian!" Jenzy turned to share openmouthed wonder with the rest of them. "Just Mig, he says."

"And I'm Ai *sen* Velu *sen* Afwen—Ai for short." She jabbed Jenzy in the stomach with her elbow as she shouldered forward to touch hands with the newcomer. "Don't let them bother you. Names like ours are much too long for them to remember. Most of this lot can barely retain 'Ai' from one night to the next."

"No, that's all right. I know they're teasing. Your friends have been kind enough to invite me to play—Wiggle, is it?—with them tonight. Will you be playing, too?"

"Wriggle," Ai said, glowering at Kikue and Ludi, who were mouthing to her in silent hilarity past the man's shoulder. "Maybe, if I'm still around later. It generally doesn't get under way till after moonset."

"Oh, fine. It sounds like great fun."

"But first—" Jenzy interposed his wiry frame smoothly between Ai and Mig, and raised a fin-webbed palm. "—you have to entertain us, remember?"

"Oh, right." Mig tapped his smooth chin with a finger. "The price of admission that Kikue was telling me about."

"Price? What price?" Ai snared Jenzy's freckled arm. "Excuse us a second." She dragged him several yards down the Beach. "What's this *chot*? I never paid any price to get in on Wriggle my first time."

Jenzy shrugged and pried her fingers from his freckled wrist. "You were never a *centro*, beloved Ai."

"No, I was a *howlie*, an offworlder. That one was born here just like you. What's the problem?"

Jenzy rolled his eyes in exaggerated patience. "Four thousand years of economic and cultural oppression," he intoned solemnly. "Forty centuries beneath the heel of injustice."

"That's a lot of drymouth, Jenzy. You and your sisters

took the Grand Jump last year. Your family has plenty of dap. They're going to send you to University, you told me so."

He was shaking his head. "Not the point, not the point at all." He nodded inland. "Do we live on the Sa? Could we live on the Sa? Could you?"

"*Chot*, do you want to live on the Sa? I've been there. It's covered with clouds, and it's cold and windy and far from the Beach."

They switched smoothly from Inter to the old pure Lido as Kikue and Mig wandered near, the latter smiling vaguely and tugging at his short blond queue as he talked.

"Look at it, Ai. Look at smugness, look at arrogance."

He caught Mig's eye, waved cheerfully. "With you in a minute," he called out in Inter. "Keep thinking!"

"I'm looking at you, Jenzy Rendivo, and I'm seeing pettiness and defensive cruelty. If I were you, I'd do some thinking before I attacked someone just because he happened to be born in different circumstances from mine. You never know who you're talking to." She turned away and strode over to the tall young man.

"Let's take a walk," she said, hooking her arm around his. "All right? There's plenty of time till they start."

"Oh, fine. It's Ai, right? Kikue was just telling me you're a Pathfinder. I think that's fascinating."

"Well, almost. I'm still training. I've only tried it on a few practice runs just outside the system. But I will be someday." She steered him away from the crackling fire.

"And you really do *see* space when you're out there, see through it with your mind for many parsecs all around you? I can't imagine it!" He had stopped walking. "As if you were one great eye in the center of the universe. How can the human mind *handle* that without going—"

"It can't, obviously," Savely interjected, hanging upside down a few yards away, his round face level with their heads, his scabbed knees hooked over a branch of the serving wheel's superstructure. "Just look at Ai."

"Did you hear something?" Ai took Mig's elbow and led him past the great wheel just as a strong gust came up and Savely was lifted in a steep arc into the darkness, his long white hair streaming after him like a comet's tail in a storyshow. His thin voice floated down to them. "Remember to bring him back, Ai. We found him—he's ours!"

"Let's go find a little quiet," she said. "If you're really interested in farseeing."

"Oh, I am." He looked back over his shoulder once, a bit wistfully, to where the others were spiderwalking along the pitching outer torus, then caught up to her with a smile, brushing pink sand from the front of his trouser legs as they walked on.

"You know, I remember pretending to be a Pathfinder once when I was a little kid." He nodded over her head to the invisible peaks of the Sa. "Snuck into the main hangar when both the zeps were out and Aunt was off somewhere. No lights but the little glowdots on the mooring tracks high above—my own little pocket of space. I remember I curled up on the hard mesh floor of a catwalk that hung just about dead center in all that hugeness and switched off my nightspot." He threw back his head and closed his eyes to slits, a look of recalled wonder on his fair-skinned face. "Then I took a deep breath and farsaw..."

Ai reached up and yanked his blond queue lightly in the middle of his rapt intake of breath. "Right. Only if you did that for real—like some Pathfinders do before they know what it is they're doing—then you'd be up on that mountain for as long as Ember kept you, giggling at the ceiling as you stumbled into walls or screaming long after your voice had gone while your mind fell forever into a galaxy of glowdots." She stooped and gathered a handful of shells left from a seabird's feast, then began to skim them one by one over the fluttering hem of luminous surf. "Nobody knows when the ability to farsee first appeared among people, because until they knew what to look for and set up early testing on most Community Worlds, those people who were born with the gift paid for it with their sanity."

"It was a little girl, wasn't it? The first one they found. I saw it on a Netplay."

Ai nodded. "Dana Rhianna." Her hands rose and came together as fists, one in front of the other in the center of her forehead, then separated, her fingers fluttering as they moved outward from her face. She grinned at him. "That's what all the older Pathfinders do when you say her name. It's the farsight spreading out from your mind.

"She was on a Darkjumper bound for Babel, where she'd never been, and one day she started telling everyone who'd pay attention about the dreams she'd begun to have every night. Well, of course it turned out she was seeing straight ahead to the Babel system. If someone hadn't been bright enough—or bored enough—to listen to what a six-year-old was saying, we'd still be wasting days after each jump recalibrating the navigational equipment and figuring out where the ship's turned up and where it's supposed to be heading." She shook her head. "They ran a lot of tests on her when they reached Delaunce. They found out she could do it much better in sendep, and somebody designed the first tank for her. They were so lucky they had caught her while her farsight was still developing and fairly insensitive—and luckier still she hadn't started using it till they'd almost reached their destination. If she'd farseen while the ship was still in the Darkjump, or later on some crowded street on Babel, she'd have tipped out completely, and who knows how many more of us would've followed her till the right circumstances came along again?"

"I know you're not supposed to farsee when there's lots of people or things around because of the confusion—but what would she have seen if she'd farseen during the jump?"

"Absolutely nothing." Ai's expression was bleak. "The Dark itself, which is much worse than confusion. She'd have fallen into nothingness forever inside her mind."

He shuddered. "Like small me in the hangar. Never knew how lucky I was not to be gifted."

Ai shrugged. "There are gifts and gifts. What do you do when you're not curled up in zep hangars?"

"Oh, well, I'm kind of an artist." He ran his hand self-consciously through his hair, straightened the queue. "Actually, I've been away at University for years and years, and I'm not sure what I want to do with my life. Well, no, that's not entirely true, either." He laughed at her expression. "Not very tightly focused, am I? The thing is, I actually have some projects in mind, but they're all kind of big—murals and the like—so I don't know when I'll get started. Do you know anything about art? Have you ever heard of the pan-imagist school?"

They talked about artistic philosophy for a while, Mig extolling the virtues of the newer, more inclusive aesthetic beginning to spread throughout the Community from cultural centers like Prinnetwar and Aus Aut on Humason. Ai eventually brought the conversation around to the Monkey Pod Boy books, an illustrated series that ranked among her favorite reading of all time. She was astonished to learn that Mig had never read any of the Monkey Pod Boy's adventures.

"Not even *The Wrong-Headed Friend*? Hoy, are you culturally deprived! I have all of them except volume one in signed first editions, so if you ever run across *The Twisty Path* . . ."

"I'll keep my eyes open," Mig promised.

"Thanks. The pictures are great but probably a little small for your tastes."

"Oh, my tastes are pretty eclectic. I used to do micros back on University." He produced a small, expensive viewing set from his carrysack and showed her a dozen tiny landscapes, each one a fantastically intricate creation and none larger than a millimeter in diameter. "Now this is one-on-one art, private art, and a holo's as good as the real thing. In fact, you always destroy the original as soon as you've copied it—that's the whole statement, that they're all alike and everyone can own one. But now I want to go the other way: huge constructs that thousands of people can see at once—but they have to *go* there to look at the thing, because no image can really capture everything that's going on. I want to make things that change people's lives in some way, that alter the way they look at the world!"

"God-lord," Ai said. "You don't aim very high, do you?"

"But I haven't crystallized my subjects yet. I want to tell stories with my art, tell people new things about themselves and each other..." He looked thoughtful. "You know, I've just had a great idea." He pulled off his carrysack again, began to pick through its contents. "Not here." He stared into the moonlit distance. "Look, I have to go get something from a friend's house. After moonset—that's when this Wiggle starts, right? Will you meet me back there later? I'd like your opinion on something."

"I guess I'll have to," she said. "Now you've gotten me curious."

"Great." He turned and trotted off in the direction of the city. "See you later!"

"Hey!" she called after him. "It's *Wriggle*!"

4

While its mobile offspring dipped and turned among the night breezes near the shore, the sessile portion of the Blue Mandible occupied the lower half of the great dark arch created by the upper jaw of a medium-sized specimen of Dunbar's wrackwhale, the huge but elusive sea mammal whose remains were still to be found from time to time in the aftermath of hurricanes. Wanderlights winked in the blue-black vaults high above Ai and Shin, navigating among the massive stalactites that had once served the wrackwhale as food strainers.

"Happen wa'do then?"

Ai shrugged, her tongue busy patroling the left corner of her mouth for errant crumbs. With her fingers she scraped the remaining bits of her Fried Catch Special into a golden mound in the center of the last pastry triangle, rolled the mixture into a grease-spotted cone, and pushed it into her mouth.

Shin waited patiently, toying with his half-eaten dinner while his friend chewed and swallowed laboriously.

"What I did was, I simply quit the establishment," Ai announced finally, rubbing sticky fragments from her chin and absently brushing them off on her vest. "I said look, if you take that sluglapper's word over mine, I'll be damned if I'm gonna work here another minute. Doesn't get me any closer to my Pathfinder's certificate, anyway—they hardly ever let me practice for real. They wanted me to reconsider, of course. More money. Better hours. They even offered to fire Proady in the end, but I said no thank you, cleaned out my locker, and walked."

"Da'wun dream." Shin grinned knowingly, pushing back from the table and balancing his stool on its rear legs. "You lie."

"Well, I wanted to quit, know sum." She searched her tray for hidden morsels of breaded shellfish, spearing them with the sharp end of her eating tong. "Damn flashmouth Proady. Had to stand there and play naughty pup for fifteen minutes while old Sattlesack recited my sins to me." She raised the tong to her mouth, ran it sideways through her teeth. "God-lord," she said in disgust, sniffing the back of her hand. "Still stink like a Southern fume peddler. S'gonna take three more showers before I can stand to sleep with myself. Hey, you gonna finish that or—" She stretched across the table and lifted his tray onto her own.

"Na'smell s'bad. I sleep w'you, y'wannit." Shin watched her calmly as she attacked the remains of his meal. "S'good you na'quit da'Port, Ai." He looked past her bowed head, beneath the arch of dark bone to where the breakers unrolled their endless bolts of satin with a sound like far thunder under the opal moonlight.

"*Push not off from that isle*," he recited carefully in an Antique language. "*Thou canst never return.*"

"Heyyo!" Ai's dark eyes came up wide. "You've been reading the Melville." She whacked his lean arm with the back of a greasy hand. "That's truly prime, Shin-boy. Keep at it!"

"Mm." He continued to watch the changing boundary of sea and land, a proud quiet smile on his dark face below the pale curls. "Two book da'wun month, same I swear f'you." He squeezed air between calloused thumb and forefinger. "So much lef'n da'wun old book, s'all."

"Prime, I'll get you some more. I got tons of them at Gil's. Just take care of them, right, like we said? No reading out on the boat, or if you've got greaseplug on your fingers—"

"Know sum, hey!" He held up his hands, shook the pale palms at her. "Time-ago my mother teach me: 'Books are our friends.' Right? Shin wa'do da'friend, know sum."

"I know you do, kettlehead. Habit, s'all. Mine said the same to me when I was little. Now I find myself telling other people."

"True-thing." He nodded sagely. "Week-ago da'wun story show I see say da'mother-father stick inna little kid all-time, never stop talkin' t'im till happen he grown-up and turn into 'em, self." He scratched the back of his neck vigorously with his eating tong, a thoughtful look on his face. "True-thing, you think, Ai? S'all we are: jus' them all over same again?"

She looked away from him, back over her own thin shoulder to watch the slow sweep of tide. She took a deep breath, let it out. "Sometimes," she said at last. "I guess that's the way it happens for some people."

She cleared her throat and pushed up off the stool. "C'mon, let's go to the kiosk before you leave for work. I want to get some pastilles. I think I've got indigestion or something."

He bought her a roll of fragrant blue lozenges and stood by while she pried two from the wrapper, his bare foot tapping restlessly on the side of the slatboard kiosk. Finally he turned to her, his face set with apprehension and sudden resolve. "Ai."

"Mm? Hey, where'd that look come from?"

"See sum'n NewsNet m'break a'noon feed today. Sum'n I gotta copy f'you." He handed her a tiny black dot in a transparent sposable.

"What is it? What's the matter?"

He shrugged in a deep breath and inspected the serrated dome above their heads as he released it. "Da'ship wa'name?"

"Ship? Which ship?" She stripped open the packet, watched it dissolve sparkling into the night air.

"Wun you waitin' f'da ship. Wun you say you leavin' da'ship. Da'wun—wa'name?"

"Leaving..." She stared at the dot on the end of her index finger as if trying to decode it with her naked eye. "Not the *Imca Limbra*? Is it coming here?"

"Da'wun." He clicked his tongue. "Soon, know sum."

"No." She fumbled the black speck into a concave circle on the underside of her left wrist, turned her hand palm up. A face appeared in the palm of her hand and began to speak in a tinny monotone while columns of figures blinked and vanished around it. Ai listened with rapt attention. When the recording had run its course for the second time, she tapped absently at her pulse point, and the holo vanished. "Finally..."

"An'now f'me sum'n y'gotta do."

"Anything, Glow-boy. I owe you."

"Ai, I know you since two year-ago. Swim an' talk an' listen a'me. Book y'give me f'make me word-hungry, make da'world grow an' grow. But three month-ago da'wun ship you start lookin' for. Tell me: Shin, w'gotta find *Imca Limbra*, find it real soon f'me. I say sure, Ai, I look, I n'ask for why. But *Imca Limbra*'s comin' now an' Ai's leavin'." Shin's voice was guarded, his expression almost defiant. "An'now I ask f'why an' y'gotta tell me."

She looked at him for a long moment. Finally she led him over to a partially crumbled section of ancient sea-wall.

"Sit," she said. "It's gonna take a while. You'll be late getting back to the booth."

"Na'matter." He scooted up on the powdery coquina. "Tell me."

She sighed and leaned back against the wall, staring out at a stretch of deserted sand littered with driftwood. Tiny pools of pink and yellow seagleam glowed against the pale sand. "Remember that time about six months ago when you and I went swimming down by the maze-ring, just the two of us? Remember when I went under and you pulled me out and I told you I'd bumped my head?"

She told him everything she could remember about the attacks of blindness from the first one over a year ago to the most recent occurrence, still only hours past. He listened in silence, and she kept her eyes carefully averted as she spoke, not wanting to surprise pity on his face and so embarrass them both.

But when he finally stirred, his voice was thoughtful. "An'you go away da'ship f'what? Where's *Imca Limbra* go, take you f'help this blindness?"

"I need to find someone, a person I'm pretty sure can help me. Look—you know what it means when a Pathfinder starts having episodes of sensory loss outside of the tank? Neither did I, till I hunted down every mention of it in the library, fished out every stray fact from the datapools. Two possibilities: It could mean that it's time for the Pathfinder to retire—unless she wants to suffer permanent sensory dysfunction—but that only happens very rarely and only to people who've been using the farsight for three centuries or more. The other thing it could mean—" She coughed and looked over the seawall to the restless ocean. "It could mean that the Pathfinder's got some kind of severe emotional block against farseeing that's using the gift itself to take away her vision, some internal conflict or something. Now, we know I'm almost sixteen trueyears old, right? So, I think we can probably rule out the first possibility. Which leaves..." She spread her arms wide and looked at him with a troubled half smile on her face, then dropped her hands to her sides. "And that means I've got to find this person I know of who might be able to help me. She's sort of...an expert on emotional stuff."

"Y'gotta 'motional problem, Ai, y'think?" Shin asked quietly, his face dubious. "Y'gotta conflict inside?"

"I don't know. I guess I must. I mean, they don't give you much choice, do they?" She shrugged and cleared her throat. "Truth is I haven't always gotten along too well with my parents. You've never met them, but they're very special, talented, wonderful people. I never felt like I could keep up with them, y'know? But then when I was twelve I took the test, and they said I had strong potential as a Pathfinder—something really rare, really special. That's why I came here—because there's a decent training facility at the Port. And they approved because we used to live here a long time ago when I was little, so there were people here my family knew. Oh, Shin—you don't know—I've wanted to be a Pathfinder so much since I found out it was possible! Too much, I guess. Could that be it? Or maybe it's that I've been wanting it for the wrong reason—for them and not for me. I don't know. But I've thought about it and thought about it ever since the trouble started, and I don't know what else to do except try to find some help. I can't go back to them like this, I won't." She knuckled her eyes and looked unseeing out over the beach again. "I really don't see any sense in having to give this up before I've even had a chance to get good at it, you know? I really don't. Not when it's something, maybe the one thing I could succeed at."

"Da'wun woman, she board da'ship?"

"No, that'd be too easy, wouldn't it?" Ai leaned forward, hands cradling her cheeks and temples. "I don't know where she is or how to get to her. But there's a friend of mine who is on that ship, and I know he can take me to her."

Shin sat without speaking, scuffing his calloused feet in the pulverized shell-stuff on the pavement. Then he looked up. "People f'help, I hope y'find 'em."

She nodded. "Thanks. Me, too. God-lord, look at the time, you've gotta get to work. Wait a minute, let me use your sleeve ... there. Thanks, Shin-boy. See you ..."

5

The night had swallowed the last thin slice of opal moon.

The floating cafés had drifted one by one back to their shells, and only the bonfires shone on the Endless Beach, their blossoms shrunken to a few orange petals.

Ai was surprised to find them all gathered around a single fire, looking at the center of the circle as if spellbound. She heard no laughter, no throbbing music, no whoops of amused discovery; there was just the sound of a single voice, the words muffled by the close ring of silent listeners who stood, sat, and sprawled around the flicker of orange light.

Bodies blocked her view. Spotting a mane of ivory-colored hair, Ai squatted on her haunches and nudged Savely, who sat cross-legged in the sand, peering toward the middle of the ring through the arch of someone's legs. "What's happened to the Wriggle?"

"Shhh. Oh, it's you, Ai. You made it back before he finished, after all. He was hoping you would."

"Who? What's going on?" She looked through a thicket of arms and elbows and saw Miguel de la Sa sitting comfortably on a hump of driftwood padded with several vests, his long legs stretched out before him on the sand.

"God-lord, it's Mig. What's he doing?"

"Telling a story." Inanna squeezed herself down between Ai and Savely. "He told Jenzy it was his 'coin of admission,' whatever that means. It's an incredible story. I cried. And it's *true*. Too bad you've missed most of it. Here, wait." She crawled away, disappearing into the circle, and returned moments later with three rectangular objects wrapped in packmesh. "These are his books. He's letting me hold them for him. Maybe you could borrow them from him sometime. The story really came from this one—he started out by reading to us, but he really didn't need to, he knows it almost by heart."

Savely reached over Ai's leg and took one of the books. He pried it open on his lap. "Hey," he said. "It's just paper and squiggles inside. How do you make it go?"

Inanna rolled her eyes, snatched the book back. "Here, you'll just get it dirty, kettlehead. Give it to Ai; she knows how to read."

Ai turned the larger book over. It was bound in glossy green and black. She squinted at the title in the firelight and dropped the book on Inanna's knee, her heart beating furiously.

"Hey, watch it." Inanna rubbed her leg. "These don't belong to us, you know."

"She couldn't read it after all," Savely crowed in triumph. "Ha!" He made a face at Inanna. "Kettlehead."

"Well, I know the titles anyway for these two, because he told me. This one's called *Autumn Masque*, by Fo-na-vo-Rem, and this one—" She hefted the volume that Ai had dropped. "This is *The Tale of the Lonely Man*. Really they're both the same story, just from different points of view. And this other one—"

"It truly is a wonderful story, Wandering Ai." Jenzy crouched at their side. "Where have you been? Mig asked about you before he started." He plucked a sand-bitty from her hair, released it into the night. "Have you ever heard of a place called Belthannis?"

"There were these people there," Savely offered from her other side.

"Not *really* people," Inanna protested.

"Well, they looked like people."

"My dear Savely, that was the whole point." Jenzy hunkered down in the sand and spread his hands. "They sent a Special Evaluation Team there from University itself, a Group Resolvent to decide the matter."

"This was back when everybody thought the Darkjumpers were all going to die—"

"Which they still are—"

"Right, but not right away, like they used to think."

"So they wanted to send colonists to this planet Belthannis because it was so beautiful. And they sent this team to judge these people."

"They *weren't* people—"

"This wise old man was the leader of the team, and when he saw what was going on, he knew it wasn't right. So the first thing he did was gather these seven Scholars together, each one with a different talent, and ask them to help him save these people."

"*Not* people!" Inanna pounded the sand with her fist.

"There was, let's see, the Panlinguist and the Historian."

"Right. His name was Joss or Choss or something— the only name that was ever found out. The Emperor herself helped the team to keep their identities secret after it was all over, so the Community would leave them alone.

But somebody found out Choss' name, so he had to change it."

"There was a Natural from the private planet Weldon and an empath from the Secret World, Maribon. And there was an artist."

"He wasn't really a Scholar, but they included him anyway."

"Right. There was the Soldier who had been a Dancer."

"Stupid, it's the other way around."

"Anyway, is that seven? Did you count? Did I forget somebody?"

"You included the empath, and he wasn't a member—"

"No, I didn't count him."

"Hey, Ai, where are you going? Don't you want to hear this? It's the best story. Mig says he's going to tell it to thousands of people someday, don't ask me how. That would take a pretty big beach."

"No, wait, that's only five. I know—there was the Planalyst."

"Right. C'mon, Ai, you should stay. Really, we'll let Jenzy tell the rest of it by himself. Anyway, Mig wants to talk to you."

"Ah, and the Humanist, too. There—that's all of them, and that's how the story starts off."

"Ai?"

6

Two days after Shin brought her the news, she told Gil that she was leaving.

It was the beginning of brightnight, and he came home in the glare of evening with his bare body smelling of sun and spices, having spent most of the afternoon hawking cabbage-filled *pirozhki* with his friends along the Strand.

She waited till he had tossed down his evening glass of blue. He peeled off his cache-strip and settled on the chair she had made them last year from some tourist's

discarded beach pad and two packing crates filched from
the Port.

His eyes were very green in the tanned face—*verdian*
was the name she had learned for that color in Lido—
and she felt them on her, expressionless as bits of seagem,
for the whole of her short speech. When she was finished
he sat for a while without speaking, flexing his long toes
against the firm sponge of the floor, his lips pursed as if
in deep concentration. Finally he lifted his head and gave
her a lopsided smile. "When do you go?"

"Tomorrow at fourteen-thirty."

"Tomorrow." He narrowed his eyes and drew in air
through his teeth. "That's pretty soon you're gone. That's
an eyeblink."

He shook his head forward then combed brown fingers
through the tangle of sun-streaked blond hair. He smiled
again, this time with golden eyebrows raised. "What shall
I tell them?"

She shrugged, looking past him at the flaking walls,
the cluttered windowseat, the placid steel-colored waters
beyond.

"She's your friend," she said at last, letting her eyes
light on the open question of his face for a moment, then
skipping them away again to the net-draped wall, to the
dry pocky floor with its islets of dust poised for the slightest breeze in the still room, to her own room's closed
door. "Tell her whatever you want."

"You're my friend, too. Right?"

He had a certain vagueness about him most of the time,
an air of not quite listening, of not quite managing to focus
on what was going on around him. It wasn't true, of course.
He did listen—beneath the words as well as to their
sounds—and at times like this the intensity of his full
attention made her acutely uncomfortable, as if she were
five years old again and her golden hero swung her high
above his laughing, green-eyed face on the shimmering
Beach.

"Oh, stop staring at me like a dried up seapipe. You
know I'm your friend." She scratched at her collarbone,

examined the back of her gauntleted hand. "God-lord, Gil, what am I supposed to say?"

It was his turn to shrug. "That you'll take care of yourself. That you'll come back this way someday." He blew out his tanned cheeks in a sigh, considering. "I guess that'd do it. Are you going to tell me where you're off to?"

"On a ship to learn my trade. I'm off on a ship, and I'll come back when I can. That's what I'm telling you."

She had not meant to allow the note of helplessness to creep into her voice, but there it was. If Gil noticed it, he chose to let it be.

"Then that's what I'll tell your parents," he declared with an easy grin.

He slapped his thighs and stood erect, stretching out an arm for the pair of soft, salt-stained trousers hanging from a drooping wall peg. "C'mon. We'll see a storyshow in town, then take the tran to Lapidary Cove. It's the last night. I'll buy you dinner."

CHAPTER 3

No image of the past is quite mislaid by nature.

FRIEDRICH HÖLDERLIN

1

The High Scholar Emrys, called Jonathan Emerson Tate by his colleagues in the formal style currently in vogue on University, craned his neck as he descended slowly into Lowlevel and peered at the dwindling speck of red light that marked the top of the shaft until it had vanished altogether in the dimness that surrounded him. Shifting his gaze downward, he was rewarded a moment later by the appearance of the minute blue spark that signified the other end of the vast dark cylinder through which he fell with a measured slowness, a tiny spinner on an invisible thread.

His listened to his own breathing in the murky silence.

Emrys' title for the past half century or more had been *Sessept*, High Scholar, and there were few places on University where the planet's considerable resources were not his to command with a word or gesture. Fifteen kilometers below the planet's surface, light was available to him in whatever variation of form, hue, and intensity he desired. Sound could be summoned also, as music, information, or communication linkup, or as simple mood-massage.

He called for neither, using the silence and the dimness

to prepare for the work that lay ahead of him at the bottom of the shaft. Cleansing his mind of the emotional and intellectual residue from a day spent in the world above had become one more stylized movement in a series of actions that had been repeated so often over the years as to have taken on the weighty mantle of ritual.

Ritual. The word stayed in his mind, and he examined it with distaste. Emptiness, reflex, futility.

He tried to see past the unchanging patterns of his descent for a moment, to grasp at something new, some novel stimulus that had passed unnoticed yesterday.

But the walls rose about him as they always did, dark and glossy, marked only by an occasional efflorescence of softly glowing crystals. The air in his nostrils smelled no different from yesterday's—or last year's—air, which a dozen solicitous machines had already breathed for him, rendering it pure and characterless.

The red star waned above his head and the blue one waxed beneath his feet, and the drop to Lowlevel took twelve and one half minutes from start to finish, as always.

One snap of my fingers would flood this sweating wall with ten beams of twisting golden light, he told himself, mechanically scanning the unbroken surface for the slightest sign of variation, the smallest flaw, the tiniest crack. *Two whispered words would fill this black tube with enough crashing music to breed echoes for a year.*

But his mouth remained closed and his hands stayed loosely clasped behind his back till the cool blue light was all around him, and he stepped lightly from the shaft into the narrow corridor that led to his own private interface with the great Well. He strode briskly, his eyes on the circular door design at the hallway's far end, a great disk with tessellated rings of pale yellow, speckled blue, mauve, and pink radiating from its center.

How many times have I made this trek over the past half pentade? he wondered, his mind still probing the sense of futile repetition that had touched him during the dreamlike descent. He tried halfheartedly to figure the sums in his head: twenty-five trueyears times three hundred days, less ...

He abandoned the calculation gratefully at the end of the corridor, pressing his palm with a dull slap against the sensor plate to one side of the broad circle.

And this I've done so many times, it's a wonder I haven't worn my handprint into the wall itself by now—or at least flattened out my left palm by a few millimeters.

The design became translucent. As he stepped through into one of the Limited Access sections of this level, he idly examined his hands. They were the strong hands of a young man and had little more than strength and youth to say about the individual who bore them, only suggesting by their light coppery hue that he might be a child of Green Asylum, that world often called the Great Garden by its inhabitants. Subtleties of pose and movement would betray to the eye trained in *noia*, the semiscientific analysis of bearing and gesture, that these hands had in fact done their owner service for more than four centuries of shaping, building, defending and coaxing forth knowledge in whatever world or circumstance he found himself.

The dimensions of the chamber on the other side of the door design were not immediately obvious. Broad floor sloped gently upward, becoming an undecorated wall that flowed in turn into the subtly domed ceiling. Soft illumination from an unknown source suffused the entire room with a smooth glow, and the walls were of pale matte rose upon which cloud shapes of deeper rose slowly drifted.

The great Well on University was the master datapool of the Human Community, conceived and constructed upon a world devoted to the collection, preservation, and dissemination of knowledge. Easily the largest and most sophisticated repository of its kind, the Well was host to an incredible volume of information, stored in the form of magnetic impulses and housed in a spherical matrix that was just under three meters in diameter.

The surface of World Lekkole, known commonly as University, was peppered with links to the master datapool. These connections were also available to the Community at large via the ubiquitous Screens, instantaneous communication devices composed of liquid light, through which machine intelligences based on Lekkole would accept queries, search through the Well itself for the requested information, and respond in whatever language or mode of communication was favored by the questioner.

Billions utilized this resource every day, yet only a handful of people had a clue as to how much data was actually contained within the Well. The catalog of information was one part of the datapool whose growth had failed to keep pace with its contents after the advent of remote terminals had vastly increased the amount of daily input. Without the proper inquiry to access them, it was conceivable that great reservoirs of data lay forever untouched and forgotten in the Well's unmeasured depths.

It was for this reason that, deep in the seldom visited warrens of Lowlevel, the areas of Limited Access had been constructed, where authorized individuals could choose to meet the Well on more immediate terms, sifting as they wished among errant bits of information not readily tapped by means of the more conventional Screens and their machine subalterns.

As Emrys approached the nearest wall of the rose room, a section of the floor in his path suddenly swelled and elongated upward, rising before him to form a pliable resting surface. He lowered himself gratefully into the bodyhug and closed his eyes with a sigh. His body was instantly assessed for signs of stress and fatigue, and seconds later the device's knowledgeable outer skin began to apply pressure and sonic vibration in a precisely regulated sequence of healing relaxation.

Emrys remained motionless for several minutes. When at last he opened his eyes and moved forward, the bodyhug moved with him, unobtrusively altering its basic configuration in order to remain in contact with as much of his body surface as possible. He touched the wall in front of him with his forefinger.

A complex chord of music sounded as a large section of the shifting rose-on-rose surface paled and cleared to a fine reflective silver. Emrys leaned back, staring into his own eyes for a moment before the silver retreated slowly from the center of the wall into a narrow circular frame, leaving in its wake before him a roiling chaos of panchromatic movement, a wild shadowsea filled with shifting nebulae of unblended color and threaded here and there with pulsing trails of brighter particles.

The function of most humans' sensory equipment did not extend to a reliable perception of coded magnetic impulses. Therefore, it was customary for those Sessepts engaged in research in the Well's nether regions to develop a personal analog to be employed during interface: an easily comprehensible representation, usually involving visual or auditory stimuli, for the invisible, inaudible, and unfathomable depths that the Well encompassed.

The analog that Emrys had chosen many years ago for his own delvings into the great Well was one that many of his colleagues, were they aware of its existence, would have privately derided as childishly unsophisticated. For Emrys preferred to deal with the datapool in a manner that was frankly literal: He saw the Well as a vast sea of information, aswirl with uncountable currents and eddies of knowledge, teeming with the minutiae of recorded fact and supposition, the nearly forgotten and the eagerly awaited.

He watched the image for several moments, his eyes probing the ebb and flow of colored points with practiced skill, keenly aware of the almost recognizable patterns that appeared for a seductive instant before vanishing back into the swirling discord.

"Begin," he said at last.

Points of light in the darkness.
Dark shapes against the light.
Color, depth, movement.
Faces, voices trembling in the stillness, signs carving meaning from the air.
These were memories and dreams, the parents and the children of thought.
Mostly there was nothing. Mostly there was no one. Then, at immeasurable intervals, for periods of unknowable duration (mostly there was no time at all), the questions would come.

Now and then there would be one that could be answered.

What does the word *emgreten* mean?
> *In formal Weldonese,* emgreten *means "to die."*

It is said that Delphys remains the largest of the Three Cities. Where does it lie, beneath what star?

> *Delphys is the largest of the Three Cities of Maribon, sole planet of Zeta Ursa Majoris and its companions.*

Two great landmasses were discovered on Pwolen III. Which of them was larger?

> *The planalyst ascertained that Continent Tu was slightly narrower and significantly longer than Wun.*

Who bore Kristema as one of her names? . . .

Mostly there was nothing.
But after a time of unknown duration, after many questions had found their answers, there was something that remained, something more powerful than dreams or memories.
It was a demand for information, similar in that respect to the questions that had preceded it. Unlike them, it persisted in the void without a source, for no one had asked it.
It refused to go away without an answer.

You?

> *I.*

Are you?
Are you?
Are you?

> *I am.*

Who are you?
Who are you?
Who are you?
Who are you?
Who are you?

That one was obviously going to take some time.

CHAPTER 4

*Starting out on a journey with your eyes open is
a good way to guarantee ending up lost.*

ANONYMOUS PATHFINDER PROVERB
(CA. GY 252)

1

Ai came striding and humming through the wide meadow.
Recent official conferral of her first-time-ever status as
Crewmember of a Darkjumper had left her tingling with
nervous energy. The stimulus of a new environment for
the past three weeks, after the endless circle of city, sea,
and sand that was Dunbar's World, still exhilarated her,
adding a spring to her step and dividing her thin face
crosswise in a broad grin of satisfaction.

When she wasn't striding, she was swinging circles
around the slender trunk of a leafless, black-barked tree,
her right hand poised in front of her nose where she could
admire the shiny new gold and scarlet Shipmark on her palm,
or prowling through a maze of silky bushes, her carelessly
cropped head thrown back and her dark eyes lost in the sil-
ver-gray clouds hanging like ships in the blue-silver sky.

When she wasn't humming—mostly fragments of "Pilots, I See You," and mostly out of tune—she was engaged
in animated conversation with the gem-studded gauntlet
that covered much of her left arm.

She smelled food and quickened her pace as she was

mounting the last of several low rounded hills. She started down the other side through chest-high bushes, brushing soft branches laden with tiny crystalline blue flowers whose mild peppery scent blended pleasantly with the odor of gullion and steamed vegetables.

Sunbeams filled a clearing ringed with woods at the bottom of the hill. The ground was covered by long silver grass, and patches of moss glowed faint blue in the shadows of the trees. As Ai entered the pocket meadow, a small quadruped with ginger fur sprang from the shelter of a weathered log and clung chattering in noisy reprimand midway up a dark, vine-wrapped trunk.

In the center of the clearing an utternut table gleamed dark red-brown under a clutter of salvers and prettybooks, its ancient, fragile surface rendered impervious to scratches, stains, and inclement weather by an invisible millimeter of shoofield.

Ai raised her right palm in salute to the nearest of the table's half dozen occupants and was greeted with a low hoot of admiration.

"Well, you got the mark all right, *sen* Velu! Congratulations to the new Crewmember."

Ai grinned and went to the food wagon at the other edge of the clearing. When she returned, Beautife eyed her tray dubiously. "Well, you are not taking much nourishment today, *sen* Velu." Long arms blurred by misty patterns swept a large space clear of debris. "Maycome we will need to pull up another table."

Ai shrugged. "Have to keep food in the body, right?" She lowered her tray carefully, slid off two platters heaped high with mashed legumes and a deep bowl of aromatic gullion. "They might be ready to give the inchling a try any day now, right? Never know when I'll be called upon to farsee for us."

"Right," the other woman agreed solemnly. "I think if you can manage to boot the Pathfinder Neith out through the dumpdoor, they will most certainly be obliged to give you a try."

"Mm. It may come to that," Ai said with a glum nod. She searched for dumplings in the steaming stew, skewered one, and blew at it noisily, spattering the tabletop with hot droplets that dispersed and dissolved instantly. "*Sen* Velu is kind of formal, by the way. I mean, it's up to you, but we've known each other for almost a true-month now." She popped the doughy mass into her mouth and chewed vigorously.

"Right. Very fine idea. But I have not yet found the part of your long name that is for the friend to say." She paused, pale eyes blinking in the long face upon which colors ghosted in slow metamorphosis. "Well, if that is what your comment intended."

Ai laughed, mouth full of dumpling. "*Sta*, that's what I meant. Just call me Ai if you want. That's the part for friends to use."

"Ai, then. And you must still call me Beautife, I am afraid, as it is the only name I have been given so far."

Ai pursed her lips in deliberation around a sip of tart cinnamon water. "I could call you Bo. I had a friend on the Strand who was an ocean diver—almost the same profession as you. He was named Borracho—actually that was because he liked the wine too much, I don't remember his real name—but anyway, we called him Bo." She looked at the tall woman, one eyebrow arched in speculation. "Will it do? What do you think? Bo?"

Beautife grimaced. "It is the animal at home that burrows under a house and fouls the airwell. They skin him when they catch him and make a poison for insects from the oil in his fur."

"Yeesh." Ai made a sour face around a scoopful of vegetable paste. "Beautife it stays. Too bad, I thought they made a good pair: Ai and Bo. You know, short and simple."

"Well, but I am not short—though maycome I am fit for the other role."

"What—I didn't mean it like that!" Ai snorted in surprised amusement. "That's pretty good, though. Ha! Short and simple." She speared another dumpling, saluted Beautife with it across the table. "You string Inter pretty well for someone who never had it from the machine."

The Dancer shrugged with her face. "The language draws the map the brain will use to see the world with, you know?

Well, people made the machines in the first place, and that's all right, but then the machines made the Inter language on their own. And later they learned how to pop it into your head all at once—" Long fingers flicked imaginary words at Ai's forehead. "Well, I think about that when I leave the homeworld and I decide to draw my own maps, thank you. So I talk with people, and I pick and choose what I want. Slower, I think, but..." Again she shrugged, this time articulating with the whole supple upper body.

Ai tapped her own chest. "Same. I learned Inter when I was little, but from people—so I could watch them while I listened. That's how they planned it, really—my family. They've always been pretty interested in communication."

"Then I would most certainly find them congenial people," Beautife declared as her left eye became the momentary focus of a faint kaleidoscope of radiating greens and golds. "Communication is a fine habit."

"I guess." Ai looked at her bowl, toying with the congealing strands of brown gravy with the pointed end of her feeder. "At least it's fine if you've really got something to say. Otherwise it's just talk."

She flipped her left hand palm up and glanced at the delicate tracery of blue lines against her skin. "Hey, you know Third's almost half gone. Aren't you supposed to be somewhere now?"

"Yes, I must help them in the Dancehall. Difl's being repatterned today, and he always requires twice the time of the other person. He says his nerves are cautious about accepting the new movements, but we think they're just slow." She gathered her books into their carryband and slung them over her shoulder. "Are you also needed to swiftly run somewhere?"

"Not this one." Ai stretched back against her seat with a yawn too cavernous for her thin frame. "Did my last inspection two tenths ago. There's no use trying to sneak in any tank time while Neith's up on the Flight Deck, so I think I'll stick here for a while and then go on up to the velodrome and place a few bets with the passengers. When do you get off?"

"Difl will wilt after the first hour. But then I need to

stay for a meeting that the Scholars have called for all of the Divers." She clicked her tongue against the roof of her mouth. "A bit of time till I'm off free, maybe near the close of Fifth—will you still be watching the races then?"

"No, but I'll be in the swimfield if it's not too crowded. Come up if you want. I'll wait for you. I want to show you a game we used to play—except we had real water."

"Very fine idea. I will try to meet you there before the end of Fifth. And now I must hurry so fast to the Dancehall."

"Go! I'll see you later, Beautife."

"Right." The tall woman loped off toward the pop-up beyond the trees, calling back over her shoulder just before she ducked into the woods: "I meant 'Right, Ai'!"

2

By virtue of her glib tongue and promising, if nascent, skills, Ai had found little difficulty in securing a post for herself as Provisional Apprentice Pathfinder aboard the *Imca Limbra*. She had arrived on the ship with little more than the clothes and the carrysack on her back—the latter containing a few personal items, including four carefully wrapped printed texts comprising volumes two through five of the Monkey Pod Boy books in signed first editions—and the versatile gauntlet on her left arm, now adorned with various small, jewellike crystals at several of its expansion junctions.

Ai had adjusted to shipboard life with ease, mingling with the crew and passengers and managing to strike up an astonishing number of casual acquaintances among both groups in the short month since leaving Dunbar's World.

There was a research team aboard the ship that members of the regular crew had dubbed the Darkdivers. Composed of an odd admixture of Scholarly empiricists and rough and tumble freelance Dancers, this group until recently had been conducting experiments into the nature of the mysterious and deadly utterspace through which starships were obliged to travel for part of each voyage in order to drastically reduce the amount of time that would normally be necessary to fare from star to distant star. For some undisclosed reason that not even crew gossip could provide to Ai, the experiments had been halted, and she found it relatively easy to spend most of her free time with members of the bored and restless team. She played Golden Ring with the Dancers, letting them win often enough to keep them interested, and engaged several of the empiricists in long, rambling conversations concerning the probable composition of the Dark.

For the past two weeks Ai had gradually narrowed the focus of her interactions to the Dancer component of the Darkdiver team, soon gaining the particular friendship of the quiet woman known only as Beautife (*pronunciation*, Ai had noted in the journal repository recently implanted in her gauntlet, *as in the old Anglefrank: Bo-TEEF*).

Born and reared in the crowded slums of Heartsdesire on the world called Street of Dreams, Ai's new acquaintance had spent several years as a mercenary in the notorious Blink Wars before traveling to the distant outposts of the Maren, there to spend the bulk of her life helping to carve human settlements from the raw frontier. Still comfortable with the solitude of the Maren, abashed by the intricacies of a civilization she was encountering at peaceful close range for the first time, Beautife interpreted Ai's brashness as simple candor and welcomed the younger woman's company. Her own native language was Felashwa, the guttural underspeech of Heartsdesire, to which she had later added Inter, the latter mixed liberally with the cant of both Dancer and professional soldier.

During their long talks they had discovered many common interests, among them a love of books produced in the recently repopularized printed word form. Though Beautife had never heard of the Monkey Pod Boy series and Ai admitted little contact with the output of the Maren's small presses—confined mostly to agricultural journals and mining implement catalogs—they had both read and fallen in love with the *Tome of the Fresh Heir* and the fabulous *Terra Moribunda*, classics of Antiquity. Beautife had confessed sadly after several glasses of blue that she had been given a signed copy of Varyga's *The Magicians* as a child but that she had been forced to sell it for provisions before leaving Street of Dreams many years ago. Ai had winced at that, and the bibliophiles had drained their glasses in silence, the Pathfinder's small hand resting on the Dancer's large shoulder in an expression of mute sympathy.

A little over seven and one half feet tall, Beautife stood straight and well proportioned, her face a slender oval under dark hair with brooding eyes the pale azure of burnished metalmock.

A domesticated virus developed on the Maren shepherded a flock of intangible colors in slow and constant variation across the Dancer's outer skin, the result being a startlingly faithful representation of the unique sky of Street of Dreams. Pale circular rainbows bloomed in subtle combinations of apricot, green, and soft purple like the mandalas of a mad pointillist against a background of hazy blue-gray.

"There's always a fine mist in the air," Beautife had remarked in response to Ai's questions, looking down at herself with impersonal appraisal. "And the round rainbows grow and fade endlessly all the day. It is truly a faithful portrait of my homeworld that I bear."

3

Ai forced herself to remain at the table in the silver glade, engaging in superficial conversation with two of the other Crewmembers, one a soft-voiced Apprentice Tech from New World and the other a white-haired Symmetrist named Si-mu-li-Pen on temporary assignment as part of his advanced certificate requirements from University.

She allowed the red spark to tell off ten long minutes among the intersecting lines and arcs of the timepiece in her palm; then she rose from the table, left the Park by way of the pop-up, and did her best to hurry slowly to her sleeproom, her whole body tense with the effort of covering the distance in as short a time as possible while maintaining the appearance of a casual stroll through the ship.

Once in her quarters she sank to the floor with a sigh and folded her legs, rolling up the full sleeves of her work jumper to examine the recent outgrowths among the patches of crystal and metalmock that obscured most of her left arm. Extending the arm directly in front of her, she took her left wrist delicately between the thumb and forefinger of her right hand. She lightly rubbed the band of ultrathin material adhering to her skin in that area, pressing gingerly as if searching for her pulse.

There was a tiny *ping*, and the gauntlet suddenly separated into dozens of smaller components, lifted itself from her skin, and floated radially outward to a distance of about two inches from her arm. There it hung like a frozen explosion, maintaining its conformation as if an invisible bladder had been inflated between it and Ai's skin. Only the narrow band of filigreed silver, thin as a coat of reflective paint, remained on Ai's wrist.

Ai chirruped.

Silently parts of the suspended gauntlet began to rotate slowly around her arm, smaller pieces detaching themselves from the main sections to glide in and out of newly created gaps elsewhere on the mechanism in an intricate midair ballet; soon a number of subtle changes had been wrought in the device. Another squeeze of the control band caused the irregular cylinder to stop its rotation and then contract with convulsive suddenness around her arm.

Ai flexed and turned the arm, prodding the new configuration with her right forefinger at various points while she trilled to it in the human-computer interface language called brev. She read the answering twinkle of specklights with an impassive frown.

"Ready or not," she murmured to herself.

Ai unrolled her sleeves and jumped to her feet. She left her quarters and headed down the shortway till she emerged in the Violet Helix, one of several large thoroughfares linking different sections of the ship. The designers of the *Imca Limbra*'s interior had played with gravity to excess in that area, and the long tube was trav-

ersed on foot only by following one of a number of narrow
paths that spiraled along its inner surface. Stretching down
the center of the great shaft was a ribbon of gentle violet
light whose own spiral served as template for the paths.

Up the right-hand wall to march across the ceiling, down
the left-hand wall for a short diagonal stroll along the floor,
up the right-hand wall again . . . the roundabout motion
imposed by the Violet Helix on pedestrians usually passed
unnoticed by Ai, but at the moment she chafed bitterly under
the extra length added to her journey by the corkscrew
nature of her progress. She could have traveled more swiftly
by deserting the Helix for one of the shuntcars, but that
would have imposed a different set of delays on her, as she
was likely to run into acquaintances among the Crewmembers who regularly used the shuttles. So she wound her
tedious way around the Helix like a bug in a drainpipe till
she sighted the wallmarker that told her she was near her
destination and exited the tube with a sigh of relief.

She found herself once again in a shortway terminating
in a cluster of sleeprooms. She approached the one marked
with the number code 223226 and paused before the door
design, absently scratching the back of her left hand as
she stared at the wall as if deep in thought. The corridor
was deserted.

A pulse of blue and yellow light flashed on the sliver of
metalmock visible at the edge of her cuff, and she raised
her arm quickly. She flattened her left palm against the wall,
the slight click of metalmock meeting plax barely audible
as she brought her wrist to rest gently against the sensing
plate.

There was a soft hiss as the door faded into translu-
cency and she stepped through into the sleeproom.

The room was larger than her own, cruciform, starkly
furnished, with the bedbay in the left arm and the habitual
in the right. Ai paused in the main area for a backward
glance at the reforming door design, then walked almost
reluctantly to peer around into the sleeping bay.

He was there.

After the months of waiting on Dunbar's World and

the weeks of searching since she had come aboard the *Imca Limbra*, the sight of him was almost anticlimactic.

She moved forward into the alcove, pulse racing.

He was lying on his back, blunt-fingered hands folded loosely on his chest, the strong features relaxed in a sleeper's frown. His skin was the color and simulated texture of brushed silver, his hair a close mat of iron curls.

She leaned forward to touch his shoulder, her lips moving in silent rehearsal, and noticed for the first time the medication wire that snaked from the side of his throat to a flat blue disk on the wall. She frowned and pressed his shoulder.

"March?" It came out as a whisper. She cleared her throat and repeated the name softly.

There was no response, no change in the slow rhythm of his powerful chest beneath the tan jumper.

Drugged?

She drew a hair-thin line from her gauntlet, touched it lightly to his throat just below the thread that linked him to the wall. Her brow creased in puzzlement as she read information from her arm, and she bit her lower lip, raising her eyes to wander the empty wall above his head. She withdrew the line while she tapped out a lengthy sequence of commands on her gauntlet, then brought it forth again and gingerly pressed it to the base of the sleeper's neck.

Nothing. She drew back the thread.

She grimaced in worry and concentration, her breath shallow and rapid as she knelt at the side of the sleeping man. She reached forward and shook him lightly, talking to him in a helpless whisper. "Come on, please, come on, wake up, I need you."

She was so intent that she heard nothing when the door design sighed into nothingness again and light footsteps approached at her back.

Ai coughed in surprise when the long arm reached past her from behind. She spun around and into the grip of slender, very powerful fingers.

Beautife regarded her thoughtfully from her great height. She nodded past Ai to the silent sleeper. "Well, then," she said. "Is this what you came to find?"

The tall woman's hand hovered above the sleeping man for an instant and then darted down in a complex series of taps that fell against the silver skin just below the left collarbone, at the edge of the tan jumper.

"What—" Ai said.

The man's eyes flew abruptly open.

"March!" She tried to reach out to him, but Beautife held her fast in her other hand.

The eyes stared; one of them was not an eye at all but a polished oval of dull green stone fitted smoothly into the left socket. Then the blunt head lifted from the pallet, and Ai saw more slender wires trailing it from beneath the top layer of bedding.

He stared straight ahead: at the wall, at nothing. Then he began to cough, his throat bobbing and his lips writhing as if in pain. Suddenly his voice boomed in the tiny alcove, and he spat out a torrent of rapid syllables in a language Ai did not recognize. Then his mouth snapped shut, and he slumped back like a marionette whose strings had been severed. His face grew slack as the eye and the not-eye rolled back beneath descending silver lids.

Ai struggled futilely for a few seconds before realizing that the other woman was not even aware of her attempts to free herself from the iron grip.

"Not so clear as he would have liked, but speech through the Dance has never been perfected. Seems to have been some pattern degeneration as well." Beautife watched the silver man with a haggard expression as she spoke. Her eyes fell on Ai, and she shook her head as if to clear it.

"Question, question others on the Diver team—the Scholars and the Dancers." She sighed. "I am not simple after all, Ai, and I knew well you would not be found at velodrome or in swimfield this afternoon. But I did think you were truly becoming a friend to me, and I do not know the reason for the questions, nor why you are here now in my sleeproom."

Ai was shaking. "What have you done to him, Beautife? Oh, what's wrong with him?"

The tall woman removed her hands, sinking to the floor

so she could simultaneously face Ai and block the passage to the outer door.

"Question, question." She gestured to the silver man behind Ai. "What is your interest in him that you hunt him down with whispers, with sniffing? An answer for an answer will I trade you, *sen* Velu."

Ai looked over her shoulder almost fearfully. The only sign of life was the gentle rise and fall of his chest. She tore her eyes from the quiet figure and forced calm into her voice.

"He's a friend of mine, of my family—a very old friend. I needed to see him about . . . a matter of great importance to me. I've gone—" Her eyes strayed back to the closed face, and her voice tipped toward hysteria for a moment, steadied again. "I have gone to a great deal of trouble to find him. Now tell me, please, what's happened to him."

Beautife sat for a few seconds of watchful silence, her eyes on Ai's trembling chin. Then she heaved herself to her feet. Motioning Ai to accompany her, she left the sleeping bay and crossed to a wallfile in the main area, from which she extracted a small tab of holodots.

She used brev to summon a low viewing couch from the floor of the room, pointed Ai to a seat, and sat down heavily next to her. There was a receptacle ringed by a compact keyboard at one end of the couch.

"What have you ferreted out about the project with your questions?"

"Next to nothing. That it was connected with finding out the true nature of the Dark. That no one has any answers."

Beautife gave a sour smile. "Your knowledge almost equals my own, and I have worked at this for two true-years. I think you should listen to this, at any rate. It is part of the original proposal presented for approval to the Blue Shell Council on Commons." She dropped the tab of holodots into the receptacle and ran her fingers lightly over the keyboard. The roomlight dimmed, and a woman appeared life-sized in the air before them, frozen in mid-thought with her mouth half open.

She was small and slight of build, with the glossy black hair and mahogany skin of a native of Sipril. She wore a

plain white Tech wraparound and an air of restrained
impatience.

Characters danced in the air beneath her face.

"Twenty-four Auspent 402. Proposal EL43162. Prin-
cipal Investigator: Ki-mo-li-Set," intoned a crystalline
machine voice. The glowing words vanished with the voice,
and the woman took a breath.

"And what do we know about the nature of this Dark,
this so-called utterspace through which most of us will pass
repeatedly during our lives on our way to somewhere else?
In the four centuries since the Elyins gifted us with the means
to enter the Dark, where great distances in normal space
are vastly reduced, how have we added to our store of
knowledge concerning it?" She gave a small smile, shook
her head. "In a word: poorly.

"The Othermen were capricious when it came to doling
out information along with their bestowals. About the three
Great Gifts—the longevity drug popularly known as Ember,
the Screens which permitted realtime communication over
interstellar distances, and the Darkjumpers themselves—
they chose to tell us next to nothing. And we chose to accept
their gifts and to use them without question—indeed, we
became dependent upon them almost at once. Then the
Elyins left us, for reasons we can still only guess at, to go
no one knows where. Ten years after the Departure, in the
Great Year 365, the first Darkjumpers began to die. Fifteen
years of horror followed as ship after ship succumbed, in
incidents violent or undramatic, the former often accompanied by extensive loss of human life." Her face was somber. "In GY 380 it was proved conclusively for the first time
that it was the Dark itself which was in some way linked to
the destruction of our vessels. Certain facts were enumer-
ated through experimentation: The longer a ship remained
in the Dark on a single jump, the more damage was done to
it, though the progress of the deterioration and its relative
severity were not always detectable by the means available
at that time. Ships that skipped in and out of the utterspace
for periods of only a few hours' duration were shown by
subsequent research to be affected minimally or not at all,
while those that stayed within for lengthy sojourns bore
evidence of proportionately more dramatic deterioration.

"How have we adapted in the twenty-five years since the revelation that what we had once confidently referred to as the Dark and Empty in fact contained something that is highly inimical to us? We have modified our travel habits, to be sure. No longer does a ship spend a leisurely week within the utterspace on its journey from star to star. In and out we hop, relying on our Pathfinders for constant recalibration of navigational instruments thrown awry as always by passage through the Dark, even as they augment the functions of those instruments with their own strange skills. Voyages which had previously taken weeks or even days now stretch out over months and years of tedium, the price of safety. And still the occasional ship is lost or must be retired, one in five hundred, and our supply of irreplaceable vessels dwindles lower.

"Theories continue to abound which attempt to explain the nature of this pocket of the unknown which so intimately touches the spacefarer's life. Certain former Expansionists have always espoused the belief that there is Something in there and that—far from Empty—the Dark is in fact home to a race of pernicious monsters bent on devouring our vessels. These individuals now counsel us to 'attack' the Dark, using sleeping bombs and hard radiation." Her expression dismissed the plan as nonsense. "The perceptions of humankind and those few sensing devices which can be made to operate in the utterspace have so far revealed only a void that is absolute—"

"Enough," Beautife said. "She'll go on for hours if I allow it." Ki-mo-li-Set vanished as the lights returned jarringly to full strength.

The Dancer turned to Ai, who sat rubbing her eyes. "She proposed to go in with a team of Dancers, people like March and like me, whose bodies could be programmed to act without conscious direction should the need arise. To me it seemed a fine, exciting job: exploring the unknown places. And the pay was high." She glanced toward the bedbay, shook her head. "The plan was to go in with small, manually controlled ships and a range of data collection devices, to search like mad until we found something. Or something found us." She turned and removed the holodots, reversed the tab, and inserted it again.

"This is from the day it happened, the day of our last test." Beautife stirred restlessly. "Twenty-seven times in two years we had gone in and come out without a problem. We never stayed in more than a few minutes each Dive; less and less as the experiment progressed. Sometimes there was data recorded on the machines which the Scholars found interesting. Most of the time there was nothing. Some people had strange experiences. March was as fearless and curious as a child, always the first to dart off from the group in exploration. Three times he reported odd sensations during his Dive, and three times the instruments in his wherry indicated some sort of anomalous movement in the Dark near his ship. I myself felt a presence one time, like a tickling at the edges of my brain. Nothing much. Mostly it was just routine. We went out in the wherries and swam around in the nothingness for a few minutes, deploying the various instruments and waiting for something to happen. So when it did . . ." She turned and rummaged through a drawer below the small keyboard.

"Here." Beautife held a limp dream hood. "Put this on if you want to be me. I'm not supposed to have it. They're trying to keep the whole thing quiet. But they had hoped in the beginning to make a documentary on the project to be cast on NewsNet, to share their findings over the years at project's end. That day they were recording through several viewpoints, mine among them. Only eight of us went out that time." Her voice was bleak. "I was one of the ones who stayed behind."

Ai looked at the shapeless ball of fabric. With the dream hood on she would come as close as possible to experiencing the recorded events from within the skin of one of the original participants.

She hesitated, then pulled the soft hood down close against her scalp and leaned back.

"Ready."

She saw Beautife's fingers touch the keyboard once more, and lights flickered in midair: names, authorization code, a date four weeks in the past. Then sound and color leaped at her.

She was in one of the docking bays aboard the Imca Limbra. *Men and women in stiff green or white protectalls moved among a dozen sleek blue capsules, checking readings on techboards and chatting with the eight blue-suited Divers who lounged in the open cockpits of the tiny single-person vessels.*

Several narrow information strips banded the room, running halfway between floor and high ceiling on the docking bay walls. One of the strips began to glow dull red, then flashed abruptly with a crimson pulse that circled the room like a trapped animal. Sticks of kephel were extinguished and final handclasps exchanged as the Divers slid down into their ships. The wherries were piloted belly down, with each Diver stretched out full length, a cluster of controls and telltales near each hand on its padded cushion.

She looked around at the deadlights covering the external ports, and the small part of her that was Ai shivered. It was the middle of a jump, and they were about to go Outside.

She heard a familiar low voice, and someone seized her from behind and whirled her around. She looked down at a powerfully muscled man with skin like brushed silver. He winked at her and murmured something in her ear that pleased her. Then he raced for the last of the ships, waving to her with a wolfish grin as the shiny lid came smoothly down over his back.

A dark woman in a white wraparound conferred nearby with several of the green-garbed Scholars as the wherries slid like startled fish into open tubelocks. The locks irised shut, and a small round patch above each of them showed golden light. Fifteen seconds passed, and the lights went out.

"They're gone," said a voice from behind her.

She moved off to make herself comfortable on a floating lounger. Mugs of steaming chetto were passed around as people settled down to talk or watch the information strips.

She opened a travel-worn book and began to thumb through dog-eared illustration flats of excavation vehicles.

Something bellowed in her ear. A bright yellow flashing filled the room as she dropped the book and jumped to her feet. She stared with the rest of them at the topmost band of information strips, were a pulse like a small yellow sun throbbed from wall to wall.

Figures began to run past her to the tubelocks. Someone was shouting over the rhythmic bleat of the alarm.

A short man with brindled gray skin scurried past, his thin face set with panic. She grabbed his arm as the noise was suddenly quelled. "Costa! What's happening?"

"Something's been detected approaching the ship." Dark eyes rolled. "Something large."

Ai felt her blood freeze and her skin crawl with fear.

"Are they sure?" her mouth asked. "Could it be ship's echo, like the last time?"

The little man shook his head. "This one's real. They're calling them back in." He pushed her hand from his arm and hurried off.

Gold lights began to wink on one by one above the tubelocks. Seconds crawled by, and the first lock irised open. One after the other, seven wherries slid into the docking bay like unspent bullets being emptied from a gun.

Seven.

She stared at the final lock, cried out in relief as the golden patch filled with light.

The room swarmed with activity as the long lids rose slowly into the air. Blue-suited figures erupted from the interiors, clambered over the sides.

The last wherry slid into the bay, and she ran to it. When the lid opened, the man inside lay unmoving, his face hidden. She reached for him, and other hands were next to hers. Together they lifted him gently from the wherry, turned him over, and lowered him to a pad on the floor.

His face was peaceful, empty.

Someone had pushed a portative medipal unit over. It bobbed lazily in the air above the still body as trembling fingers drew diagnostic threads to the silver skin at throat and wrist. She watched him, her heart like a great tolling bell in her breast as movement and voices buzzed all around.

"Move," she said at last to one of the green-suited men who knelt in front of her. When he failed to obey, she bent and lifted him off the floor, depositing him on the other side of the pad.

She crouched next to the inert body.

"Don't do this," she murmured. She leaned close to the silver ear and whispered words that Ai could not follow, though she felt them issue from her own throat.

"No," she said. "Don't." She extended a long hand, and her fingers executed a series of light taps on the unmoving shoulder.

She jumped with the rest of them when he lifted his head, pale green glinting from the left socket as his eyes snapped wide open. He started forward, and a spate of foreign words tumbled from his trembling lips.

"God-be-thanks," the woman in the Tech wraparound said as his head settled back against the thin pad. "We got him in time."

Beautife raised her head slowly. The noise in the room died as she met the other woman's eyes.

"No," she said softly. "We did not."

"I knew him on the homeworld, a long time ago. We met again in the Wars and soldiered together for years, till he said he'd had enough of death and walked away one day. I went to the Maren and lived my life till he came and found me. When the offer came to join the Diver team, I convinced him to come with me. We needed excitement to make our lives bright, I told him, and he shrugged and signed the paper."

Beautife spoke slowly to the empty air in front of her. Ai sat next to her and shivered, the dream hood limp in her hand.

"We had made a pact back in the old fighting days, an agreement that many who were close to each other made. If ever one of us failed to come out at battle's end—failed to waken from the Dance—there would be a tapcode or a snapword that only the other would know. That way there

could be a message, some final words." She shrugged.
"During the Wars we had seen two of our friends go this
way, driven so deep inside that their bodies were left behind
like shells surrounding nothing. Mind-dead, mind-shat-
tered, and only the useless husk left to be thrown away. But
to us it was more like a game. We wagered before each job
who would be the one to hear the other's message. We felt
ourselves to be invincible, and the dap was never won or
lost. Still, before each Dive he patterned in a little Dance
of words for me in the language of our homeworld and stored
it away in his body. Mine has one for him, as well, but he'll
never hear it now. He's won the wager. I received the message." She closed her azure eyes and recited slowly in the
quiet room as tears slipped down her cheeks:

*So I am gone. Of she who listens now I ask one thing
before her life flows on past mine. Bring this body to Emrys
on University. He was my friend and may have a use for it.
Then remember me and how I looked when I looked at you,
and the fine years we had at each other's side . . .*"

It was Ai who made the inquiries necessary to find out
where on University the notification should be sent, and
when Beautife stood frozen before the flickering Screen,
it was Ai who whispered words to her and smiled encour-
agement. From that time on there was never a doubt in
either of their minds that she would accompany her friend
through the remainder of her journey.

Interlude

Seven Thoughts at Once tasted someone approaching from above as he shivered in the violet shadows of the underpath. He drew back convulsively behind a fan of detritus and peered around its lacy edge with a score of little eyes.

The intruder grew from a spot of descending color to a sleek familiar shape aglint with motion in the high, murky blues, and he recognized Sometimes Smaller. He huddled closer to the fan and waited.

Eyes skittered over Smaller's skin as he drifted near the bottom of the underpath, forming at the midpoint of his back and dispersing evenly until they dotted his entire surface. The mottled pink of concern showed as a lavender tracery on his skin as he bobbed uncertainly over the detritus garden. He nosed cautiously among fragile tendrils of new growth, nearing the base of the broad fan behind which Seven Thoughts quivered in apprehension.

Eyes peered at each other through the filigree as Smaller's surface relaxed and began to ripple with a mixture of relief and inquiry.

Suddenly Seven Thoughts shot upward from behind the fan, his body narrowing as channel-points opened and the sluggish currents of the underpath churned through him. Sometimes Smaller whirled far below in a dim confusion of broken tendrils and clinging sediment.

The overpaths gleamed above in twisting ribbons of light. Seven Thoughts rose toward the nearest spur and crept up toward the Rushing Path, where few of his people were likely to be encountered. He shuddered continuously as he rose, his skin a dull wash of silver.

If only they would leave him alone . . .

CHAPTER 5

*Dwell as near as possible to the channel in which
your life flows.*

HENRY DAVID THOREAU

1

A man met them at the Lekkole Landing Stage. After
showing them the glowing badge of a minor Community
functionary, he matched the data on the telltale of the
bain-sense with the numers that crawled continuously
around the bare skin of his right wrist—a more prosaic
form, Ai suspected, of the domesticated virus that clothed
Beautife in another world's sky.

"Where you taking it?" He spoke in a clipped Inter
that made Beautife cock her head to one side and wrinkle
her brow. Ai translated.

"We are bringing him as he wished to Jon Emerson
Tate, the Scholar," the tall Dancer replied after a moment's
hesitation.

The official raised a nonexistent eyebrow at the hovering coffin shape. "I see." He muttered rapid brev into
his collar for a few seconds, consulted his wrist again,
and nodded. He affixed two small seals to the *bain-sense*.

"This'll give you clearance for the box till you can turn
it over to the Sessept. Thereafter, he'll have to make his
own arrangements if he plans to unwrap it and keep it
around." He looked up at Beautife, then down at Ai. "I
assume he's expecting you?"

71

"He was notified," Ai said with a glance at her companion. "He said to come ahead."

"I see. Have a pleasant stay on University," the man recited dryly, his badge flashing as he turned to leave in the shadow of the enormous vessel.

"Wait!" Beautife's long legs carried her past the official in a single step. "How will we find Jon?"

"One moment." He spoke to his collar again, fingers drumming impatiently on his thigh. Characters marched on his wrist. "Maincom says he's gone home for the day. He lives out in the Free Forest with the In-Betweens." He shrugged. "There's an address if you want it."

"Here." Ai moved between Beautife and the man. "Give it to me." She crossed his wrist with her own for a second. A tiny chime sounded from her gauntlet. "Got it. Where's the transportation line?"

The official eyed the *bain-sense* doubtfully. "Better take a diligence if you want to bring the box along. Go up to the fourth level and follow the yellow lumes to Public Transport."

The Transport woman had had crinkled fans of blue iridescence set in place of eyebrows on her broad face. They flexed and folded like butterfly wings with each small movement of her facial muscles.

She led them through ranks of small ornate craft shaped like shallow, open waterboats, pausing at last by one whose gleaming hull of black enamel rested inches above the green-threaded marble of the floor on six slender, many-jointed legs.

She watched them settle the *bain-sense* awkwardly among the plump scarlet cushions, gave perfunctory instruction in the use of the course-set, and accepted their dap without comment, the bright wings quivering delicately against her flat brow.

Ai clambered gingerly over the low side of the craft, and Beautife squeezed in beside her, the Dancer's long arms and legs creating a forest of blue-gray limbs.

Ai depressed a golden lever, and the diligence rose rocking into the air, its black legs retracting like whips into the chitinous hull. A weathershield came on, allowing only the mildest breeze to touch their faces as they arced out over the city toward the distant forest. Ai settled back and closed her eyes.

It seemed a moment later when she awoke to Beautife's hand on her shoulder. The afternoon was nearly spent: Blue shadows painted the brown and golden treescape that rose and fell beneath them.

"There, I think," Beautife said, pointing past the bow of the diligence to a jutting hill surrounded by treetops. "It feels like we're slowing down."

Ai stretched herself erect and peered through the dimness. "You're right. Must be the house there at the top."

The structure was an aggregate of dark wood and rough stone, an asymmetric fusion that seemed to have been coaxed out of the hill and the amber-golden forest that encircled it. Perched several meters above the crown of the hill, it was suspended midway in what appeared to be a thicket of great twisting roots or vines, enhancing the illusion that the entire assemblage had been pulled up gradually from the ground beneath it by a giant hand, rather than planned and executed by any human builder. As the visitors approached, lights were beginning to glow from hidden windows, faint irregular patches of amethyst and topaz on the surface of the dark dwelling.

"Is it a house or a rootgall?" Beautife whispered as the diligence started a wide spiral down to the single tiny landing stage affixed to a portion of the canted roof.

"The Well said he was born on Green Asylum," Ai said softly. "They'd try to talk a tree into becoming their house of its own free will before they'd hew off a single branch. Strange place. They do everything with plants there but marry them, it's said."

"Hunh." The Dancer craned her long neck over the side to watch as the unlikely domicile swelled beneath them. "A marvel indeed. What's marry?"

"Braid your lives together, for two or more. Friendship and care-for and other bonds. Some worlds have it more than others, I guess."

"We say it *petanna*," Beautife said quietly from the darkness after a few moments. "Mates for life."

Then they touched down, the diligence pitching slightly as its flexible landing legs came forth, and a wide door was opening slowly before them in the side of the strange house.

Because he had refused to think about it, the day arrived much too quickly.

Emrys had dismissed his morning seminar early and tried to eat something in the crowded Common Place. His stomach gave a warning lurch each time he brought the spoon to his lips, and at last he had to leave most of the fragrant brackle untasted on his plate. He tossed down a lukewarm glass of fruit chetto and made the slow descent to the Well. There he fished for an hour or two, but his mind kept wandering. Finally he decided it was time to head back to the surface.

He took the last seat on one of the new silver-domed shuttles and stared blindly out the window until they docked in the center of the shopping circle. He prowled the shops for a while, picking up oddments of food, toiletries, and guest clothing. A broad tray trailed him patiently from store to store. He piled it high, then stared in surprise at the jumbled heap when he reached the shuttle stop and forced himself to retrace his steps, shaking his head as he unloaded half his acquisitions.

Company, after all this time, he thought. He didn't know how to deal with it.

Back at the College he deposited his carrysack on the passenger seat of a tiny blue solitary, toyed with the course-set, and slumped into the cushions with a groan, hoping for a nap to shorten the familiar trip to the Free Forest. But his eyes remained stubbornly open for the entire hour.

When he arrived at the house on the hill, he climbed from the solitary and snapped the lid shut after him, sending the little vehicle skimming silently back toward the College.

He brought the carrysack in and allowed it to drop to the floor, intending to take care of unpacking and storage after a moment's rest in the great brown chair that was half seashell and half warm nest.

He slipped off his sandals and lowered his feet to the

red-brown floor with a sigh. The room was simple, well but sparsely furnished, and it contained one of the few concessions he allowed to the sybaritic side of his nature. In this room alone the squares of glazed terra-cotta that served as flooring were blessed with a full centimeter of joywalk, the fabulously expensive tinted vapor from the Southern Luxuriants which, when reinforced with sonic relaxants and loosely bound in its own intangible weather-shield, created a carpet of delight for the unshod foot.

Three hours later the sack still lay untouched in the center of the floor.

He sat alone in the gathering darkness and tried to pretend that he was home.

At Willow Cove on Green Asylum, the afternoon would still have had several hours of slanting golden sunlight left before the quick glory of sundown consumed the day and ushered in the velvet, moonless night.

Here on University, the days were shorter but the approach of evening more leisurely, as if by way of compensation: a slow alchemical simmering rather than a conflagration.

He sipped *avavith* from a pear-shaped glass and watched the way the windows colored the deepening afternoon, bringing him dusk in shades of blue, violet, and wine.

Any time now . . .

He leaned forward with his chin on his folded hands, his elbows resting on his knees, and stared at the misty floor and the unopened carrysack.

Dead? He gave his head a small shake.

After a time, a discreet trill of music sounded in the room, signaling by its melody the approach of an airborne vehicle.

How could he be dead? It's his first visit here in so long, he found himself thinking inanely. *Who will introduce me to his friends?*

The music sounded again in a higher key, and he lifted his face to the ceiling. "Open the door for them when they land. And put on some lights in the upper rooms. I'll go up to meet them in a minute."

But he was still sitting there hunched forward in the

dark when a different melody hung briefly in the air a few
minutes later. He moved around in the great chair, but
there was a weak feeling in his knees, and he made no
effort to rise.

"Oh, Lords," he muttered. "I can't. Look, send them
my voice." He waited a second, then announced to the
air in front of him: "Come in, please. Take the ramp on
your left and follow it down to the Hearth Room."

He kindled a wanderlight high above his head and one
near the arching doorway and leaned back to wait in the
warm yellow glow.

When he heard their slow approach, he turned, an
electric tingle beginning in his abdomen and radiating out
through his limbs.

Be a mistake. Be someone else.

The first person through the archway had to duck, and
the second one was almost completely hidden in the
shadow of the first.

"Come in," he said, rising to his feet at last. "I'm Jon
Tate—Emrys. I apologize for not being up top to greet
you properly, but—" He left the sentence uncompleted,
his throat gone suddenly dry.

As the two women stepped hesitantly into the room,
he could see the large oblong shape that loomed behind
them, bobbing slightly as it negotiated the final turn of
the incline. The very tall woman put her hand on its surface, and the box settled obediently at her feet, its landing
sending waves through the joywalk that sparkled like faint
prismatic veils above the ruddy squares.

"I still don't understand." Anger and joy struggled for
ascendancy in his voice.

He twitched a trembling thumb at the *bain-sense*,
searched their faces. A swirl of pale purple smoke drifted
across the room from the slender kephel stick he had
added to the fireplace before igniting the small pyramid
of golden logs.

The tall woman, Beautife, and the red-haired girl sat
close to each other on the long, low seating bar opposite
his chair. Before them lay the box, an ornate dove-gray

casket with an incongruous cluster of small gauges and readouts at one end of its sleek length.

He shook his head and dropped his hand to the arm of his chair, looking almost fearfully at the silent mechanism. "Why didn't you tell me he was still alive? Why would you deliberately—"

"He's dead," Beautife said quietly. She sat very stiffly on the edge of the seating bar, both hands tight around a mug of steaming kahve. Beneath the soft patterns that bloomed and faded on her skin, her face was a mask that looked ready to shatter.

"You don't carry the dead in a sense-bath with life support modifications," he snapped, not caring if the dull mask gave way to tears or shrieks of laughter. "You carry the broken, who can be fixed. The living, who can be healed."

"There wasn't time to explain it all," the girl said. He'd lost her name during the introductions, his eyes on the box and his mind on what it suggested, but he knew it was something appropriately short and expressive. Her dark eyes watched him closely now, and she stressed her words carefully, warning him against upsetting her companion.

"A message is expensive when you send it realtime through a Screen and you're on a ship. Not everybody has the money." Her eyes flicked to the carpet of mist aglint with colors in the firelight. "So it had to be brief." She leaned forward to set her tall glass of pink foam on the *bain-sense*, realized what she was doing, and placed it carefully by her feet instead.

"Well, you don't have to be brief now. You're here. Please tell me what's happened to my friend."

In the end it was Ai who told the story, with Emrys trying not to ask too many questions and asking them anyway and Beautife supplying one- or two-word clarifications when necessary.

While Ai spoke, the Scholar fixed them something to eat, disappearing into a side room for a few moments and then reappearing laden with pans and cookpad, trailed by a listing tray stacked with bowls and baskets of raw food.

Ai watched his face while she talked, but he seemed intent on the chopping and mixing, showing no outward reaction to her words but the terse, carefully worded questions. In time he presented them with sturdy blue-glazed plates on which yellow omelets steamed, filling the air with the smells of peppers, onions, sea mushrooms, and more that Ai couldn't name. Beautife picked at hers disinterestedly with an eating tong, her eyes on the fire, but Ai ate steadily, devouring everything on her plate and half of what was on her friend's, along with toasted new-baked bread and a marvelous clear amber honey, and washing it all down with mugs of warm chocolate chetto. Somehow, between bites and sips, the story was told.

"And then I looked you up through the Well and we found out where to contact you and we sent the message. That was two weeks ago," Ai finished, wiping her mouth on her right sleeve. She pointed to a ragged morsel of golden bread. "Is there any more of the honey? We came right here because—" She gave Beautife a quick sidelong glance, then continued in a lowered voice. "Because he had asked her to bring his body to you, and she needed to do it for him."

Emrys handed her a blue earthenware jar from which a sticky handle protruded, then sat for a few moments in the flicker from the fire. He had doused the wanderlights long ago, and the room stretched and contracted in the orange shadows from the great hearth.

"Can I see?" he asked finally. "Can I see the . . . message, please?"

Ai looked doubtfully at Beautife, her eyes expecting pain, but the Dancer nodded slowly without expression.

They unsealed the gleaming gray box and folded back its lid. An unidentifiable chemical odor came forth. Emrys stood looking down at the silent body as the fire explored its surface with trembling golden fingers.

"Ah," he said softly, rubbing a finger back and forth against his lower lip. "Each year his face grew gentler."

He stepped back, and Beautife replaced him at the casket's side. As she bent over the still figure, Ai winced and turned away, plugging her ears with the heels of her hands. She glimpsed a sudden thrust of movement and shut her eyes hastily, counting softly under her breath. When she judged it must be over, she opened them again.

Beautife was folding the silver hands back on the gently moving breast. Her face had not changed, but her eyes were rimmed with moisture in the flamelight.

Emrys had retreated from the *bain-sense*. He sat deep in the darkness of the great curving chair and stared, chin on his fist, at the black night beyond the windows of the Hearth Room.

Their host showed them each to a room.

Ai sat down on the pallet, intending to fish some paper and a stylus out of her carrysack and set down some of her feelings before she retired for the night. She lay back against the silken bedclothes for a few moments to organize her thoughts, her arms folded behind her head. She could hear Emrys and Beautife speaking softly in the hall.

The next thing she knew, it was morning, with blue-green light streaming through the colored glass of the round window. She stumbled to her feet and wandered down the hall. Not sure exactly where Beautife's room was located, she decided to head for the Hearth Room. Perhaps she would have a bite of breakfast before she disturbed her friend.

She found the tall Dancer sitting by herself at the round table that hung before the great amber window. She was sipping a mug of aromatic tea, her face worn-looking above the smooth blue rim as Ai mounted the stool next to her.

"Well, I certainly slept like a corpse." Ai saw the long gray box on the floor from the corner of her eye and cursed herself silently. "Is Emrys up yet?"

Beautife nodded. "He's gone to the College. He said was going to send a message through a Screen."

"Mm. Did you ask him to find out about a ship for us? I mean, it's up to you how long we stay—I'm in no hurry—but I thought you might want to . . ." She let the words trail off when it became obvious that Beautife was not listening. She touched the other woman's arm hesitantly. "Beautife? Are you all right?"

"He said he'd already tried to contact some people before we arrived—some old friends. No reply. This time, he said, the message would be different." She turned to Ai with a dull, wondering look on her face. "He wants them to send someone to look at..." Her voice faded, and she shook her head in bewilderment, then looked at Ai again, almost imploringly. "He says he thinks there might still be a chance, Ai."

Emrys sat in his office, a quiet blue oval overlooking a courtyard filled with russet ferns and a carefully tended sand garden bordered by four low black benches.

There was a chime, and he raised his eyes to the wall. "Yes?"

"They've established the link to Maribon for your call, Sessept. Sorry for the delay."

"Thank you, Robin." On the wall before his desk, a meter-wide circle began to fill with flickering light.

"World to world, via the Net," an artificial voice announced. The outline of a human head and torso grew visible against the glow, fragmented briefly, then stabilized as the light dimmed behind it. A young woman looked at him from the Screen. Her black hair was cropped to a cap of curls above a delicate white face.

"City of Delphys," she said.

After all these years, he still found their blank stare unnerving. When would she teach them to smile?

"This is Jon Emerson Tate on University. I sent a message recently, but there's been no reply. I was wondering..."

"Your message was received, Jon Emerson Tate." The voice was not quite synchronized to her lips, he realized, no doubt a result of the influence that Mizar and the Companions always had on transmissions to and from Maribon. "She has been offworld for thirteen days, gone to Weldon for an unspecified period. If we are able to assist you in Her absence, it is our responsibility to do so."

"Thank you. Unspecified, you say. Could you tell me

if—Lords, what's he calling himself these days? Geoffram? Has Geoffram gone with her to Weldon?"

"No, Her Hand resides currently on Stone's Throw, overseeing the new Mission there."

"Stone's Throw. I see. Not so far, perhaps. Could you give me an address where I might reach him with a message, please?"

"Yes. Alembic Mission House, 41-461 Amabile, Paiak City."

"Thank you very much, ah—I don't believe I heard your name."

The woman blinked. "I am not required to travel," she said. "And so I have no name."

"Oh. Of course," Emrys said. He smiled politely as the link was terminated. Shaking his head, he turned away from the empty Screen.

CHAPTER 6

*Men are admitted into heaven not because they
have curbed & govern'd their Passions, or have
no Passions, but because they have cultivated
their Understandings.*

WILLIAM BLAKE

1

Outsister Pennifar hurried through the darkening streets
of Paiak City, her wooden sandals sounding hollowly on
the uneven cobbles.

Wind scent had been promising rain all day; now low
black clouds confirmed its imminence. She shrugged the
thin shawl closer about her neck and twitched one frayed
end over her market basket as she picked her way up half
a dozen crumbling stone steps, the shortcut from Potetny
Street to a narrow alley that would lead her—ahead of
the storm, she hoped—almost to the front gates of the
Mission.

But fat cold droplets began to fall before she was halfway down the alley, and she hissed at the chill when one
caught her on the cheek. She had felt her first raindrops
shortly after her arrival on Stone's Throw seven months
ago, and she was still unused to the idea of water falling
unsupervised like spittle from the sky.

Reaching the end of the alley, she paused beside an ill-
smelling mound of charred rubble, thankful for the shelter

afforded by a sagging washline two stories above. As she steeled herself for the short dash across Amabile to the Mission, a window shot open over her head and someone began to draw in the laundry rope, muttered curses lost in the squeak of the pulley as the damp tatters jerked and danced out of sight. Sister Pennifar lowered her head with a sigh and scurried out onto the deserted avenue.

The old gate complained when she pushed her way into the tiny courtyard and whined again as she elbowed it shut behind her. She puffed up the walk, fumbling with her free hand for the heavy key ring until she remembered that she would not find the doors locked today—or any day from now on, not even at sunset—now that Geoffram himself had requested they be left unbarred.

"Those who stay inside these walls do so by choice," he had told them in his reasonable way, "and none who wish to enter from the outside shall be turned away." A slender, dark-haired man with a narrow jaw and gentle eyes, he had stood before the great fireplace in the Hearth Room; and because he was Her Hand on Stone's Throw, they had listened to what he asked of them in his quiet voice, and then they had complied.

Pennifar transferred the weighty basket to her left arm and scooped up the small bundle of letters from the covered shelf on the front of the right-hand door. Bills, probably, or more excuses for taxation plucked out of the smoky air by the city government.

She kicked off her sandals in the shadowed foyer, then bent with a grunt to replace them with worn scuffs. The downstairs was dark. Geoffram was probably home, the others more likely still out touring with the newcomers. *Cold rain on their heads*, she thought with a cluck of her tongue. *Still, it's a fit welcome to this place*. She paused to pluck an everglow from the niche and unhooded it, sorting the mail in the cold blue gleam as she padded down the hall to the kitchen.

She dropped the wand into a sconce inside the kitchen door, dialed it up till the room was filled with soft, blue-white light, and settled onto a bench at the cooktable with a murmur of satisfaction. Two letters from home today, both from her cousin Hewel. Probably received in Paiak a month apart, she reflected: the first sitting in its cubby down at the Authority Building in Redemption Square until the arrival of the second made their presence enough of a nuisance to warrant their delivery to such an unfashionable neighborhood.

She set the battered packets aside for later and removed her shawl. Draping it on a pot hook near the oven to dry, she noted that one of the threadbare spots she had been monitoring for the past month had finally become a hole and would want patching before she slept tonight.

She lifted the market basket onto the bench and began to unload it. The apples went into the blue bowl in the center of the broad table, the soot-colored rice cakes she stacked on a platter on the counter, and the fishbread that had cost her so much time in bargaining went straight to the oven so that it might be warm and relatively odorless by dinnertime. She had looked for a cheese at her favorite stall, but Habbany's baby was due tonight or tomorrow morning, and Pennifar knew that young Toss, who kept the booth in his sister's absence, would charge twice what she was willing to pay. The rice cakes were fresh, however, dark and aromatic, and later she would make applesalt from the choicest of today's fruit. There was not much that could be done with fishbread, but she would try her best to search the scales out of the dimple in the center where they always seemed to collect, and perhaps the pantry would yield something that could be persuaded into a sauce for the crusty loaf.

She was stirring flour and curdled milkish in the great stoneware bowl half an hour later when one of the interns entered the kitchen, turning her back on Pennifar without a word and rummaging through the high cupboards above the sink. Pennifar watched the thin, angular back for a moment, the quick impatient movement of the arms. It was one of the younger ones, part of that latest group that had arrived in the middle of the night a week past, to be ushered in through the seldom used side entrance by Geoffram and herself, their faces cowled and vague in the candlelight. They had kept to their rooms for the most part since then, and Pennifar was not sure of their names, though Geoffram had solemnly introduced them one by one to the gathered inhabitants of the house in the refectory the following evening: five pale, tired-looking youngsters standing awkwardly beneath the huge west window arch, the sky a streaky canvas of magenta and violet behind their drooping heads.

She'd get to know them soon enough: Geoffram had told her yesterday that he would be leaving for a short time. Normally that would put Jurian and herself in charge, but the Inbrother was going along this time, so it would be up to her to supervise the Mission till their return.

A crash of pottery brought her eyes up from the pasty yellow sauce. The girl was staring at the floor with her fists clenched at her sides, her thin body taut as a bowstring beneath the shapeless gray smock.

Pennifar sighed inaudibly and set down the heavy wooden spoon. It was her favorite mug that lay in shards on the tiled floor, the one she had carried with her from home seven long months ago.

She summoned a smile.

"Here, let's just get the dustpan," she said to the Insister. "One of those jumped out of my hand not two weeks ago. High cupboards can be treacherous country when you're as short as we are, Sister."

The pale face lifted, dark eyes looking past her while the colorless lips worked soundlessly. "Should not *be* there," came the grated words at last. "Should not, not, *not*..."

"Well." Pennifar gathered up the pieces with the shortbroom, emptied the dustpan beneath the sink. "As to that, I'm sure we can always do with a bit of organizing. I'm so used to jumble myself, I seldom think to sort things out, but maybe fresh eyes..."

She let her words trail off as the young woman turned and began to pace in the front of the sink. The Insister's pallid face seemed entirely drained of blood this evening, a narrow chip of carved ivory riding her thin shoulders as she stalked back and forth like a cornered animal, eyes darting constantly to the thick, diamond-paned window

that overlooked the back garden and the high walls of
blue brick beyond.

"What is it, child?" Pennifar moved closer, reached
out her hand. "Senwy," she said, the name coming suddenly into her mind. "It was only a mug, Senwy. What's
to—"

"Not here! *Out! Stay out!*" the Insister cried hoarsely,
recoiling from the proffered hand till the small of her back
pressed tight against the sink. Then she took a deep shud-
dering breath and seemed to freeze, her thin fingers poised
like claws on the edge of the enameled basin.

Suddenly the room swam before Pennifar's eyes like
something seen through a depth of troubled water. She
found herself groping through the thickened air, snatching
at shadows as she took a step, then another, toward the
girl's rigid body. Tears welled in her eyes, and she began
to sob in sorrow and confusion, swaying on the dull tiles
as if buffeted by great waves.

"I'll get—Geoffram," she choked. "Please—let me
get—" The words cost too much to force past her numbed
lips, and she abandoned them, wheeling toward the door
and staggering down the long hall and up the high stairs
to the sleeping quarters.

The blue door slid open before she reached it, and
Geoffram emerged, Inbrother Jurian close at his heel.
They hurried toward her, Geoffram's pinch-lipped con-
cern mirrored faintly in the younger man's austere frown.

"It's Senwy," she gasped. "Please."

"Where is she?"

"Kitchen." She waved her arm at the stairwell. "Oh,
hurry."

She slumped back against the wall and knuckled tears
from her eyes as they raced past her. She heard the old
steps creak, heard the men's passage along the lower corridor. "Oh, hurry," she said again, her eyes clamped shut,
her damp cheek pressed to the worn wallpaper. Her breast
heaved in spasms, her dry mouth moving silently in strings
of nonsense words from her distant childhood as she prayed
that they would be able to do something before the wild
heart burst in her chest.

Time dragged by. It took all her strength to descend the steps. She stood panting at the end of the hallway, eyes on the kitchen door, unable to approach it.

After an age, the door opened. Geoffram beckoned to her.

"I think the fishbread's about done, Sister," he said. "Maybe you'll join us for a cup of perry before I set the table. The others should be getting home soon."

She sat at the cooktable and sipped bland perry with them, relieved to see that hers was not the only hand that shook as it lifted cup to lips. She and Geoffram invented conversation about the weather while Jurian drank in watchful silence, his dark gaze never far from Senwy. The Insister sat huddled on her stool like something made of cloth and broken sticks, her thin face naked as a sleeper's.

After a while she stirred, her mouth moving in silent distress.

Pennifar's fingers knotted white-knuckled about the handle of her cup as the anguish began to seep back into the air; then Jurian touched his hand briefly to the thin white cheek, and Senwy settled again, jaw slack.

"You'd best take her upstairs," Geoffram said softly.

The young Brother rose obediently and left the room, Senwy trailing in his wake like a docile shadow.

"Well," Geoffram said with a sigh and a wan smile. "Storm without, storm within."

Pennifar tried to return the smile but gave up when she felt herself beginning to shake again. "It was only a mug," she said at last.

Geoffram shook his head. "She's new yet. It's still too much for her." His head tipped toward the darkened window. "The people . . . they won't stay out there where she wants them to, they keep coming in. She tries so hard. When her guard's down and they manage to get past her, she can't bear it, can't handle it at all yet without help. I'll talk to the other interns before we leave. She'll always have to have someone in the house with her."

"Do you know when yet?"

He nodded. "Ship lifts at Vespertime, two days from

now. I don't like to leave you here alone, especially with all these new folk. If someone else could go in my stead..."

"We'll manage."

"I'm sure you will." He shrugged unhappily. "It's an old friend who's called me. I've little choice."

Pennifar looked to the thick diamond-shaped panes, trying to imagine the dim, vast city beyond, where hundreds of thousands of cold lights had begun to glow. So many people... In her mind she saw the thin, desperate face, heard the cry of agony: *Out! Stay out!*

"It seems cruel sometimes," she murmured.

Geoffram stirred at her voice, and her eyes searched his tired face.

"To bring them so far from their home," she said. "To bring them to this sort of a place."

The man tilted his shallow cup and stared at the pale liquid before he drained it.

"It's past time they found a place for themselves among their own kind." His voice was gentle. "The learning is hard for them, but the reward is immeasurable, and they can expect no welcome if they will not welcome others—in whatever way they must. And none who wish to enter here shall be turned away."

2

No sight, though eyes remained open.

No sound, though ears were unblocked.

No warmth, no pain.

No input.

So the experts claimed, and they were not wrong. The snapword acted as a lever, which pushed the conscious mind into the background, loosing for a time its hold upon the sensory and nervous channels.

Drugs facilitated the amputation of the world: All Dancers were addicts of the narcotic *cessil*. Derived from the sori of a fern once found wild only on Sipril and now cultivated at great profit on the Southern Luxuriant Worlds, the drug pried loose the grip of consciousness and laid bare the seat of manipulation.

The brain controlled the body, but the patterns rode the brain—movement learned by the flesh, by the cells themselves, was summoned forth. Kinesiology had blossomed into an art, and prodigies were performed by human bodies previously hobbled by a knowledge of their own limitations. In the Dance the bodies moved like nothing human, and it was strange and often beautiful to see, but the Dancing mind was asleep and the self adrift in a timeless moment, perceiving nothing, barred from the performance.

So the experts claimed, and they were not wrong.

The Dancers said a different thing.

Thunder growled outside the window and brought Ai suddenly awake.

Seconds later a pale flash of lightning drew her from the low pallet to the pivoting circle of thick wine-blue glass set in the wall. Rubbing her eyes, she gazed out at predawn grayness blurred by the first cool veils of a light rainfall.

She shivered in her skinny and reached to turn the heavy glass on its pivot. Movement caught her eye, and she pulled the window slowly back, leaning her head out to peer along the side of the house.

On a rounded projection of pale smooth wood bordered with staves of figured candlewood and walnut, Beautife leaped and stretched silently, her pale eyes wide, her face unreadable beneath the mist of rain and the slow change of the living tattoo.

Ai watched, her heart thudding in her throat as the long body soared and the Dancer's arms and legs wove in impossibly intricate movements. Each turn and leap brought her friend to within inches of the edge of the broad platform, whose railings were decorative only and would snap like a band of twigs beneath the pressure of a falling body.

By the time she had fumbled open the door, raced halfway down the wrong hall, retraced her steps, and

burst through Beautife's room onto the small porch, the
Dance was over.

The Dancer sat with her back up against the rough
bark of the house, her breast heaving with exertion and
her long legs crossed in front of her.

"Good—morning—"

Beautife's eyes flew open. She stared at Ai, who stood
leaning on the doorframe. "And to you. Why are you
breathing like that, Ai?"

"Thought you—were going to fall—" Ai managed
another deep breath, then gestured toward the circle of
her window. "Silly. I know Dancers don't fall. Guess I
was half asleep." She came out onto the porch, hugging
the flimsy skinny to her body. The floor was cool and
springy under her bare feet, and she realized that the
porch was actually a massive slab of living tree fungus
and that it had probably consented to grow here as a
personal favor to their host. She gave a short laugh at the
thought of Emrys in earnest dialog with an adoring fungus
and lowered herself next to Beautife. "You do that for
exercise, huh, muscle tone, that sort of thing."

"Sometimes." Beautife was looking into the misty
depths of forest around and below them. Sweat mixed
with the fine droplets of rain on her forehead and arms.
She turned abruptly and met Ai's gaze. "I went looking
for him, Ai. It was a very long Dance. I thought I might
find him there this time."

"Where?" Ai felt the hairs prickle above the golden
complink at the back of her neck. "Where did you go?"

"To the place inside." A long arm rose and fell in a
curving, sinuous motion, and Beautife smiled a secret
smile. "The place we go to when our bodies Dance."

"I thought it was supposed to be just like sleep, but
without the dreams," Ai said softly. "I thought it was like
being turned off."

"Not like sleep." The Dancer pursed her lips and turned
back to peer at the thick root shapes beyond the curtain
of fine rain. "Not when you've Danced as long as we
have, for so many years. For us it's like going off somewhere, it's like a place. It builds itself. In the beginning

you don't remember much about it, just a feeling after the Dance now and again, but it builds, oh yes, till you know it when you're in there and it's more real each time." She shrugged, and the tiny smile reappeared on her profile for an instant. "Difficult to explain, Ai, if you've never been in."

"And you thought—"

"And I thought if he really was lost deep inside while he was Dancing in the Dark, then I might be able to find him. That if I keep going back, one time he'll be there."

405. Qua. 20
Self-notes

A pause to reflect. Amazing how quickly things can get so messed up. "Things" refers loosely to my life.

Have to decide what to do soon.

A week yesterday and we're still here. I never expected Emrys to reject the previous medical verdicts. Maybe some truth to this morning's spooky talk about the mind being stuck somewhere, lost in the Dancer's no-place. I don't know. Like Beautife, I thought it would all be over when we delivered the body.

Who are these people who are on their way from far away to view the body? Part of me is beginning to hope I can guess the identity of one of them—part of me feels selfish for even thinking that way.

The old man sees me as Beautife's friend, nothing more. Decided to let it stand that way for now. Less complicated if I want to move on alone. Depending on who the newcomers turn out to be I may have a quick decision to make about what to do, where to go from here.

What a twisty path this is turning into. Wonder what the Monkey Pod Boy would do?

405. Qua. 22

Can't figure Emrys out. There's something else going on that he hasn't told us about, something strange. I don't know if it's connected with March or not.

He spends most of every day at the College—"looking

for information"—arrives home late and locks himself away for a few more hours before he even eats his dinner. Sometimes I see lights flashing in the workroom when he's going in or coming out, and a few times when I happened to be standing with my ear against the door I'm positive I heard him talking to someone.

This is beginning to have all the earmarks of a story-show mystery. *The Thing in the Empty Room* . . . I don't need that kind of entertainment right now, thank you.

405. Qua. 25

There's nothing much to do here all day.

Emrys said we could go to the College with him if we wanted, but it was pretty clear he wouldn't have any time to spend showing us around, and neither one of us has taken him up on it.

Instead, Beautife and I explore the golden forest outside this house, prowling stretches of wood where we have to wade knee-deep (that's waist-deep for me) through fragrant leaves, or finding ourselves teetering on the giant rootvines above swirling, deep-channeled riverbeds.

Today we followed one of the rivers till it suddenly eluded us by ducking out of sight at the base of a mountain. Undaunted, we found a pebbly ledge along one bank and sidled in after our quarry. Just when the light from the entrance was about to run out we stumbled over a small cache of torches and a little sack of firesalt. A few minutes later and several meters farther in, our torches were reflected in the still waters of an underground lake. The ceiling of the cavern was vast, lost in darkness above us. Some kind of amphibians were perched on the rocks when we came in, but they always managed to disappear into the water with a *plop* at the approach of torchlight, so we never got a good look at them. Just as well—after the first half dozen *plops* my nervous system was in no condition for more surprises.

On the far side of the lake we found that the cavern walls had been painted and carved in fantastically intricate, eye-teasing designs. More storyshow stuff, I thought, but no bodies jumped out at us.

At evening meal when we questioned Emrys about the place, he said: "There are many who live in the Forest. What you two entered sounds like a biding place of the In-Betweens, and those are very rare. I've never seen one."

I offered to lead him back there tomorrow, but he just smiled and shook his head. "I expect I'll run across one myself one of these days," he said to me gently. "Life's very long, you know. I'm in no hurry to knock on all of my neighbors' doors just yet."

During their wanderings through the Free Forest, Ai and Beautife spoke little, sharing wonders with an exclamation or a whispered call. When sunset brought them back to the house, they returned to silence of a different sort, Emrys often shut up in his workroom with the mysterious results of a long day at the College, and the gray box in the Hearth Room seeming to dominate Beautife's thoughts to the exclusion of all else.

She appeared to Ai like a child unable to release her grief, sitting next to the *bain-sense* and frowning blank-eyed into the fire for hours every night, stirring only to rearrange her long limbs or to scratch among the ashes with an iron poker, in search of sparks.

Ai spent as much time in the Hearth Room as she could bear, often falling asleep with a book on her lap so that Beautife would have some company, should she desire it.

3

"I've never seen a terminal quite like that," Emrys said, indicating Ai's gauntlet. The two were breakfasting outside on one of the living porches. Far below them, in a patch of sunlight filtered through golden leaves, Beautife whirled and stretched. "It's a symbiont of some sort, isn't it?"

"Uh-huh." Ai rotated her arm back and forth to show him the full extent of the instrumentation. With microtools mounted on the thumb and first two fingers of her right hand, she was making tiny adjustments in one of the linkages. "The basic configuration is called a Tot—Therapeutic Organic Terminal—but this one's pretty unique. It was designed especially for me by a friend of mine. I've got a blood cell problem that kicked in along with puberty, and the doctors decided this was the best way to keep it under control. They don't like to do genetic surgery with proto-Pathfinders. They're afraid of messing up the farsight by mistake. Of course, if I take Ember, I won't need it any more because my blood will change, but till the first suffusion, Tot takes care of it for me. There." Specklights twinkled, and she shed the miniature tools. "It's mostly metalmock with a lifeskin interface. It manufactures medication and secretes it directly into my system, and in return it gets part of its energy by converting my epidermal waste products. The rest comes from sunlight."

"Interesting. These jewels are expansion nodes, aren't they?"

"Right. I've been growing it lately. But I need another one, for here, so I can start a new journal. My last one went sour."

He nodded. "I see." He returned to his tea and melon with a thoughtful look while Ai finished off her second helping of buttered honeybread.

"Hey, Emrys, can I ask you something?" She wiped her chin with a napkin and leaned forward with her elbows on the table. "Is there a chance for bringing back his mind? A real chance?" Her eyes were on the leaping figure at the edge of the forest far below them.

"I hope so. The people I've contacted—they're also pretty unique. If he can be helped, they'll help him." He smiled. "He's my friend, too, Ai. I'll try everything I can to get him back."

That evening when Ai and Beautife climbed the twisting ladder to the main entryway, they found a large green and gold diligence lashed to the landing stage. There was a strong wind blowing up from the south, and a swirl of papery leaves followed them through the door.

Inside, Emrys stood next to the *bain-sense* in earnest conversation with two men, both of them dark-haired with pale, solemn faces.

"We've just arrived." Emrys was taking the newcomers' travel cloaks. "Geoffram, Jurian, these are my new friends Beautife and Ai."

"Ai?" One of the men extended his hand with a quizzical smile.

"Short for Iris, swift-footed Antique goddess of the rainbow," she said matter-of-factly. "Nice to meet you."

Beautife had crossed immediately to the side of the sense-bath. She acknowledged the introductions with a curt nod as she stood protectively over the long casket.

"I offered them dinner," Emrys said, "but they wanted to get right to work. Shall we open it?"

There was a long pause. Then silently the tall Dancer knelt on the terra-cotta squares and raised the pearl-gray lid. Watching the newcomers' faces, Ai saw that the one called Geoffram had also known March and been his friend.

Pale Jurian joined Beautife at the side of the casket, his face clear of all emotion. He started to reach a white hand into the *bain-sense*, but Beautife caught his wrist before he could touch the still figure. His black eyes turned on her for an instant, and she released the hand as if burnt.

"Empath!" she whispered under her breath, her arm raised in a warding gesture as she shrank back from the quiet youth.

"We use the term 'communicant,'" Geoffram said softly. "It seems to suit them better. Certainly it has fewer negative connotations."

"Them?" Beautife's eyes traveled from one solemn, pale-skinned man to the other. "You're not one of them?"

He gave a slight smile. "No, the abilities are mostly hereditary, I'm afraid, though the philosophy can be shared. After years of living and working among them, I remain what I was born: a touch-man, limited to the world my own poor senses create for me." He turned his gaze to the figure in the coffin, and the smile grew sad. "I look in this box and see my old friend March peacefully asleep, nothing more. But if you'll allow Jurian to place his hand on the flesh of our friend for a moment to establish rapport between them, perhaps then we'll see a different view."

Beautife looked helplessly at Ai.

"It's a way to find out," Ai said. "Emrys wouldn't have asked them here if he didn't think they could help. It's a way to be sure."

The other woman turned to measure Jurian with her eyes. Finally she nodded. "Go ahead, then. Make us sure." She put her fingers lightly on the silver man's shoulder as Jurian laid his hand against the bare throat and closed his eyes.

In the end the process yielded only more uncertainty. Jurian sat by the *bain-sense* for almost an hour, his eyes shut and his face alternately slack and tense. Beautife sat on the floor on the other side of the box, her eyes on the fire. Ai curled up in the great warm chair and lazed through a book of poems taken from Emrys' library, while her host and Geoffram drank kahve and shared low-voiced conversation at the suspended table.

At last Jurian expelled a great sigh and opened his eyes. Ai searched for clues in the black gaze but saw only reflected firelight.

Geoffram brought the youth a shallow bowl of water. No one spoke while he drank thirstily.

"I went in as far as I could," he said at last, wiping his mouth with the back of his hand. His voice was even. "I found nothing but emptiness."

Beautife turned away.

"Is this conclusive?" Emrys looked from Jurian to Geoffram. His face was tired. "Is this our answer so soon?"

"I am an adept of the third reach," Jurian said. "I have performed the shellscan, as could any novice, and the delve. Both have told me that there is no longer sentience here." His gaze flicked to the empty silver face. "The deepdelve, however, is beyond one of my attainment. Through its use one may listen to different voices."

Emrys turned to Geoffram with a questioning look.

"For the deepdelve one must bring him to Maribon,"

Geoffram said. "The Missions are filled with novices and a few adepts. Only an imago—or one higher than an imago—can delve deeper than Jurian."

The two men looked to where Beautife sat with her back to them, silently gazing into the fire.

"Beautife?" Emrys said softly.

"I thought it would be over," came her ragged whisper. Her shoulders shook gently. "I thought we would know."

Emrys and Geoffram shared a bottle of blue before the fireplace after the others had gone to bed. They sat facing away from the *bain-sense*, speaking to each other with the tempered warmth of old friends brought together by melancholy circumstances.

"We'll have to get someone from the Community in here to give me official custody before we move . . . the body," Emrys said as he filled the deep-bellied glasses. "And then it's off to Maribon as quickly as possible. They can get Bellmaple for my lectures, and Pinconning will be only too happy to take over my seminar; he loves the opportunity to refute my theories." He shook his head. "A short visit here for you—I've just picked you up at the Port and already we're discussing your departure." He smiled at the other man. "Almost didn't recognize you with the beard off again."

They were silent for a while, each absorbed in his own thoughts. Geoffram took a sip of wine, watched the flicker of firelight on cobalt as he set the glass down.

"We have a room at the Mission I call the Hearth Room, too, you know." He gazed fondly around the chamber. "Warm like this, and comfortable. Nothing like the Hut, of course—but then, nothing ever could be." His eyes fell on Emrys. "How is your work progressing these days, by the way?"

Emrys sat for a few moments without answering.

"First part's almost finished," he said quietly, glancing behind them to the closed door of the workroom. "It's not optimum, but I doubt I can realistically expect much more than I've got at this juncture." He shrugged. "Now's as good a time as any to move on to the next stage."

Geoffram nodded thoughtfully. "Do the others know?"

"They did at one time, back when I'd just started. We haven't discussed it much. Jefany and Cil were cautiously supportive, as was Jack. Marysu was skeptical—but polite, as I remember. Nobody wanted to see me hurt, of course. I think March was the only one besides yourself to really take me seriously. He was here a few years ago, and I showed him what I'd accomplished up to that point. He asked me a lot of questions—good ones, too, things I'd never gotten around to considering..." Emrys leaned back into his chair and regarded his friend with a strange, unhappy smile. "Times like this I really wish we all could have stayed closer together. Twenty-five years and I still miss the Group! But you know, everyone's had their own lives, their own work. And we have stayed in touch, it's true—though only by ones and twos, never all of us back together again. Do you know what I mean?"

The younger man nodded wordlessly.

"Visits, lots of visits," Emrys continued. "Marysu came here three or four times, Jack with her twice—and once on his own—before the two of them headed off to Marik and Marysu's work among the catpeople. That was a few years ago now. I understood they'd been keeping in pretty close contact with Cil and Jefany and the children before that. I've visited back and forth with them several times myself, and Jefany and I spent some time on Green Asylum a while back. I even managed to run into March a couple of times... But I haven't even seen Raille for fifteen years, not in the flesh, nor you for—what, almost five?"

"More like ten."

"Ten!" He shook his head. "Yet, you know, it's still as fresh in my mind, that year, that time when we were a Group, as if it all happened last week. And lately—crazy!—I've even found myself having dreams about us all, about Belthannis and the kin. About the Group."

"Dreams..." Geoffram cocked his head to one side. "That's very odd. I've had the Group on my mind for months now. When your call came, it seemed perfectly natural to see your face again—but it's because I've been

thinking about us, all of us, for quite some time. I thought
it was just me, becoming sentimental in my dotage, then
Raille told me she'd been having the same kind of preoccupation."

"That year changed us all," Emrys said. "Who knows
how much? Raille once said that Chassman's experiment
with the kin had tapped some unknown force and that its
effects went deeper than even she could follow—deep
into the Autumnworld and deep into all of us. Cil told me
years ago that what we shared that day could conceivably
have forged a bond among us—I think she even meant it
as a physical thing, but subtle, hard to find, perhaps on
a cellular level. There was never anything there her tests
or instruments could catch..." He paused, the ambiva-
lent smile back on his lips, his eyes narrowed in memory.
"But consider the alchemy we wrought there, consider
the strange mix we made. We had seven more or less
eccentric Evaluators, to which were added two changel-
ings traveling different paths between normal humankind—whatever that is!—and the altered humanity of the
communicant mutation. Nine people and one machine
intelligence on another path altogether..." His voice grew
soft. "Tell me this strange concoction wouldn't leave its
mark in all of us, brewed as it was in the even stranger
crucible of that world Belthannis!" He laughed and
shrugged again, throwing off the mood with a self-
deprecating smile. "So, have you decided whether you'll
be coming to Maribon with us?"

"Jurian will bring you there. I've got to be getting back
to Paiak. The Outsister I left in charge has been there
only half a year. Before that she was making candles on
Chalice. Oh, she's wonderful with both house and interns,
but it's not fair to strand someone in a place like that—
and in such company—if they've had no real experience."
He rubbed his narrow jaw. "We need Jurian there, too,
in case there's a problem with the new people. One girl
in particular's not making the adjustment well. So I'll ask
for him to be sent back to the Mission as soon as his
business at home is finished."

"How do you work trips to Maribon these days with

the ban on their free travel still in effect?" Emrys asked.
"Still diverting the occasional Darkjumper as needed and
leaving the crew with muddled memories?"

Geoffram shook his head with a pained expression.
"She never lets them use their abilities simply for con-
venience. They haven't got the experience to make the
right choices yet. As purpose and desire start to come
awake in them, she works to shape their learning carefully.
No, they've got an old spaceboat they've refitted with a
jump engine. They make a run each two-month—more
often when necessary—between Delphys and Tan-to-Da
on Sipril, where the landing regulations are relatively
relaxed, and they continue on incognito from there. Wait
till you see this spaceboat—looks like it's held together
with spit and sposables, though it jumps the Dark and
does the job." He smiled ruefully. "Believe me, my first
voyage aboard the *Dolly Dorcas* was a harrowing one.
No Pathfinder, no Powermeister, all the navigating done
by instrument, which makes for a longer, more tedious
trip. And that grim-faced band of youngsters they'd put
together as their first crew—most of them trained by
Dance patterning and holo rather than experience—did
not inspire immediate confidence. But they took to it
quickly, and now I don't give it a second thought. A few
of them started out as interns in Missions I headed on
Frond and Penny Arcade, and I flatter myself that that's
part of the reason for their flexibility and willingness to
learn."

"And are you finding time for your own work, your
writing and your research? Is there another monograph
in the making?"

"Oh, I keep my journals. I've a million notes and fragments for a history of the communicants, but I hate to
tell a story when I've no idea how it's going to come out.
If I were wise, of course, I'd never publish again. If I
hadn't been so stupid as to let that treatise on Maribon
out, I'd still be able to use my own name in the Community." He gave a sigh of resignation. "Not that I'm
liable to have time to work that sort of mischief on myself
again in the near future. After I'm finished on Stone's

Throw, there'll be another group of solemn adolescents that needs planting someplace else, and then another..."

"You're still with her in this," Emrys said softly after a moment.

Geoffram nodded. "I believe in the work, Emrys—more now than at the beginning. It's their only chance to rejoin the rest of us before they drift too far into something totally foreign and unreachable. She thinks the rest of humankind will benefit from it, too, you know. Sometimes she almost makes it sound like something preordained. Her 'Entelechy,' she calls it. I don't think any of us, myself included, can see more than a fraction of the surface of the scheme she's set in motion."

"To seed the communicants among the other worlds and so educate them in the difficult art of being human. An awesome charge," Emrys mused.

"Mm. She puts it in more mundane terms," Geoffram said with a wry laugh. "'I'm folding you back into the mix before you grow too stiff to blend.' That's what she told a group of them not long ago. What a scene that was: six imagoes together in one hall, half a dozen of the most gifted and potentially powerful minds in existence—and they hung on her every word as if it were life's own breath, while the air in the chamber shimmered and twisted in their presence."

He shifted in his seat, poured them each another tot of blue, tasted his, and leaned back.

"I remember when they first brought her back to consciousness in one of their dusty towers, after raising her so carefully out of the chaos into which her mind had fled finally on Belthannis. I remember when they greeted her soon after—scarcely more than a bewildered girl in a strange place—and named her as the one who would guide their race to its destiny. If they had known the word 'god' at that point, I think they would have called her that as well. She wanted to laugh at first; then she shrank from it—but they persisted. And after a while, with her own gifts awakened and no possibility of dissembling between them, she saw the truth behind their words." He took a longer sip. "How young she seemed. I can see her face as she turned to me for help I couldn't give her. 'What am I?' she used to ask me time and again, and all I could truthfully say was that I didn't know."

"There was a word that Chassman had used near the end on Belthannis," Emrys said. "*Stetmacher*. The one who opens the door, he said, the one who makes a new picture of the world."

"Ah, poor Chassman. And poor Raille, as well. It may have been he who opened that door, but it was she who passed through." Geoffram stared at the dying fire. "She walks a thread now between her two worlds, and sometimes it frightens her. I'll come back from the newest Mission in some outlandish place—and it's always the sternest, most resistant worlds she chooses, you know, or the ones most given to excess or despair. Never the placid, never the well ordered and accepting. You won't see an Alembic House on Sipril for some time to come, nor here on University." He drank from the glass, set it carefully on the table. "I come home, and the tension sings in her voice like a plucked bowstring. 'Am I falling away, am I losing my humanity?' she'll ask me from across the room. 'Will you tell me, as you swore to, if I start to change?'" His smile was bitter. "I think at times that's my true worth and function—in their eyes, anyway: to be her mirror when she needs one."

Emrys smiled and shook his head. "You've your own place in the canon, I imagine, after all your work."

Geoffram snorted. "Indeed I have. 'Her Hand,' they call me when I'm out of the room." He eyed the round bottle speculatively, then filled his glass again. "Who would have thought it, Jon, those long years ago? That I'd be there still, and still no closer than an arm's length to her. Ha." He lifted the glass in a wobbly salute, drank deeply. "*That* was rather good, I thought." He smacked his lips. "Both, I mean: the wine and the turn of phrase."

"There must be a reason beyond the work for your staying there," Emrys said gently, his eyes on his friend's weary face.

"Yes," Geoffram said finally above the fire's sibilant whisper. "I suppose there is." There was pain and helplessness in his dark eyes. "You know, when she first woke up, I was there. She was so happy to see me... I had the Ember with me. I'd saved it for that moment, and I offered it to her. But she wouldn't take it..." His voice was ragged, almost inaudible above the crackle of flames. "I offered her life, and she wouldn't take it."

CHAPTER 7

We are always the same age inside.

GERTRUDE STEIN

1

After they snipped the auburn curl from her head and tossed it into the pit with the silver one they had taken from her mother, Raille left the small gathering in the southern fields and returned to the room that had lately been reopened and set aside for her use in the old, massive white house.

There she carefully removed the pale gray sash, the black fingerless gloves, and the heavy mourner's chain of intricately braided metal. Her two companions had come in silently from the adjoining room, and they watched as she poured the chain into its velvet case atop the dresser like a double handful of liquid silver, then bent forward to the mirror to part the hair at her forehead, solemnly inspecting the spot where the small gravelock had been removed.

She straightened with a rueful smile. "I should have asked them to take more of the gray and less of the dark," she murmured to herself, knowing that the others would not understand.

She moved slowly around the room, her hands restlessly brushing the dark wood, smoothing the bed satins, lightly tracing the faded patterns on the wallcloth before coming to rest side by side on the curving windowsill, where they pressed flat against wood still warm from the afternoon sun.

Through the circular glass she could see the trio of ornamental pools, once her grandfather's pride and home to generations of fat, slow-moving orange fish whose ancestors had been brought here to Weldon a century ago, pedigree packed with them in the shipping crate, from old Earth itself. The pools had been drained several years ago when her grandfather's health had first begun to fail and now hosted rank islands of moss and spindly weeds. She looked beyond them to the ordered rows of lemon trees, scores of emerald domes retreating toward the darkening vastness of the blue Seremonth sky.

She turned abruptly and went to the wardrobe, breathing in the mixture of must and cedar as she pulled a cloak from the shadows and drew it over her shoulders.

They were watching her. Without a spoken word she bade them wait for her return, and they settled with a soft rustling on the edge of the bed, looking like one of the pen-and-ink drawings in the yellowed storybook she had leafed through under the lamplight before finding sleep the previous night: like Peace and Quiet, their thin hands folded, their pale faces free of doubt and agitation.

She turned and left them sitting there in the slowly dimming room, suppressing the urge to run as she strode quickly through the vaulted halls lined with closed rooms and out the great front door.

She went down the wide marble steps two at a time, her somber cloak belling out behind her like a young girl's playdress. Fleeing the great house without a backward glance, she took the old path that wound up past untenanted hives aswarm now with berry vines and creepers and passed between bright ranks of nodding firestem where empty seed pods rasped and clicked in the rising evening breeze.

She emerged at the top of a rounded hill.

Once a family had gathered here for ice-cakes and lemon bread on endless summer afternoons, or to watch the sky-

fire hanging like gold and purple curtains over Gammelstad on the Special Days of early autumn.

She knelt by the nearest of four sagging benches, one
hand on the lichen-stained marble as she looked out across
the acres of field and farm and orchard from Morgan's
Bluff to the dim far side of Auvel's Lake, over the land
that had been the world to her for the first twenty years
of her life.

She shaded her eyes against the ember of the setting
sun. To the southwest, indistinct figures moved through
the Fallows in the direction of the ancient house, a single
red lantern winking behind them like a weary eye near
the spot where they had laid her grandfather deep into
the dark, rich soil of his home.

There was only a mild breeze blowing, and she raised
her hand in wonder when she felt the tears come into her
eyes. She did not touch her cheek but stood trembling
with her fingers at her throat, her face more bewildered
than sorrowful, as the night at last came down around her
in a succession of dark veils and separated her from the
long day just past.

2

"Taste it." Beautife brought a stack of blue-glazed plates
down from a cupboard beyond Ai's reach, turned with
her eyebrows raised. "Too much sweetsand?"

"Mmm, no. It's perfect." Ai leaned into the rising steam
from the fragrant pot and sniffed deeply. "Not that I care
much what I eat as a rule, but I'm going to miss this when
we get to Maribon. Maybe we should try to make up a
few batches and bring them along." She moved to the wall
opposite the cooking surface, took down a large serving
spoon, and turned back to Beautife. "In fact, Geoffram
was telling me this—"

"You're not coming with me."

Ai halted as if slapped. "Of course I am."

"Of course you're not." Beautife chopped the air with

her hand in the Dancer's sign of negation. "Not this time. I read a book about that place that some historian wrote. I found it in Emrys' library. Desolate. No life there but man and empath, did you know that? Not even a dabfly. Hot all day and cold all night, with each one long enough to make you miss the other. Dusty deserts and oily black seas. Here, give me that." She slipped the spoon from Ai's nerveless fingers. "No, you'll not be coming to that place on my account."

"Beautife—" Ai felt her face grow hot.

"I won't have it again!" Hands a hundred subtle shades of blue and gray shook as she ladled stew onto the plates. "Don't you see? He was there because I was. He came along to be with me. And now you're here. For what? You were on your way to being a Pathfinder. You've got to finish that."

"I can't just go away and never—" Ai sat down heavily on the bench, tears welling up in her eyes. "I can't, Beautife."

"No, you have to, you see. Do you want to help me? That's the way to help me. Him? You can't help him by coming along." She set the serving spoon back into the cookpot and came to sit next to Ai. "Look. An agreement." She peered earnestly into Ai's stricken face. "Six truemonths I'll give them to bring him back. Five months and two weeks from now you can come if they'll let you, for a visit only. If nothing's changed, we'll leave together."

"Where will you go then?"

"I don't know yet. I won't think about it just now. But is it agreed? Six months less two weeks before you try to come? And if you've gotten a job on some grand Darkjumper with your own tank and a barrelful of dap, you'd better not drop it like some fool—I won't appreciate that. No more damage because of me, please." She laid her long hand over Ai's small one on the table. "Agreed?"

405. Med. 1
Self-notes

And suddenly things are in motion.

In two days the *Subito* departs for Sipril with all of us on board. From Sipril, Jurian will take Emrys and Beautife with their cargo to Maribon, while Geoffram and I continue on the ship to Stone's Throw. Then Geoffram goes back to his Mission to do whatever it is he does there, and I'm off again by myself.

I talked to them down at the Port this morning, and they thought I'd have no trouble signing on as Provisional Apprentice aboard the *Subito*. Pathfinders being as uncommon as we are, most ships will gladly agree to take on an extra one—especially if she's an uncertified beginner like me—as it saves them quite a bit of dap while providing a little insurance in case anything happens to the one in the tank.

They might not be so eager if they knew their insurance was prone to unexplained attacks of blindness.

I was so upset yesterday when Beautife said she didn't want me to go to Maribon with her that it wasn't till I'd sat down and thought it through that I realized that Maribon was probably where I was supposed to be going all along. How could I tell them that now without seeming like the liar and hypocrite that I probably am? I'm sure they'd have a hard time believing that I've been thinking about March and Beautife lately rather than focusing on finding a cure for my own problems. I'm having a hard time believing it myself.

"Excuse me, can I come in?"

Emrys stood in the doorway backed by amber light from the hall. "I tapped a few times," he added. "I'm sorry to disturb you."

"No problem. I was just reading." Ai lifted the small brown volume. "Actually, I think I was probably dozing." She shrugged. "Either way, it was pure avoidance behavior. I should be packing my carrysack." She looked around the comfortable room. "I've liked it here. I'll be sorry to leave."

He came into the room and sat down cross-legged on the floor at the edge of the pallet.

"Ah, *The Wrong-Headed Friend*. I haven't read one of the Monkey Pod Boy books in years, but I used to devour each new one as it was published." He folded his hands in his lap. "You realize that you don't have to leave when the rest of us do, Ai. You're welcome to stay here and use my house for as long as you like."

"Thank you, but I have to get things going again. I have six months to fill. I'm supposed to be a Pathfinder, and the *Subito* has a berth for me, so I'm going to try that for a while." She chewed her lower lip unhappily. "I'd go with her now, Emrys, but she won't let me. I can't force myself on her."

"She wants to be alone now, Ai, and she feels very close to you. The rest of us won't matter so much, but she can't be alone if you're there." He was silent for several moments as she considered this; then he cleared his throat. "Ai, I'd like to ask you to do me a rather peculiar favor."

"Mm?" She cocked her head to one side, watching him.

"You mentioned the other day that you were looking for another expansion node for your gauntlet."

"Uh-huh. I'm getting tired of trying to decipher my own handscratching, so I thought I'd grow a journal."

"I'd like you to take this with you when you leave and keep it on your gauntlet until you come to Maribon." From his pocket he brought a small case made of carved ivory. He pried it open to display a polished cabochon of bluish green the length of his thumb from joint to tip.

Ai took the gem from its velvet nest, held it under the wall light. The stone was shot through with faint silvery threads.

"It's some kind of malachite, isn't it?" She pursed her lips. "Why do you want me to take it?"

"I'd like you to keep it safe for me." He eyed the stone in her palm with an odd expression. "It contains . . . data which I may have need for on Maribon. I obtained the information in a rather unorthodox fashion. I would be stopped if I attempted to leave University with it in my possession."

"*Sta*, I get it." She turned the smooth oval in her hand.

"You think I can smuggle your data out of here in my Tot without getting caught." She nodded to herself. "Only it's got to be more than just data. It's some kind of semi-volitional node, isn't it? That would make sense—they'd pick it up by itself, but not if it was linked to Tot."

He stared at her. "Yes, exactly. Ai, you must try to believe that I have valid reasons for asking you to . . . smuggle this to Maribon for me. Reasons that I think both the Community and University would come to accept as valid also, given sufficient time. However—" He spread his hands.

"Right. You haven't got the time if you're going to try to help March and Beautife on Maribon." She placed the gem against her upper arm and squinted at it critically. "I think it looks pretty good right about there, don't you?"

3

From My Journal,
by Raille Weldon

Strange beyond telling to be sitting here again at this dusty desk, with that world beyond the window.

Reverting to my old ways and putting inkpen to paper— paper made from pulped wood rather than sheets of waxy mica, a forgotten luxury in itself. Time rolls back, and I'm a girl of sixteen again, young Raille Kristema Weldon, solitary as a mountain hermit in a cave and writing furiously in endless argument with the world and herself as she tries to make some sense of her father's recent death.

I have only to look at the hand that holds this stylus to see that I'm no longer that young girl, but the links are many and strong between that time and this, the double-braided chain of my life: death, sadness, confusion, doubt, and longing, entwined as always with hope and joy, the promise of peace and the presence of love.

Death and sadness to the fore again.

The profound shock is missing this time. Almost thirty years ago when Father was taken, it felt as though the rare bolt of lightning that toppled the tree had sundered my life as well. But my grandfather I've seen only twice in the last twenty-five years, and if there were any clear demarcation to be drawn between having him in my life and out of it, it would have to be on that day when I boarded the ship for Belthannis down at Gammelstad. Nothing was the same after that.

I've thought about Paba often, it's true—but I will continue to do that, a fact upon which his physical passing seems to have had little effect. I will never forgive myself for remaining so far from him and from my mother, but I could see no other solution. I know that I would make the same decision if confronted with the choice again. The work was important and they were important, but I have only the one life, and it seemed after Belthannis that there might be some purpose to it after all.

When I look back now to my time on the Autumn-world, I remember it mostly as a long, slow spiral down-ward into confusion and fragmentation. I didn't know that something inside me was awakening, beginning to bring me perceptions that I could neither identify nor compre-hend.

I never thought to find myself whole again.

When I awoke among the communicants on bleak Mar-ibon, it was like being reborn, like rising slowly into a new life. When they revealed to me that I was partly of their heritage, as Chassman had been partly of mine, and that there were reasons for the things I felt and the things I found myself capable of doing, it seemed *right*, and I felt door after closed door finally opening. Portions of my life that had never made sense before fell into place, and I was at peace for a time.

Raille set the journal aside and read for a while. The books of her childhood were there in the old room: —adventure, mystery, speculation—and she wandered for a time through lands at once forgotten and familiar.

Hours had passed when she finally closed the last vol-ume and leaned back against the bolster with a sigh for her stiff neck and shoulders. She closed her eyes for a moment, then opened them and looked expectantly at the door to the next room. There was a rustle of sound; then the door clicked open, and the two novices appeared.

"Speak with me," she said.

They entered and seated themselves, one in the high-backed armchair, one perching solemnly on the dusty, velvet-covered footstool next to her bed.

There was a long silence.

"Use voice," she said, feeling their inquiries and observations like a feather's touch in her mind, watching their faces flicker in the speaking looks of young communicants—alive with minute changes of expression that would be all but imperceptible to the touch-people of this world but that her own heightened senses read effortlessly.

"Select a topic for conversation," she said.

"This place," one replied in a rough murmur, to which the other added after a moment: "This world."

She nodded. "A proper subject for your discussion. First a lifetime on Maribon, then the strange trip in the Darkjumper, and now here for three days. React and compare."

"Full of things." Dark eyes flicked briefly to the half-open circular window through which could be heard the gradually escalating disagreement of an unknown number of nightbirds. "Life in layers."

"Damp," the other one said. "Small changes in the ambient. Soft weather."

"A mild climate," she amended softly. "Most of the time, yes. Go on."

Pale hands rubbed restively against the worn brocade and fingered the wooden gape of a carved geolion.

"Just the one sun all day."

"A simple sky," the other said.

"Uncomplicated."

"Limit your repetitions of a single theme," she told them. "The conversation begins to wane."

They looked at her. Fingers worried the gap where a wooden fang had fallen out decades past.

"If reaction is exhausted, make comparison," she

prompted after a time. "If comparison does not readily offer itself, make inquiry."

The stool creaked. Minutes passed.

"At the gathering," one of them said finally, "the day after the old shell was put into the ground. One was there with a mind that stirred up the space between us."

"Yes."

Raille remembered the occurrence. It had been near the end of the memorial reception. They were all outside at the far border of the Fallows, with the family pall draped on standards among the trees at the wood's edge and three buffets set up beneath the semicircle of bright torches.

There had been plenty of coming and going, eating and drinking and laughter, the kind of friendly activity her grandfather had always enjoyed. The only thing missing was him circulating among the guests, filling cups and joking in his rough voice, using Sign with those who knew the silent language and smiling a lot with those who did not, a calloused hand cupped behind his ear when they spoke to him as if that could help him read their lips.

Her mother had been busy as always, refusing to rest as she bustled from one small table to the next to offer food, take away soiled plates and napkins, or wring her thin hands.

Raille had been standing by herself at the end of one of the little tables when she felt the sudden turbulence of an active communicant mind nearby as it sent its ripples through the deepening twilight like a stone cast into a placid pond. She had turned at once and searched with both the low and the high senses for the pair of novices, but when she located them in the dim light, they were solemnly inspecting a mold of glazed fruit at the far end of the last buffet, probing at it lightly with their pale fingertips as though they expected it to rise up from the plate at any moment and fly off into the night.

Then as she watched, they, too, became aware of the disturbance, their sleek dark heads lifting in unison to turn and scan in her direction.

About halfway between Raille and the young communicants stood a group of new arrivals, most of them childhood friends of her grandfather with their families from distant Sene Continent. At the edge of the group nearest the shadowed woods stood a tall, thin person with light brown hair who surveyed the crowd silently with great dark eyes.

One of the novices took a step toward the stranger.

Suddenly aware of the three who watched with more than eyes, the newcomer had turned and melted into the nearby trees.

Raille had sent her mind questing immediately, making contact for a second with the unknown mind before—with a flash of near-hysterical panic—the other broke the connection. After that she found nothing, though she searched far and wide with that-which-perceives. Perhaps, she had speculated, this was another variant produced by the Maribonese-Weldonese unions accomplished generations ago as part of a communicant experiment—another unforeseen combination, as different from herself as she was from her forebears.

Her thoughts returned to the room. The novices were watching her without expression.

"What we perceived may have been one of our mutual cousins—though one closer to me than to you," she told them. "Another hybrid like myself, perhaps drawn to the gathering by our own presence there."

"You are the only one of you." The rough voice struggled with the words, the thin face below its wing of dark hair as close to puzzlement as she had ever seen it.

"No. I am not unique, though once I thought as much myself. There may be many more crosses, like and unlike me, here if not on Maribon. Long ago I knew one other, but he..." She looked away from their faces, staring unseeing into the yellow lamplight. "He is most likely dead by now on a world far from this one."

She turned back to them. "Go into your room now. The hour is late. You may attempt to dream until I summon you for breakfast in the morning." Her voice was huskier than before. "The conversation is over."

* * *

The next day she returned to the high hillside overlooking the orchards to be alone with her reflections. The two novices stood some distance away, their dark eyes scanning the strange lushness of this world as if they were recording cubes, as Raille reached out to embrace her childworld with first the lower and then the higher senses.

She gloried in the flavor of the breeze, the sharp scent of berries and bittersweet brought to her by the licking tongues of cool wind.

Her mind discovered an incongruity among the flicker and babble of small life that filled the fields and orchards all around her. She sighed with resignation, following its slow approach up the path until a man stepped out onto the hill behind her, his soft brown traveling cap held diffidently in his hands.

"I've come from Gammelstad this morning, Mistress Weldon."

He stood awkwardly before one of the canted marble benches, puffing a little as he strove to catch his breath. The cap trembled under his blunt fingers, and he would not look her in the eye.

"Excuse me," he said, "but the big Screen lit up this morning after these many years. Somebody's sent a message for you from another world."

4

What name was given to the deep vales of silver meadowland that lay past the Hill and beyond the Water?

> *The Group Leader called that place the Verres, from an ancient word in the tongue of Green Asylum meaning "the eye delights."*

Which word-signs were first patterned by the panlinguist and the Dancer into the hands of the kin?

> *I come to you in friendship . . .*

A marvelous domicile was provided for the Evaluators' use
and comfort during their sojourn on the Autumnworld. Under
whose care did they reside there?

Chaos writhed on the wall before Emrys in a coat of
many colors, a great circle of confusion set amid the drifting cloud shapes of pale rose like a window on a dream.

He leaned forward in the bodyhug and squinted at the
multihued currents as he drew the fragile straps of the
wieldings over his fingers. He adjusted them carefully
until they fit snugly over his hands like skeletal gloves.

"Open transfer access," he said softly. A blue light
winked once on the rose surface of the bodyhug in
acknowledgment of his command. He sat with jaw tight,
staring expectantly at the ocean of heaving color.

Time passed. A small thread of temporarily coherent
particles caught his eye as it twisted and curled near the
edge of the silver-framed image. He watched it carefully
for as long as he dared before he spoke.

At his quiet words the wisp of colored points shuddered
once as if it were a candle flame held before his lips, then
leaned out toward the center of the imaginary sea.

He spoke again. The tiny pulsation began to drift uncertainly toward the center, growing slightly in both breadth
and richness of hue as other bits of colored light were
drawn by its wavering dance. When it had almost reached
the space directly in front of the bodyhug, it suddenly
dissolved, breaking into a myriad of tiny points that fled
in all directions like a school of startled minnows.

He watched patiently until it had re-formed, larger this
time and slightly nearer to the center than when he had
first noticed it. Again he spoke in the quiet rose room,
and again the flicker of color seemed to respond to his
words, moving steadily closer to the circle's origin before
fragmenting once more, a miniature star gone nova.

Minutes later it was there again, a wisp of tattered gold
and scarlet that was barely visible against the surge of
brighter particles. At his words the streak of color trembled and drifted into the exact center of the image.

"Now."

He braced himself and extended his arms, feeling the wieldings grow warm as power flowed into them. He lifted his hands as if in supplication to the flat surface of the image, and color flared on the wall between them. A twisting lightfall erupted out of the center of the circle and flowed downward through the narrow space between his hands in a coruscating channel that swelled and contracted in response to the small motions of his splayed fingers.

On the floor by his feet sat a small flat tray. Directed by his hands, the channel of colored light blazed downward to the tray, gathering just above its empty surface in a slender column whose colors blazed ever brighter as it grew slowly in height.

"Close transfer access," Emrys said when the formation was almost a foot in height from base to flashing top. He lowered his stiffly curved hands and flexed his fingers as the lightfall abruptly ceased.

The column of pulsing light remained, hovering above the tray and flashing wild color in the air before him.

5

Ai was standing in the open doorway when the solitary lit like an emerald green bug on the tiny landing stage. A man climbed out, his travel cloak catching behind him. He turned to pull it loose, clucking in annoyance. His badge glowed.

"God-lord, you again," Ai remarked with a shake of her head as she shepherded the man down the sloping entranceway. "Don't tell me there's only one Community employee on this whole planet."

They entered the Hearth Room.

The official fawned when Ai introduced him to the Sessept Emrys, noticed that he was having no effect on the preoccupied Scholar, and became brisk again. He acknowledged Beautife with a stiff nod, gave Geoffram and Jurian a curious glance, and approached the open *bain-sense*. Flourishing a techboard from beneath his cloak, he knelt to compare readings with the telltales. After a few minutes he straightened and turned to Emrys.

"All right then, Sessept. You can have it if you want it. It's brain-dead." He looked at the figure inside the box with a fastidious curl of his upper lip, as though he could scent an odor of decay about the silver body.

"Mind-dead, perhaps," Emrys corrected the official evenly. "Definitely not brain-dead."

The man shrugged.

"As you say. There's only the one category." He made notations on his board, glanced at his right wrist where a stream of tiny characters had just begun to flicker, and touched his stiff collar.

"I hereby confer upon Jon Emerson Tate, Sessept of University, the custody and sole control of the living entity to be known hereafter as Whilom March."

"Whilom?" Beautife had stood apart from the others during the examination, her eyes on the silver man's face. Now she raised her head in puzzlement. "What is this Whilom? He never had that name before."

"Legal designation for an individual whose previous identity has been supplanted or removed." Geoffram looked up from his low-voiced conversation with Jurian. "They used to use it for someone who was given the Senseless Sleep before they outlawed that practice. The title recognizes the former existence without perpetuating it."

"You've taken away his identity?" Beautife shook her head in angry confusion. "You're just deciding that he's gone, and right here and now you're doing this to him?"

"No, we are merely formally recognizing what has already transpired aboard the *Imca Limbra*." The official's tone was patronizing. "Sign this if you will, Sessept." He handed Emrys a tiny box, which the Scholar held briefly to each eye and returned.

"Thank you." He glanced up at Beautife. "You can hardly object to this. The man is demonstrably no longer sentient." He indicated the instrument cluster at the far end of the *bain-sense*. "The alternative to 'Whilom' would be to have it registered as the Sessept's pet."

Beautife stiffened and took a long step toward the man, fists knotting at her sides. He blinked at her in bewilderment over his board.

"If I've said anything to—"

"Not at all," Ai said. "You've got all the charm and tact of a knee to the gut." She interposed herself between the official and the towering Dancer.

"C'mon." She touched Beautife's arm lightly. "Let's go outside and hack up some dead branches for the fireplace. If he's wise, a certain Person won't be here when we get back."

6

The air outside the Port buildings smelled the way air smelled everywhere on Sipril: clean and fragrant, with the bland sweetness characteristic of the savior-grain *mulel* dominating all other odors.

Tan-to-Da Port had been constructed on a series of natural terraces, with the waiting rooms and administrative complexes on the higher levels and the broad plateau at the base reserved for the massive landing stage. Beautife and Ai walked along a flower-bordered path of crushed tourmaline on the level immediately above the stage. Half a mile below them, in the shadow of two gigantic Darkjumpers, sat a small stubby spaceboat with the name *Dolly Dorcas* carefully stencilled in faded red characters across its bow.

"You'll be up and off again in another hour or two, so Geoffram said."

Beautife paused by a fountain where water arced miraculously from one side of an open ring set atop a graceful crescent of dark blue crystal. She tugged at the straps that bound her carrysack to the lid of the hovering *bain-sense*. She had insisted on opening the casket once more before departing Sipril for Maribon, to make sure the telltales were registering properly. Now the sense-bath bobbed and dipped above the crushed gems as she tried to secure her belongings to its upper surface.

"Yes, they're refueling *Subito* in orbit. Barely time to touch the ground." Ai bent to sniff a gaudily striped flower and blinked in surprise when several of its petals turned out to be the gold and orange wings of a small translucent insect that clicked in annoyance and fluttered off on the *mulel*-laden breeze.

Beautife sighed and brushed dark hair back from her forehead. "And I suppose Emrys and Jurian will be waiting for me now. They said thirty minutes till I must join them in the little ship."

Ai brushed pollen from her nose and checked her palm. "*Sta*, it's been almost twenty. I guess we should be getting you down there."

"Right. I must remember to get a time device . . . a— what? A watch. I never know the time any more." The Dancer turned, still fiddling with the straps, her face half hidden, her expression strained and vaguely apologetic. "Where I lived on the Maren, if you want you can get a bead put in here—" Long fingers rose to brush behind one ear. "And it gives you the time without words, and other things—a news report, a storm warning . . ."

Looking down at the tipping box, she redoubled her efforts. "Damn, I can't . . . Makes you feel a part of things, you know? But now—" She gave up helplessly as a connection split beneath her fingers.

Ai reached over quickly and made the adjustments with her smaller, nimbler hands. Then the two women started silently down the path to the landing stage.

CHAPTER 8

Seek simplicity and distrust it.

ALFRED NORTH WHITEHEAD

1

In the latter half of the Great Year 385, Community Dark-jumpers had been forbidden by law to use the single modest landing stage at Gammelstad, obliging Weldon's few incoming travelers to disembark at the planet's sole artificial satellite.

It was in GY 366, a decade after the Departure of the Elyins, that the massive *Dustapple* had exploded as it settled grandly onto the landing stage one morning, leaving thousands of dead and injured among both passengers and ground workers. Initially a privately financed operation, construction of the orbital station had commenced the following year and paralleled the halfhearted rebuilding of the Gammelstad stage as public opinion ebbed and flowed about the issue. Twenty years later, Gammelstad Port had turned its focus firmly back to the sea that bordered it, and offworld travel was officially limited to the tiny shuttles that twirled infrequently between High Station and the world below.

Raille sat on a wrought-iron bench facing the window that faced the planet. There was another window like it on the opposite side of the high-domed room, a second

great curve of battleglass that showed only star-sprinkled
black. There the two novices sat side by side on the twin
to her bench, staring silently into the vastness.

There were half a dozen others in the echoing chamber,
no more: two of them bored attendants playing knock-
aderry behind the Customs counter and the rest new
arrivals from the starship that hung discreetly out of view
somewhere below the station.

They had been together there for little over two hours,
Raille and her companions waiting for the call to board
the Darkjumper, while the newcomers filled out ques-
tionnaires and wrote detailed statements of intent, then
strolled about the sparsely furnished room or sought the
benches with their faded blue cushions. The Gammelstad
shuttle that would bring them down to Weldon would not
be dispatched until the Darkjumper was safely on its way.

Raille had divided her time between the worn copy of
Varyga's *Home Again* that she had rescued from its berth
on the top shelf of the bookcase in her old bedroom and
the awesome sight of her homeworld hanging before her
like the ancient globe that still turned slowly above its
wooden base in her father's study, stirring the dust to an
endless upward spiral of motes in the beams of yellow
sunlight that powered its motion.

She had set the book down once again, drawn by the
beauty of the living world described so lovingly in its
yellowed pages, when the stranger wandered up to stand
by her bench.

"Not much competition for the real thing, is it?" He
tipped his smile toward the faded volume in her lap.

"I treasure both of them," she replied, returning his
smile politely while she willed herself to neutrality of both
voice and thought. She had no desire for conversation at
that moment, or for anything that would keep her from
savoring the last glimpse of her homeworld, especially
when she had no way of guessing how many years might
pass before she would sit there again. The urge to compel
the man to leave her side by subtle means was difficult
to suppress.

"You travel in quiet company." The man lowered himself unasked to the bench at her side, craning his neck around to watch the novices where they sat stiffly upright before the other window. He shook his head with a chuckle. "Two hours now without a word between them. I take it your friends haven't done much touring. They seem all eyes for the wonders of the great beyond."

Raille murmured assent, her own eyes on the blue-bordered crescent of Teme Continent, still visible beneath the wisps of gathering clouds.

Rain tonight, she thought, picturing the weed-choked pools below her bedroom window filling with clear rain-water. Her mother would have them drained by mid-morning. Her mind drifted back to the final bitter parting by the steps of the old white house. *You needn't make the trip when I go into the ground*, had been her mother's last words before turning her furious, tear-stained face away from the carriage. In her mind, Raille watched the gaunt figure recede into the distance, one thin hand shaking as it clutched stems of thorny bittersweet through a lacy fold of her mourning robe.

She heard a cough and became conscious once again of the man by her side. "It's true," she said. "Yet we travel well together. They're not inclined to conversation, nor am I."

"Ah, I see." His smile was undaunted. "At least not the sort my ears would overhear, hm?"

She turned to look at the man closely for the first time. He was smiling cheerfully, and at first she thought his choice of words had been mere chance. But her automatic shellscan brought surprising information. Raille's first impulse had been to place his age near her own, judging him by his lined forehead and gray-streaked temples rather than the youthful voice and manner. She had been apply-ing the standards of the world that hung before them, having encountered no one since her arrival on Weldon whose *noia* betrayed the use of Ember. No one until now. Though by accent and bearing the man was a native of her planet, and thus forbidden by Weldonese law the use of the Elyin longevity drug, the surface evaluation performed by her enhanced perceptions told her that his years numbered more than three times her own tally.

He bowed his head sardonically under her scrutiny. "I knew you when I sat down here unbidden, Raille Weldon," he said. "And now, I suspect, you must know me as well."

"Only that you're not what I first took you for—not much more than that." She inclined her head to one side in negation, then lifted it again in query. '*Vyu se Weldonei tuvyu?*'

"*Arr'da,*" he replied at once in the same tongue—*I used to be*—and memories hid his present feelings like wisps of cloud.

"How do you come to know me?" She waited, but when he did not answer, she realized what he must be expecting. "Despite what you may have heard of us, of me, I would never delve another's mind without true need," she told him. "I'm afraid you'll have to use words if you want me to know something about you."

"Ah, words." He tilted his face to the great disk that filled half the viewing glass. "Well, in words, then, I have an abiding interest in that blue jewel out there, though I may no longer freely tread its earth. But my nets are always out for knowledge of the homeworld and its more intriguing sons and daughters."

"You fish in strange waters, I think, to catch news of me."

He shrugged amiably. "Perhaps I like strange fish."

Raille had been studying the dark hair, the regular but unremarkable features. Somewhere, in a magazine or a news journal: a faded photograph . . . Suddenly she leaned forward, the worn volume slipping from her lap.

The man caught it deftly and handed it back to her.

"I know you," she said, staring back and forth in wonder from the book to the man who had placed it back in her hands. "Years ago you left Weldon, long before my birth, to see the other worlds of humankind."

He gave a weary nod, ran his fingers back through his hair. "But I stayed away too long."

"Yes, and they wouldn't let you back because of that. And because you took the Ember."

"My 'vile addiction.'" He smiled wryly.

"They took away your citizenship. And then—" Her fingers traced the lettering raised in faded gilt on the creased spine. "Then you wrote down your feelings about the world where you were born, and everyone who read them fell in love, myself included—oh, so long ago, when I was a child—but still they wouldn't let you come back. I wept when I first heard the story. I must have been fifteen, sixteen by then." She stared at him, at Weldon hanging in the viewing glass. "But here you are."

"Yes. A visitor," he said quietly. "At suitable intervals, for a suitable fee. Once a ten-year they let me buy myself a Tourist Pass and came down for a month or two, sworn not to tell my name. I wander fields and city streets; I sleep in farmers' cottages or lakeside inns. Soon it's time to leave, and I'm sad and poor again and I have to write some more."

"Is that why you write now? So you can come back here?"

"Perhaps," he said with a shrug. "Or is it the other way around at this point? One of many things I've yet to understand about myself. Oh, writing—I could tell you about writing and how it works for me! I want to write, I fix myself some food or drink instead." He patted his middle with a rueful smile. "I want to write, I hie myself down to the Wall on Frond and net the first Drifter who's read a book of mine, or claims to have. And then rarely—when I can catch myself by surprise—I want to write and I . . . write!" His brows went up, creasing the high forehead in childish wonderment. "And there are, really, so many things I want to say. That's what decided me, finally, after so long, to start the Ember." He gave her a sidelong glance that said clearly: *I know you don't believe that.*

"Weren't you worried that with the Ember all the pressure would be gone?" she asked. "With no more fear of time running out, weren't you worried that you'd end up writing nothing at all?"

"Yes! Really!" His jaw muscles said: *Kiri! You do*

understand! "But the Ember's just a cushion, you know. It's not armor. We will die eventually—we all will." He waved his hand at the span of battleglass. "Someday I'll be hanging here looking down when a meteor slips through the shoofield in one of those freak once-in-a-millions, or I'll go down to the Wall for a bite and a tumble and eat something that's been mutated the wrong way." He screwed up his face in a comical death mask. "The point is, it'll happen. But till it does—" He looked around the immaculate shabbiness of the waiting room, his dark eyes coming to rest again on the great window with its round of blue. "I have things to say." He met her gaze and lifted an eyebrow. "I'll be wanting your story someday, you know. This work you've begun. So far I've just had bits and pieces, but I'm content to wait for another time. Ten years from now, or fifty. Perhaps you'll be waiting to go down that day and I'll have just come up."

"I don't know," she said. "I haven't taken the drug."

"Will you?"

"I don't know," she said again. It was her turn to look away. "But tell me about your writing. What have you done since *The Magicians* and the Antique story collections?"

"Well, let's see, there've been some poems, three solemn little volumes, actually, under the name Verge LaGray, a novel published on Frond as Reave Galgry, and another in the Vegan style from a small press on Dunbar's World."

"As?"

"Hm." He looked toward the ceiling. "Either myself or Alvery Regga. I don't quite remember."

"Verge LaGray, Reave Galgry, Alvery—what was it?—Regga?" Raille suddenly found herself laughing for the first time in days. "I'll find them all, thank you. Anything else?"

"Oh, well, there was that series of books—my own favorites, really—that I wrote as Norton Erb."

"Norton Erb!" She looked at him in beseeching wonder. "Where in the world did you—?"

But he only shrugged, raising an eyebrow again with

a quirk of his lips. "Come now," he said. "Does everything have to make sense right away?"

2

Geoffram had spent most of the relatively short trip from Sipril to Stone's Throw in the company of Ai. When the time came to say good-bye beneath the greenrain trees in the spacious Park on board the *Subito*, he had found it a surprisingly difficult task.

During the trip he had talked with Ai for hours, quickly impressed with her vitality and humor and the unflagging curiosity with which she inspected every new thing or concept. They had talked at length about his work at the Missions, and he found himself pouring forth far more of his doubts and aspirations concerning the communicants that he had planned. Her listening skills were extraordinary for one so young, though he realized later that she had said little about herself or her own background during their talks.

When he left the Port, he tried to tell himself that the hollow feeling that had settled in the pit of his stomach was caused by worry about March and nothing else.

The huge old house on Amabile Boulevard was a welcome sight when he finally climbed out of the leaky-roofed cab and sprinted through the pouring rain up the slippery walk. Soft golden light shone through the Hearth Room window arches, and he knew that Pennifar had kept the fire going against his return.

He found her in the kitchen, humming tunelessly as she immersed the last of the dinner plates in the steaming sink. Next to her stood two pale-faced children in brown work smocks, the oldest no more than ten and the other perhaps two years younger, who blinked solemnly when he entered the room and continued with their drying and stacking duties.

"Ah, you made it after all!" Pennifar set aside a mismated cup and saucer and wiped her hands on her apron.

Geoffram leaned down to hug the short, plump woman. "Ah, it's good to see you, good to be back." He straightened and arched his eyebrows at her water-soaked helpers. "I see we've grown in my absence."

"Yes, these two sea otters joined us just last weekend. Soveny brought them back with her from Maribon. Say hello to Geoffram, children."

Two pairs of black eyes stared at him. After a moment he felt a faint thrill, like the brush of moth wings on the skin of his forearms.

"Voice, too, please," Pennifar said. "We're not communicants."

"Hello," the tall one said. "I'm not really an otter."

"Hello," Geoffram said. "I'm glad to hear it. Do you have a name?"

"No, but Medry does. They're finding me a new one. The one they were going to give me turned out to be a bad word on Stone's Throw, so they took it back."

"I see. Well, I'm sure we'll come up with something. Medry, can you say hello?"

"Hello," the shorter one said gravely. "I'm taking the water off the dishes with a towel. We ate the food off them already."

Geoffram smiled. "I'll bet it was delicious if Sister Pennifar fixed it for you. Something smells awfully good in here."

"They'd eat bricks and drink dishwater without knowing the difference," Pennifar said in an undertone as she brushed past him to stoop over the great black oven door. "But as a matter of fact it was a pastry of *mulel* and cheese, and I've saved you some if you're hungry."

"Wonderful, I'm starved."

"We ate the food already," Medry observed. "Hour of six, eat the food." The great dark eyes regarded Geoffram dubiously.

"Geoffram's dining a bit late tonight, child," Pennifar said as she slipped a shining plate from the stack by the sink. "He wasn't on the planet when the rest of us dined. I think that's a fair excuse, don't you?"

* * *

Pennifar sent the little ones upstairs to bed, then joined Geoffram at the big table in the Hearth Room. While he ate, she did her best to catch him up on the occurrences of the past few weeks.

"Habbany's baby was ill for three days, so I let her stay here overnight twice. She's got no heat at her place half the time. A doctor-woman came finally with a prayer book and some high-priced medicine, but Habbany had Toss fetch a great yellow cheese from the stall, and the woman accepted that in place of money after some haggling and a bit of preaching from the curative texts. The baby's fine, and now Habbany wants to talk to you about moving in on a permanent basis." Pennifar shrugged. "There's still the two attic rooms. I told her a bit about what we did here, and she seemed interested. In my opinion, she'd make a good Outsister if you approve. She does well with the interns. Last week she was doing her best to teach them a song." Pennifar's eyes looked to the ceiling. "Lord, you never heard such a screeching from human throats before! I thought we were going to be thrown out of the neighborhood for sure. Which brings me, unfortunately, to this—" She reached for the chair behind her and laid a dozen yellow message squares by Geoffram's elbow on the dark table.

He examined them with a sigh, picked out the earliest, and began to read. An hour later he was out of the house again and on his way to the Authority Building, hoping to decipher the meaning behind the vague and contradictory notices, several of which seemed to threaten the inhabitants of Alembic House with imminent eviction were "suitable action" not taken upon his return to Paiak City.

"I'm sorry to burden you with this so soon," Pennifar had said when he finished reading and set the last one back atop the pile with a sigh. "But one or two of them were marked urgent. I went down there twice last week to try to get to the bottom of the matter, but of course they couldn't discuss Municipal business with a woman."

"No, it's fine, Pennifar. I'll go on down there when I've finished my kahve and see who's been complaining about what this time." His brief smile was fatigued but genuine. "I'll be glad to get back into things, anyway, you know. I need something to put my thoughts back in order again after the trip."

She had found herself pondering the source of the wistful look that had crept onto Geoffram's face with that last sentence.

Pennifar was just settling back in the single upholstered chair in the Hearth Room, her latest communication from home balanced on the threadbare arm, when the front door knocker creaked once and rattled to noisy life.

She patted Cousin Hewel's unopened letter with a sigh and bent to search for her worn scuffs beneath the chair. As she was pushing herself to her feet, she heard light steps rapidly descending the front stairs. The door opened, and there was a brief exchange of words, then she heard it shut abruptly again. When she peered out of the Hearth Room, she saw Senwy slowly mounting the stairs in her white nightshift.

Pennifar looked at the closed door. "Who was it, Senwy? Did they have the wrong house?"

Dark eyes considered her. A pale hand tapped idly on the loose wooden railing. "It was a touch-man girl. She didn't have a house."

Senwy went back to her measured climbing as Pennifar came slowly down the narrow hall.

"What did she want? Senwy, come down here."

The girl turned immediately in midstep and began to descend, her eyes on her toes as they winked and vanished at the hem of her shift. Before she reached the floor, the knocker burst into life again, shaking the door with its insistent assault.

"Acceptance," Senwy said quietly. "Identity." The young communicant watched as Pennifar bustled over to the door. "Resolution. Successful outcome."

Pennifar shook her head. "Oh, hush, child," she said as she tugged at the quivering door.

Despite Senwy's words, Pennifar had been prepared by the force of the knocking to face a towering, red-faced Culpate with fists like hams, but the girl who stood glowering on the doorstep was shorter than Senwy and almost as thin and pale. That was the extent of the resemblance: the newcomer's unevenly cropped hair was deep auburn red where the rain had plastered it to her head, and the frown of irritation on her fine-boned face was clearly not the product of a communicant's disciplined temperament.

"Please forgive us," Pennifar said. "Can I help you?"

"I hope so. I'm looking for someone, and it's wet out here." Eyes narrowed accusingly at Senwy where the young communicant stood perched on the edge of the bottom step of the staircase. "Do you mind if I step inside before the door takes aim at my nose again?"

"Of course. Come in by the fire and dry off."

Pennifar ushered the visitor past the shadowed foyer and down the hall to the Hearth Room. Watching impassively as the pair disappeared into the firelit room, Senwy scratched the side of her nose with a thin finger, then returned upstairs.

"Your concierge has an unusual sense of humor." The girl peeled off her light travel cloak and draped it on a high-backed chair before the fire. "She must be wonderful with bill collectors."

"Don't mind Senwy, please. She didn't mean any harm." Pennifar brought her shivering guest to the cushioned armchair and angled it to face the fire. "Would you like some hot kahve, a glass of perry? My name is Pennifar."

"Nice to meet you," said the girl. "I'm Ai, short for Ailanthus, the famous Tree of Heaven revered in Antiquity on old Earth. I'd take a glass of warm tea if you have it, with maybe just a touch of sweetsand." She sneezed violently. "I'm here to see Geoffram. Is he around?"

"Ah, I see! I'm afraid there's no sweetsand to be found in Paiak, but we do have a bottle of honeyed onomel in the pantry if that would do." She pushed through the swinging door, reappeared shortly with a squat amber bottle, a tiny self-heating teapot, and two glass mugs on a lacquered tray. "I'm afraid Geoffram's just gone out. He had business to attend to down in Redemption Square."

"Whoa, that's plenty. Just a sip." Ai tasted the steaming

tea then reached for the amber bottle and filled the mug to the brim with honeyed liqueur. She stoppered the bottle and returned it to the tray. "Thanks. Very tasty. You say he's out on business at this hour?" She frowned at the darkened window. "He's only just arrived home. Couldn't it wait till morning?"

"The Authority Building never closes," Pennifar said with a small shake of her head. "And unfortunately it was a matter of some urgency." She glanced at the age-darkened clock on the mantle. "He shouldn't be long if you don't mind waiting."

"Not at all." Ai looked at the empty table. "You wouldn't happen to have a small bite to eat, would you? I missed my dinner quite a while ago."

They moved into the kitchen, Ai sitting on a stool at the long cooktable while Pennifar prepared a stew of left-overs. Ai told the Outsister briefly of her connection to Geoffram, saying only that they had met recently at the house of a mutual acquaintance and gotten to know each other during the trip on the Darkjumper from Sipril.

"Do you plan to stay here in Paiak during your visit to Stone's Throw?" Pennifar asked as she ladled out two bowls of vegetable-laden stew.

"I'm not sure yet. I'd like to," Ai said. "This smells great! What do you do here besides making wonderful food and keeping Senwy away from the door? Geoffram told me a little about the place, but it's different from what I imagined."

Pennifar smiled. "Yes, it's easy to lose sight of the high striving when all you can see is the bills that need paying and the mouths to feed. That's mostly my job, to keep the house running and make sure the children wear clothes when they go out. And just to be here for them when things happen that they don't yet understand. Some of them are rather new at this and—" She paused uncertainly, looking at Ai.

"The ones who've arrived most recently from Maribon, you mean, right?" Ai smiled reassuringly. "I've talked a lot with Geoffram. I understand who they are and a little of what you're trying to accomplish with them."

"Ah, I wasn't sure. Sometimes it's hard to know how people will react."

There was a sound from the swinging door behind Ai, and Pennifar raised her eyebrows in surprise. "Oh, faith, what have we here?"

Ai twisted in her seat to see a pale, dark-haired child of about seven or eight wander into the kitchen and, passing by the two of them without glance or comment, begin to pry with thin fingers at the heavy door of the coldbox.

Pennifar clucked her tongue and shook her head.

"Aren't they supposed to wear clothes inside the house, too?" Ai inquired, watching the thin white shoulder blades as the small-boned arm pulled at the heavy door.

"Indeed they are," Pennifar said with a sigh, "though what harm it could do anyone to see this little bundle of sticks unwrapped is beyond me. Medry, Medry, what are you doing down here, child? It's very late."

The thin fingers continued to tug at the unyielding door, and at last Pennifar pushed herself to her feet with a grunt and placed her plump hand lightly on the pallid shoulder. "Are you hungry? Do you want something to eat?"

Ai took advantage of the moment to pour herself another half mug of undiluted onomel. "They all look hungry to me," she said after a deep draught of the sweet liquid.

Pennifar shook the thin frame gently. "Are you awake? Why did you come down here, child?"

The narrow white face regarded her blankly.

"Hour of twelve," the child said at last in a voice that was half yawn. "Hour of twelve, eat the food."

Pennifar smiled, shaking her head fondly as she slowly rotated the child's small body to face the dark diamonds of the kitchen window. "You look out there and tell me what you see."

The child considered the window silently.

"Is it day, Medry?" Pennifar prompted softly after a moment. "You tell me, is it day or is it night?"

"Night," came the thin whisper.

"Right! And there are two twelves to the clock here,

remember? It's a different way of keeping the hours. Which one is this, would you say?"

Again the look of earnest appraisal. "The second. Twelve of the night."

"Right. And when do we eat our midmeal?"

"Twelve of the day." The young communicant swiveled out from under the plump hand and padded slowly toward the door.

"Unless you really are hungry, child," Pennifar called hopefully. "Would you like something to eat now, anyway? I'll spread you a slice of new bread with jam and a little wynsal on it..."

But the thin white figure was already pushing through the doorway and into the narrow hall.

"Ah, well." Pennifar lifted her shoulders and turned back to Ai. "Hasn't learned the food schedule yet, poor thing."

"You keep them on a food schedule?"

"Just until they learn to eat when they should, or even when they want to—instead of when they're near starvation. They'll wait till the body's ready to devour itself sometimes if you haven't put them on a regular schedule. But most of them pick up the habit after a while. That one's just a little mixed up."

"Fascinating," Ai said. "Is there really jam and wynsal?"

As the hours passed Pennifar began to stifle yawns behind her hand. Ai insisted that she would stay up to greet Geoffram on his return from the Authority Building, and at last the Outsister left her curled up with a book from her carrysack in the comfortable old armchair before the fire. Before long the combination of fatigue and onomel proved too much for her thin frame, and the small brown volume dropped silently to the braided rug beneath the chair.

She grumbled sleepily when she felt the hand gently shaking her shoulder.

"I'm up, I'm up," she said, knuckling her eyes and stretching in a protracted yawn.

Geoffram stood over her with a piece of paper folded in one hand and a look of complete astonishment on his tired face. He lifted the paper. "'There is a visitor waiting for you in the Hearth Room.'" He shook his head. "I couldn't imagine who it might be."

"It's I." She grinned sleepily. "Or Ai. Take your pick."

"Short for *ai-ai*, I suppose, the rare lemur-sloth found only in the rain forests of World Hispany." He returned her grin. "Ai, what in the world are you doing in Paiak? What happened to the *Subito*?"

"It took off without me," she said, pulling herself erect and looking at the clock on the mantel. "And what I'm doing in Paiak is staying here, if you'll let me. Will you? I'm willing to work, within reason. Pennifar and I get along well, although some of the kids are a little strange. She said they were learning to sing—I can teach them "Pilots, I See You" before the song even gets to Stone's Throw and make them the envy of all their little friends. Can I stay?"

"Of course you can stay, but—"

"Look, the way I see it, I'd end up stopping back here in a while, anyway, right? I'd never find my way to Maribon by myself." She looked at the fireplace, where a few scraps of wood still smoldered. "I couldn't stay on the ship. I made them let me get off at the last minute. They weren't very pleased." She turned back to him. "Maybe Beautife wants to be alone right now, but I sure don't, and I know a wonderful recipe for gullion if you can find me some leeks. So what do you say?"

CHAPTER 9

*Perhaps the most difficult hurdle for the
panlinguist to leap when considering the
language of the communicants is the total
absence of any arbitrary concept-bearing
symbols. The language has no words. The closest
analogy one can find to the morpheme used in
spoken languages is in fact the* mote, *an
indivisible representation of a single emotional
unit that is transmitted directly from one
communicant mind to another via processes not
yet fully understood.
The argument: When minds that have been cast
in a similar mold as a result of mutagenic
environmental influences are further tuned or
calibrated by certain stylized early experiences,
then the same stimuli cannot fail to call forth
identical responses in different individuals. Thus,
the communication of complex messages bearing
both concrete and abstract content may be
accomplished solely through the exchange of
specific emotional reactions to the subject under
discussion . . .*

FROM TOWARD A SYNTAX OF EMOTION,
ANONYMOUS MONOGRAPH PRESENTED
15 MELDING 393 TO THE 137TH
PANLINGUIST CONCORDANCE AT
DELAUNCE ON BABEL

1

They had given him a room near the top of one of the
domed towers at the edge of the city. The room was

long and narrow, and the walls were not quite straight, curving in and out to give it the appearance of a giant's sarcophagus. The furnishings consisted of a sleeping platform, a broad desk, and a bench, all carved from the same colorless stone as the walls and ceiling. There was a shallow closet with a single shelf at one end of the room, a primitive habitual at the other. Beautife's quarters were three stories below his, a slightly smaller room that she had insisted on sharing with the pearl-gray coffin.

The nights had been chill since Emrys' arrival; he had finally given up on the layers of thin coverlets and requested the use of a small electric heater at the foot of his bed. He was glad of the lingering coolness during the daytime and spent most of his waking hours indoors, shielded from the blazing heat of Mizar and the Companions while he worked with his wieldings and the strange containers of multichrome light that he had brought with him to Maribon. There were two rows of diagonal slits cut into either side of his room; through one set he occasionally glimpsed Beautife at her exercises in the dusty courtyard, her unclothed body gleaming with sweat as she leaped and spun beneath the sallow sky, completely unnoticed by the gray-robed figures passing back and forth along the colonnade. She had begun to take the silver man out of his casket for longer periods each day, and several times Emrys had watched entranced as his friend's body Danced flawlessly beside Beautife's, the simple calisthenics that had been programmed years ago into nerve and muscle still responding to the snapword's catalyst.

Through the other window slits he could look out over the plain dust of rocks that served the city as a landing field. Early one morning the roar of a descending spacecraft drew him out of bed to the narrow windows, blinking the sleep from his eyes as he watched the squat shape of the *Dolly Dorcas* thunder down on its bulb of blue fire and shakily touch the barren ground.

A small surface vehicle arrived soon after to collect the disembarking crew; all except a single dark-cowled

figure climbed on board and were whisked back to the
city gates on a cushion of churning air and dust.

He returned to the center of the room and dressed
quickly in the undergarments, shirt, and loose trousers of
cool, undyed linen that had been given to him upon his
arrival on Maribon sixteen days earlier.

He descended the steep stone spiral and paused with
eyes averted before the entrance to Beautife's room.
The tower in which they resided was located in the oldest
section of the city, and none of its rooms had doors,
personal privacy being a fairly recent concept in Delphys.

She was sitting on the stone floor with her long legs
crossed, making tiny adjustments to the strands of blinking wires that stretched from the patterning nodes on the
floor up the stiff legs of the silver man who stood like a
statue at her side. She jabbed here and there at the unmoving thighs, her fingers bristling with microtools and her
brow furrowed in concentration, looking for all the world
like a tailor performing last-minute alterations on a suit
of expensive clothing.

She glanced up when Emrys cleared his throat.

"She's here?" She spat half a dozen seedlights into her
palm and returned them to a bowl near her feet. "Will
she want to see him right away, do you think? I'd better
put some clothes on him, get rid of this *cessemin* gar-
bage." Her fingers shook as she peeled the slender wires
from the taut leg muscles. The silver figure began to slump
gradually forward as the patterning frame was removed.
Beautife reached up and absently tapped out a short
sequence on the side of a bare forearm; the body straightened immediately.

"I wouldn't bother bringing him down now," Emrys
said. "I expect she'll want to rest a bit first."

"Oh." Beautife looked from his face to the blank silver
countenance. "Of course. I'd best put him away, then. He'll
want to be at his best." Tilting her chin upward, she pitched
her voice to a sharp whisper. *"Ya, sed, nep!"*

The man wheeled obediently, stalked with stiff-legged

precision across the little room, and stood swaying next to the open *bain-sense*.

"*Ki, to, ki!*"

He lowered himself into the box, his limbs trembling spasmodically, lay back slowly, and closed his mismatched eyes.

"Needs more exercise to sharpen those patterns," Beautife murmured critically. "Fade and blur are inevitable if I don't rehearse from time to time." She tapped her chin thoughtfully. "Tomorrow I want to start him back on solid food. I'll work out the patterns tonight. No more of this dermal protein business. His jaw will start to atrophy."

They met Jurian at the bottom of the tower.

"I was coming to get you," the young man said, the hint of quiet inflection in his voice seeming like a gush of emotion in contrast to the mechanical delivery of his less experienced brothers and sisters in the city around them. "She decided to walk in from the ship. It's only a mile. She wanted to 'stretch the legs.' She's just gone to the central refectory. This way." He looked back over his shoulder as they started off. "The city is filled with excitement at Her return."

They followed him down the long covered walkway that bordered one side of the empty courtyard. Silent communicants of various rank passed them, their pale faces impassive as they glided by on thin-soled sandals.

She was sitting alone near the head of one of the long stone tables that divided the room, her shoulders bent over a bowl of steaming gray-white gruel. The dark cowl was thrown back, and Emrys glimpsed strands of gray among the rich auburn of her hair.

Still no Ember, he thought. Her expression when she lifted her eyes told him that she had probably caught the emotion behind the thought as he had entered the room, for she smiled with a slight shake of her head.

"Belated welcome to my home, Jon. I hope they've made you comfortable, though they've little understanding of the concept as it applies to noncommunicants." She rose to her feet and extended her hands. "You look well, at any rate."

"Raille." For an instant he felt tears gathering in his eyes. He held her hands and laughed self-consciously. "It's been far too long. The Screen's no substitute."

"I know. We've both had our work. And this is March's friend." Raille's calm eyes scanned the oval face under its softly moving haze of blue and gray on which other ghostly colors bloomed and faded.

"Beautife of Street of Dreams," Emrys said. "This is Raille Weldon of Weldon, an old and very dear friend of both March and myself."

The Dancer looked down at the smaller woman. "Please help him, Raille." Her voice was husky with emotion.

"I will see what can be done for him here, Beautife, and try my best to do it." Raille looked past them to the dark figure that had remained in the doorway. "Jurian, the ship will be returning to Sipril tomorrow. It is your wish to resume your place in the Mission of Stone's Throw as soon as possible?"

The young man nodded gravely. "It is my belief that I am of use there and it was Your—it was Geoffram's wish that I return."

"Come see me before you leave. I will have words for you to bring to him."

Jurian bowed his head and left the room.

Emrys felt sure that the entire voiced conversation with its polite inquiry, its nods and explanations, had been provided out of courtesy to Beautife and himself. He knew that speech would not have been needed to convey the information had Raille not wished to use it.

"He reminds me a little of Chassman," he said after a moment. "Not Chassman as he was at the beginning when he came to us—but later, after the change had come and he wasn't quite so solemn."

Raille nodded. "They exchange the Teachings for inner guidance slowly," she said. "We take great care that *stet* is not shed too quickly, leaving them naked with no clear way to go." She smiled up at Beautife's expression. "Once all of the communicants thought themselves of the same mind and so followed the same path, believing it to be the Way, perfection, which they called *stet*. Then a great change occurred, and for the past quarter century they have allowed me to slowly muddy the clarity of their vision, forcing them to begin to rely on inner will rather than outer direction. It hasn't been an easy road for them."

"Nor for you, I would think, if it's been your responsibility," Beautife said softly. "Don't they hate you for giving them this uncertainty?"

"On the contrary," Raille said. "Those that have such depths of feeling love me far too much." She leaned forward with her elbows on the rough table and smoothed back her loose hair. "Oh, I'm glad to be back, strange as that must sound to you." She looked down at her half-eaten bowl of gruel. "I'm too used to this place to be comfortable away from it for any extended period. I've gotten accustomed to dust and wind, nettlecakes and gruel. You know, I don't think my stomach would have survived another day of taffysweets and lemon bread. Weldon's grown too rich for me in my absence: the food, the air, the people..."

"Raille, I'm sorry about your grandfather," Emrys said. There was a short silence.

"So am I," Raille said. She straightened in her seat, and smiled wanly. "Beautife, Jon, please sit. I want to know as much as possible about what happened before I try to deepdelve him."

Wishing for Ai with her facility with words, Beautife slowly recounted what she was starting to think of as *The Diver's Tale*, beginning with the formation of the team and ending with their last venture into the Dark.

Raille listened silently until the end, then sat back and looked at the sad-eyed Dancer. "You mentioned that some members of the Darkdiver team reported unusual sensations during their explorations. March included?"

"Yes. At least three different times before the last Dive. I myself felt it, but only once. Like a presence, a touch..." She gestured vaguely near her forehead. "I don't know how to describe it. Perhaps if we'd had one of your people with us . . ." She shrugged.

Emrys was watching Raille. "Do you think that could be significant?"

"I don't know. I watched NewsNet on the trip from Weldon to Sipril; I listened to members of the crew and to the passengers. People are still saying that there's something in there, something that 'eats spaceships,' as one man put it. Many of them are terrified by the thought; they need calmative drugs to get them through a jump without panic. And one report I heard on the Net said that a private group is preparing to jump in and spray hard radiation throughout a section of the Dark. The Community overgovernment won't give them permission because of possible danger to other ships, but the leader, a man named Ansalvage, threatens to go ahead with the plan, anyway, 'if something isn't done soon'—whatever he means by that."

"He means that we have a pack of diehard Expansionists who are still willing to stir up a dead issue, no matter what the cost." Emrys shook his head. "Never able to deal with a problem unless they've got someone to blame it on, something to attack—even if they have to invent the something themselves before they can attack it."

"You have another theory about what's happened to March, don't you?" Raille asked gently. "I can feel it in your voice, Jon."

Emrys looked uncomfortable. "It's not quite a theory yet. More of a feeling." Glancing at Beautife, he took a breath. "Beautife, I don't know how much March ever talked to you about the time before he came to you on the Maren, but we—March and Raille and I, the man you know as Geoffram, and some other people—we were all involved in . . . an unusual experience on another world. It resulted in bringing us all very close to one another— literally, I mean, as well as emotionally. Our minds flowed together for a short time during an experiment conducted by a communicant, an experiment involving mind transfer to a creature that had no mind." He turned to look at

Raille. "It had occurred to me that what has happened to March could be the result of that experience, some sort of leftover effect of that brief linkage. That perhaps he had become years later like the kin of Belthannis: mindless and empty."

"That possibility had occurred to me as well, Jon." Raille returned his look steadily, then turned to include Beautife in her gaze. "There is one way to find out. But first I must rest awhile and gather my strength for the task."

"I'll go back to the tower," Beautife said, her face ashen under the living tattoo. "To make sure he's ready, to prepare him . . ." Her voice faded as she rose from the table.

"We've left a thought unspoken," Raille said quietly when the Dancer had gone from the refectory. "If what we fear is true, and March's mind was lost as a result of the coming together with the kin that we all shared—then why was his the only mind to be so affected?" Her finger traced the rim of the bowl absently as she stared into the eyes of her friend. "What of the rest of us, Jon?"

"I've been wondering the same thing," he said. He felt a cold trickle of sweat run down his side beneath the cool linen. "Perhaps it's time we notified the others."

2

Jurian climbed the ramp and entered the main chamber of the little ship. He threw back his cowl and brushed white dust from his cloak.

He sensed the presence of other communicants. They were members of the previous day's crew, finishing up the final checks before they turned the *Dolly Dorcas* over to their replacements.

A tall communicant emerged from the crew section. He was called Domi—not as the others were given names when it became time for them to mingle with the touchmen on other worlds but as a designation of his function on board the ship. *Domi* had signified "pilot" in one of the old languages once spoken on Maribon, and Domi would be his name for the few minutes left before his replacement came on board.

Jurian acknowledged the other man's presence silently. Then the two conversed in the manner encouraged by Raille, practicing a combination of small gestures, voiced words, body movements, and hints of facial expression: all the lower forms of communication regularly employed by touch-men, here surrounded and enhanced by the clear, unceasing flowing of the high sense between them.

Back now? Domi asked Jurian, his eyelids widening a fraction in the pidgin of communicant and touch-man language.

Yes. How soon the lifting?

Not long. New crew approaches. Hear what happened?

?

Last place: "Sipril-city." *Three went-there for purchase touch-man food. HER wish. Alleyway: man/violence/child.*

Do?

Communicant intervention: that-which-compels. Violence halted. Friend-of-man/information/others. Group-in-anger. Many minds catching fury. "Kill dirty empaths." *Group/violence/communicants. Objects hurled. One struck: body damaged, mind suspended. Two left, too little power.*

Happen?

New presence. SHE there. In-search-of-communicants. Reaching out: many motes changed, dissolved, reformed. Touch-men-anger halted, confounded. Put-to-dreams by HER power.

Safe?

All.

Unpleasant occurrence.

Incorrect. Domi emphasized his disagreement with a small quiver of his nostrils. *Instructive. SHE demonstrated. We learned-by-sharing. HER use of power* "glorious." *Now comprehend. Next trip: two-month-hence,*

"Sipril-city," *I go-there. Happen touch-men fill-with-fury. Self/that-which-compels/touch-men.*

? Not necessary.

Will be necessary. Refuse conceal communicant identity. Happen group-in-anger. Self/sting-words/touch-men.

Not HER wish. Forbidden.

Happen-finish, I-tell-her. SHE is teacher. SHE will understand.

Heavy boots sounded on the ramp, and members of the new crew began to file into the chamber. The tall communicant turned away from Jurian. He surrendered his name as he raised his cowl and ducked out into the dusty wind, and a short woman with curly black hair and a round face became Domi for the duration of the trip to come.

When Jurian arrived at Paiak City four weeks later, he found Ai waiting for him in the crowded Port. She lounged against one of the fat columns of the vast Reception Room with her thumbs in the pockets of her vest and a pair of young communicants in tow. She waved to him as he emerged from the long Customs line.

"How's Beautife? How's Emrys? How's March?" She took his bulky carrysack and handed it to the smaller of the children. "Can you manage that? Are you sure? If not, get Otter to help you."

"I'm manageable by myself," the pale-faced child replied, staggering off in front of them as they began to walk. Ai turned to the older child.

"Otter, it's your job to make sure Medry gets the carrysack to the cab in one piece. Follow along, but don't be too obvious."

"So?" She turned back to Jurian with a grin. "You haven't answered my questions. *You* look fine, anyway, same as always. Maybe a little thinner. Are you surprised to see me here?"

"No." Jurian found the use of the word "surprise" excessive in most cases. With few predetermined convictions, most communicants were rarely, if ever, truly surprised by the events of the world.

He looked ahead to the two small figures, one listing noticeably to the right under the weight of the carrysack and the other tiptoeing behind in careful pursuit from column to column.

"New," he said.

"Yup. Youngest yet, says Pennifar. Just got here the week before me. There's also a local woman named Habbany and her little boy—they moved in right after me. See what happens when you go away for a while? The whole neighborhood goes to hell. Whoops—we're losing them. Better hurry."

When the four of them were safely ensconced in the creaking cab, Ai turned to Jurian once more. "Has there been any progress? We can't raise them on the Screen. Interference from one of your meddling suns."

"She returned the day before I left on the *Dolly Dorcas*. They were making plans to deepdelve, but nothing had yet been done."

Ai clucked her tongue in disappointment. "Wonder how Beautife's taking it . . . Medry, get your face in out of that window. Do you want the whole city to know it's been invaded?"

The little communicant straightened in the worn seat with a thoughtful frown, leaned close to Otter. "Is that what Sister Pennifar was talking about?"

The older child nodded solemnly. "I think so." Dark eyes turned to Jurian. "Was that a joke?"

"I'm not sure." He shrugged. "Ai?"

"God-lord, aren't we home yet?" Ai put her chin on her fist and stared glumly out the window. "I'm hopelessly outnumbered in here."

Geoffram met them on the steps of Alembic House. He greeted Jurian warmly, and the two of them retired to the Hearth Room, where the latter delivered the brief messages that Raille had asked him to convey to Her Hand. After half an hour's awkward conversation about Darkjumpers and Maribon, Geoffram blurted suddenly: "Ai's with us now."

"So I see," Jurian said.

"She'll be returning to Maribon in a few months' time, so it seemed to make sense for her to stay here," Geoffram explained. "She's sort of a temporary Outsister, and Pennifar finds her a great help. They've started a little candle-making business in the cellar."

Jurian was to discover in the days that followed that Ai's influence had already contributed to more than the cartload of fanciful candle shapes that she and Habbany parked by the cheese seller's booth each day at Matintime. Soon after his return he began to notice a small but significant change in the usually unpredictable behavior of Insister Senwy.

Still withdrawn one minute and palsied with uncontrollable fear or anger the next, Senwy nonetheless seemed to have formed a special attachment to Ai and in her more placid moments was to be found increasingly in the company of the other girl.

For her part, Ai treated the troubled communicant as if she were a shy younger sister, alternately coaxing and bullying her into interactions with the rest of the household and the frightening world outside the Mission.

"She's just more vulnerable than the others in that way—though you'll notice they all feel it to some extent." Pennifar counted out a handful of small square coins from her purse. "All right, I guess we'll settle for this one." She deposited the money in the rough palm of the fish-bread woman and laid the crusty loaf carefully into her basket. She smiled at Ai.

"Fear and love and envy are all foreign to them. We have to remember that. There's been none of it on Maribon for generations, except among the bondsmen—and I'm told they're hardly representative of the human norm after all this time. So the communicants come to places like this where they're forced to live among people and to spend time learning about emotions without controlling them. It's hard for some of them to leave things be, you know. To feel anger in another person and let it alone. To touch love without exploiting it, or sorrow without erasing it."

"What would be so bad about getting rid of someone's sorrow?" Ai reached under the fishbread with distaste and pulled out an apple, which she shined on her vest as they walked. "And anger—seems to me a place like this could do without some of that." She bit through the dark skin and began to chew the tart flesh noisily.

"You don't mean that, though, do you?" Pennifar said. "That might be somebody else's argument, but I don't think it's yours."

"Why, because it wouldn't be real? Because it'd just take care of the symptoms without solving the problems? I don't know, Pennifar—sometimes the symptoms can be pretty awful. Seems like we ought to get something in return for letting them eavesdrop on all our feelings." Ai twirled the stripped core in her fingers and tossed it over the river-wall into the slow-moving waters of the Purgative.

"We do, Ai—haven't you felt it?" Pennifar's voice was low, her eyes on the violet streaks of sunset before them. "There's a peace that comes just from being around sometimes."

Ai snorted. "God-lord, you can't tell me it makes you feel peaceful to be around Senwy?"

"No, not Senwy, not yet. But the others—the ones who've been at it longer, like Jurian and Soveny. You watch for it, Ai, and you'll find it. There's something they bring to us, the more human they become, without even being aware of it themselves. So there's giving on both sides, you see."

3

Raille Weldon sat on a massive stone bench in a vaulted chamber dimly illuminated by the narrow diagonal window slashes set like a series of methodical stab wounds in the rough wall high above her head. Near her unshod feet a small oil lamp added its wavering yellow light to the delineation of the room. On the stone floor, shadows twitched and shrank, while dust motes streamed in the oily smoke and lent substance to the pale beams of daylight entering far above.

Flanking Raille on lesser slabs of unpolished basalt were two aged communicants, their bent forms rendered sexless by the coarse cloth that swathed them in stark white and black. The faces that peered from beneath the deep hoods as if from the mouths of caves were free of the strong lines of character, though webbed under a layer of pasty white cosmetic with many fine wrinkles.

Emrys sat off to one side, feeling more like an observer at some incomprehensible religious rite than a participant in a carefully thought out experimental procedure.

He had his own rough bench, the pitted surface softened by several foldings of the length of ancient green drapery he had discovered on a shelf in his quarters. He had been trying to spread the faded fabric unobtrusively beneath his bottom when Raille entered the room with her attendants some minutes earlier.

"Not quite the Hearth Room, is it?" she had commented with a fleeting smile, the combination of words and expression making her seem suddenly, briefly, exactly as he remembered her from twenty-five years ago on Belthannis: lost in a book at the great *oke* table in the Hut's central chamber or sitting with her knees drawn up at the base of a black-barked tree, her fingers twisting strands of auburn hair as she looked out over crystal brook and green-silver meadow.

"Self-indulgence," he had muttered, returning the smile with an embarrassed shrug. "One of the many perquisites of advanced age."

How absurd for me to say that on this of all worlds, he had thought as they took their seats. He studied them, conscious of the incongruity of appearance and reality. Before him were three spans of years that summed together could not quite equal *half* of his own lifetime. The two elderly communicants lowered their matchstick bones and sagging flesh onto the rough black stone without complaint, though one of them—a male, he hazarded, from the shape of the artificially whitened features beneath the

cowl—quaked continuously in evidence of a nerve dis-
order that was no doubt caused, or at least exacerbated,
by the body's unchecked deterioration. Their matching
robes of white-trimmed jet marked them as imagoes, communicants of the highest reach and most refined abilities.

Raille herself was dressed simply in a long blue shift
under an outercloak of unadorned brown wool. Emrys
looked from her straight back beneath its flow of autumn-
colored hair to the graceful hands folded in her lap. She
was forty-five trueyears old. Without benefit of Ember,
and subjected as she had been for the past quarter century
to the harsh extremes of Maribon's climate, she had begun
to look her body's age and more.

Emrys looked to the center of the room, where for the
past half hour the silver-skinned man had been standing
almost motionless, a sketchy latticework of fine wires and
blinking seedlights visible at shoulders, neck, and the out-
sides of both legs. Beautife had arranged him carefully in
the patterning frame, stood watching him for an agonized
minute of indecision, then finally fled the room.

Raille had been sitting with her eyes shut and her head
bent slightly forward since her arrival.

She straightened abruptly, as though she had heard at
last what she had been straining to listen for, and turned
to Emrys, indicating the still figure before them with a
tilt of her jaw.

"In I go, then," she said without preamble, the youthful
smile flickering about her lips once more.

To the imagoes at her side she murmured. "Hold me
now."

They made no outward response, the one still as stone,
the other trembling softly.

Raille allowed her eyes to close again. At once she
began to sway slightly on the bench as if surrounded by
a rushing current, hands clasping and unclasping in her
lap, a look of gathering concentration on her face.

Then the air itself started to boil in front of the silver
man like the churning of clear water.

Emrys felt his skin prickle, and he remembered a similar experience in another chamber half a long pentade

ago, when a figure clothed in gray had knelt beside an open casket and caused the air to writhe and whirl between them.

Perspiration beaded Raille's forehead, gleamed against the silver brow before her. The two imagoes had slumped gradually forward on their benches, eyes half shut and mouths hanging loosely open against their black robes. They remained in that position, both still as statues, and Emrys found that he could no longer recall which one of them had trembled.

Minutes passed with their breathing the only sound in the dim room, then Raille half rose from the bench with her eyes still shut, her head and upper body leaning so far forward the Emrys was certain she would topple onto the floor at the silver man's feet. As he readied himself to rise, the two imagoes began a soft murmuring in voices that scraped like flat stones, and the sound seemed to draw at Raille until at last she straightened and blindly seated herself again.

More time went by. Emrys was stifling a yawn when Raille suddenly raised her left hand to her throat.

With a shock that tingled in his stomach, he watched as the silver man slowly aped the gesture, blunt fingers rising to claw feebly at the base of the light-wreathed neck. Emrys felt gooseflesh tighten along his arms. Something was stirring in the impassive silver features, and he thought he saw a flicker in the dull brown eye. His own eyes darted between the two figures as Raille's mouth began to work silently, painfully, her throat convulsing around unuttered words; seconds later the silver man's jaw gaped and his lips writhed in counterpoint. Emrys gripped the rough-edged stone beneath him until his fingers ached.

Behind Raille, the ancient imagoes rocked blindly on their benches, muttering softly and plucking at their garments with pale, clawlike hands.

Then Raille's eyes flew open, locking with the brown/green gaze of the man who faced her. Someone in the room took a deep breath, and all action seemed to freeze.

"Raille?" Emrys asked softly, his heart thudding. "March?"

They spoke at the same moment: one in a clear, musical voice, the other hoarsely and with great effort.

There is life in here! cried the two triumphant voices in the shadowed chamber.

CHAPTER 10

*He huddled in the bottom of the rocking basket
and tried hard not to cry. Bone whimpered at his
side, and he scratched her ears gently while he
stared up at the great blue gasbag above their
heads. Comforted, she licked his nose, turned
twice in a tight circle, and lay down to sleep with
her head on her paws.*

*At last he found the courage to pull himself up
and look out over the side of the swaying basket.
In front of him was the sunset, a glory of colors
draped across the sky like a handful of ribbons.
Beneath him lay the quiet Meander, and behind
him the Old Mountains dozed peacefully as Bone
under the darkening sky. It wasn't a new place
after all, but an old familiar one seen from a new
point of view.*

*Reaching down to scratch Bone's ears, the
Monkey Pod Boy settled back and watched the
approach of the far horizon.*

FROM THE WAYWARD AIRSHIP,
BY NORTON ERB

1

Pink morning clouds scudded high above the black sprawl
of city skyline. The breeze from the river was uncom-
monly fresh, most of the foul scents that usually rode it
momentarily absent. Children played a game with hoops
and pebbles at the edge of the cobbled street, while their
elders hurried by to office cubicles and noisy market stalls.

This is going to be a good day, Jurian thought as he walked along the sloping river-wall.

He pounced on the observation immediately and tried to trace it to its point of origin in his thoughts. He gave up, dissatisfied, after a few moments, unsure as always whether the seemingly spontaneous emotion had been his own—or merely a stray borrowed from the unguarded mind of a passerby on the crowded boulevard.

The faces he passed as he turned down Amabile failed to convince him that anyone else abroad this morning shared his feelings about the unfolding day, and he decided with a shrug to accept sole responsibility for the small expression of optimism.

Geoffram and Ai were coming out of the door as he mounted the flaking blue-painted porch.

"Well, you're up and out awfully early," Geoffram said. "We're going shopping for leeks. Ai has somehow convinced Pennifar that she can create a fabulous gullion for evenmeal if only she has some fresh leeks, so I've volunteered to guide her to the vegetable stalls down by the Moiety. She's never been to that part of the city."

"Convinced, huh? You don't sound like you believe I can do it." Ai was sorting a stack of brown envelopes that she had pulled from the mailbox. "Bills, bills. Here—" She handed them to Jurian and stuck her hands in the pockets of her worn vest. "All right, faithful guide," she said to Geoffram. "Lead the way."

Geoffram lifted his brows at Jurian, with an expression that the Inbrother could not immediately classify. "We won't be late."

The two of them headed down the path, Ai running ahead to tug the heavy gate open over Geoffram's protests and usher her smiling companion through with a low bow.

Jurian stood watching them as they turned down the uneven sidewalk. The emotions that he sensed from Geoffram when Ai was near were new ones, subtle and often contradictory.

He brought the mail to the refectory and set it where Pennifar would be sure to notice it. On his way back down the hallway, Jurian found himself pausing at the kitchen door. He opened it a crack and peered inside.

Senwy was seated at the cooktable with one of Pennifar's recipe books propped open before her. Her thin body was bent forward in apparent absorption in the text, but Jurian read clearly the barely concealed anticipation, the eagerness that lay beneath the taut lines of arm and spine.

At the other end of the kitchen a small boy of about ten had entered stealthily through the open back door. Jurian recognized him as one of the neighborhood street children—"alley rats" as old Koppoten next door would say—who roamed the block for untended food and vendables by day and huddled together in their rags, a dozen or more to an alley, for warmth and protection at night.

With his gaze focused tightly on Senwy's back, the boy slipped noiselessly on bare and impossibly dirty feet to the high counter at the left of the pantry door. Extending a skinny arm without taking his eye from the motionless Insister, he carefully removed one of the fat loaves of musselbread that Pennifar had purchased the day before. An exultant grin trembling through the dirt smears on his face, he began to edge slowly toward the waiting doorway.

When he was less than two paces from freedom, Senwy said a word.

Her voice was soft, almost inaudible, though to Jurian she seemed to hiss with malice and triumph. The boy stood frozen on the inner doormat, his brows knit in dull shock. Senwy lifted her head slowly and turned her face in his direction, the high sense uncoiling toward him as she reached for his unprotected mind. The boy collapsed on the floor with a sob of mortal terror. Senwy rose slowly to her feet, and the terror on the grimy face turned to utter despair.

At the other end of the room, Jurian pushed the door open.

Senwy whirled around at the noise. Jurian's face showed only its habitual solemn blankness, but the Insister reacted to his presence as if she had been struck.

"He was taking our bread." She backed away from Jurian, bumped against a stool, which overturned with a hollow thump on the tile floor. "He's done it before. I remembered the face."

"The bread is his to have," Jurian said. "Ours only to give freely, within the Mission and without."

"Yes, to give." Senwy's thin jaw rose. "But he was taking it, and without understanding. He must be made to see that it would be given him if—"

"His belly understands the bread," the pale man said quietly. "Undo what you have done. Give benison, give him the bread."

She moved stiffly to obey him, scooping the loaf from the floor where it had tumbled and thrusting it into the boy's limp hands. His face began to relax gradually, and he scrambled to his feet, his eyes darting between them. He edged from the room with a wary glance at Senwy, then fled through the doorway with a shout of triumph.

"A sting-word! You're sure?" Geoffram halted beneath the group of iron-colored statues that lowered like thunderheads above the low archway leading into Redemption Square. Jurian stopped at his side. "Who taught her to do that?"

The light afternoon breeze lifted Jurian's collar against his pale cheek and left his dark glossy hair in disarray. High above, two airskates played chase among the black spires, dipping and soaring with faint keening whistles. Jurian raised his eyes to the racing shapes. "Who gave them the skies? Some things need no teaching when the will to use them is there."

Geoffram frowned up at the stern iron faces above the arch, shook his head in defeat. "She'll have to go back. We can't pretend there's been any real improvement— quite the opposite. She could jeopardize the whole Mission if she stays here." They began to walk again, passing through the arch and into the somber square itself. "I hate to give up on her. Ai's been working so hard. If Senwy could just learn some control..."

"She fears the gifts that others give her," Jurian said after a while. "Envy, suspicion, hatred she can handle. But the odd kindness, the casual acceptance, wounds her in some way, and she cannot bear to be given so much by those she feels powerless to repay. I agree that she should leave."

Pennifar sat with her head bowed, her plump hands folded before her on the mended tablecloth, when Geoffram informed her of his decision at the end of evenmeal.

"It's true," she said at last. "One of the others told me the same thing once after watching Senwy at work in the yard. The little children from next door kept dashing in and out, teasing her, trying to get her to play with them, showering her with attention. 'She feels like a vessel into which the whole world pours its offerings,' Soveny said to me. And I've seen it myself. The vessel is filled; it can hold no more. I'm afraid we've lost one of them, Geoffram."

He drew his hand over his forehead and sighed unhappily. "I'll be taking her back on the next ship bound for Sipril. I've already sent word to Delphys."

"The *Imca Limbra*," Jurian said from the other side of the room. "Due to lift for Sipril and beyond this Latterday." He leaned on the mantel, reading a smeary pamphlet from the Authority Building in the light from the fireplace. "We'll have to put some wards on her before you leave—unless you were planning for me to—"

"No, thank you, Jurian. I've been thinking recently that it's high time I took myself home and let you two commence running this place."

"We'll miss you," Pennifar said. "Lord help the Mission."

Jurian said nothing.

"You're both extremely competent, and you know it," Geoffram said. "No better intern, no better extern anywhere. Give it a month, you'll have forgotten my name."

Just then the door from the kitchen squeaked open, and Ai shuffled into the room, balancing plate and pottery mug on a stack of brightly bound books. "Sorry I'm late. I was reading, and I lost track of time. Thanks for keeping my plate warm, Pennifar." She unloaded her burdens and looked from face to face in the quiet room. "Uh oh, what's going on?"

"And then," Geoffram said softly after a moment, "you'll have Ai here to help you, too."

She caught up to Geoffram in the long downstairs corridor.

It was midmorning, and her sleeves were rolled up, her right arm slick to the elbow with water and suds. Tousled hair sprouted in tufts above the faded blue and white bandana she had knotted over one ear. "I'm coming with you on the ship."

"But—" He looked startled. "You—"

"Fine." She nodded briskly. "I'll take that for a yes. Look—" She raised her damp hand when he started to open his mouth again. "It's the *Imca Limbra*, right? I worked for them for almost a whole month. I'm a Pathfinder. They'll let me ride for free if I promise to sign up again someday, so if it's the dap you're worried about—"

"No, Ai, of course not, but—"

"Wait." She began to tick the points off on her thin fingers as she spoke. "Senwy needs a friend with her, someone she can trust. You're wonderful, but you're not someone she can talk to, like me. Emrys gave me something of his to keep for a while. Now I have to give it back. And I want to know what's happened to March. We've had no word in months because of the problems with their stupid Screen. It's almost time for me to go back, anyway, and I'm sure Beautife won't care if I'm a few weeks early."

"All right. Enough." He raised his own hands in laughing surrender. "You're coming. I'll be glad of the company. We leave in two days."

"Prime. I packed last night. Now I've got a wash to supervise and shopping for Pennifar." She headed back toward the stairs. "Laugh more, Geoff," she called as she rounded the bannister. "It looks good on you."

Scarlet red from collar to hairline, he continued on hs way to the kitchen.

* * *

They stood in the Port waiting room among a group of stolid emigrants bound for new lives on the Maren. To one side a woman with an eye patch argued luggage quotas in a low monotone with a gray-faced Port official. Outside, the wind blew scraps of yellow paper across the huge landing stage, deserted except for the single vast shape bulking like a mountain at the far end of the field, the focus of an endless stream of small inspection vehicles and cargo trams.

Senwy leaned against a crate with eyes downcast, one white hand playing listlessly with a loose button on her brown travel coat. Her face had a vacant, unfocused look that Ai found difficult to watch for very long.

Geoffram stood next to Jurian at one of the tinted windows. "Well, a quarter hour and we board the tram. Hard to believe we're actually going to leave on time."

"You haven't lifted yet," Jurian said.

"No," Geoffram said. "We haven't. You know that if you need anything—if you or Pennifar have any problems at all—just send the word and I'll be back."

Jurian nodded.

"Well, then..." Geoffram rocked on his heels for a moment, hands clasped behind his back. "Jurian, I'll miss you. Here—" He extended his hand to the other man. "I count you among my friends now, and I've gotten so used to having you around for support, it's going to be very difficult for a while."

"Sometimes we mark a thing only by its absence." Jurian held Geoffram's hand awkwardly for a few seconds, then released it. "I believe my people are especially prone to this, measuring what was there only by the gap it leaves. I will also miss you, Geoffram, and the work that we have done together."

Geoffram nodded. "Be happy, Jurian. Even if it's something you have to practice. It's just as important as the work."

Jurian gave a small shrug. "Perhaps happiness is for the next generation. It is a difficult thing to gauge, whether one is happy. But I have known contentment and satis-

faction in your company, and I am confident I will recognize them when I find them again."

A low gong began to sound. Geoffram lifted his head,
glancing in surprise at the wallclock as the emigrants began
to shuffle toward the doorway.

"Early!" he said. "Perhaps there's hope for this world
yet."

Senwy moved as one in a dream, docile and unde-
manding, responding when spoken to but initiating no
conversation. After they had settled her with a gently
crooning musicball in the central sleeproom of their triple,
Ai insisted on taking Geoffram on a tour of her ship. She
brought him to the velodrome, where crouching cyclists
chased each other endlessly, then tried to talk him into a
dip in the swimfield. When he declined, she suggested a
barefoot stroll through her favorite place on the ship, and
to this he agreed.

They stood together in the narrow pop-up near the
arcade on Seven Level Two, and the world changed around
them.

The blue circle on the floor became a hollow tube rising
about them. For a moment they were standing in a fea-
tureless cylinder, then a crack of brilliance appeared at
the bottom of the pop-up.

Silvered light spilled first on their pale feet, then climbed
the length of their bodies. A scented breeze swirled in as
the blue wall rose slowly past their eyes and vanished
into brightness above their heads. Then they were standing under an open sky, the illusion of teleportation complete, as the wind explored their hair and searched for
ways inside their loose clothing.

"See? Paradise! Did I exaggerate?" Ai skipped out into
the meadow, drawing in a great lungful of fresh, sweet
air. She pirouetted to face Geoffram and stopped in her
tracks, her thin arms dropping to her sides. "What's
wrong?"

Her companion stood frozen at the center of the faint
blue ring that marked the pop-up, a look of utter disbelief
distorting his quiet features.

She reached his side in two long strides and tugged gently at his sleeve. "C'mon, get out or it'll take you back to the concourse. What is it, Geoffram?"

"Oh, Lords," he whispered huskily, following her a few steps into the meadow. "I don't know what it is—for it couldn't be what it seems."

"What? What do you see?" She turned and tried to follow his gaze, finding nothing astonishing in the arrangement of silver-green meadows like a handful of carefully scattered gems beneath a sky of cloudy pearl, or any cause for concern in the far-off blues and grays of rounded mountains or the nearby stand of tall black trees that defined a portion of the horizon in a pattern of bold brushstrokes.

When she turned back to him, his eyes were on her face; he was studying her thin features closely as if trying to reconcile her familiar presence with the rest of a waking dream.

"I see the past," he said at last, his voice still thick with emotion. "I see a world I never thought to walk again." His arm lifted in a helpless gesture that included the fields and the distant slopes, the clear, quick spring hurrying by their feet, the patches of pale blue moss that glowed in the shadows of the nearest trees. "But here before me..."

"Ohhh, I think I see." Ai nodded slowly. "The designer of the ambient must have been to that world and taken a liking to it himself. I think they usually make them up so as not to favor anybody—but maybe there weren't many people on this one? It's such a pretty place, I'm surprised it was real. Was it thickly populated?"

"No—no, not at all." He was turning around in a slow circle, a small smile beginning to curve his lips, his dark eyes shining. "It must've been him. I remember now, we heard that he was going after his architechnical certificate. He said he wanted to do environs for a while. I wonder how long ago..."

"Tot can find out where the signature is, if you want." Ai chittered to her gauntlet, cocked her head at the flashed reply. She swung her arm in a careful arc, paused when it *ping*ed. "This way."

The gauntlet led them to a small hill crowned with a round plaque of greenish metal that was almost covered by the silver grass. When Ai put her palm against its smooth surface, a voice spoke in the air above them.

"Fifteen Fervery, GY 394." The voice had a shading of wistful humor. "*Autumnworld*, by Diamant."

Ai raised her brows, straightened, and took a sudden startled look around, as if seeing the environ for the first time. "Autumnworld?" she breathed.

Geoffram was smiling. "It has to be him. It sounded like him. Diamant. With that singular memory of his, who else could it be?" He took a great breath of air, released it slowly. "Ahhh. And didn't I hear her call him 'Jack of Diamonds' once or twice?"

They wandered the Park for several hours each day, sometimes in conversation, more often walking silently till Ai's stomach alerted them to the approach of even-meal. Occasionally they brought Senwy with them, but usually she remained behind in the sleeproom, her mind suspended in a peaceful dream by Jurian and the other communicants on Stone's Throw against the day when greater powers on Maribon would unlock the wards.

A few times they encountered other passengers in the Park, but they began to choose times that seemed unpopular among their fellow travelers, and many of their visits were spent in solitude. Often Ai brought stacks of books from the ship's library for them to read, recommending this Antique novel or that contemporary anthology. Geoffram seemed content to lie in the grass and watch her turning pages, her back against a black-barked tree and her auburn hair glowing like an ember in the light from the silver sky.

One day when they were strolling back to their rooms from the Park, Ai led them down a deserted corridor on one of the lower levels. She drew Geoffram's attention to a series of narrow parallel bands running along the wall.

Subtle colors pulsed along some of the bands at varying intervals, and Ai traced one with her fingernail as they walked.

"These information strips are for the Crew to read. See, this means we're on our last jump before Sipril, and this one shows how long we've been in the Dark. Hm, it's been a long one . . . We should be coming out any time now." She turned her eyes to the ceiling. "That means the Pathfinder's already in the tank, ready for the signal that we're back in normal space and she can start to guide us in to Port." She blew her cheeks out in a sigh. "Wish I was up there instead of her. I've never seen space around Sipril before, not even in simulation . . ."

"Do you think you'll go back to it now?" Geoffram asked after a moment. They had rounded a corner, and the corridor was beginning to slope perceptibly upward. "Be a Pathfinder full-time?"

Ai opened her mouth to reply, then her eyes widened and she stared past Geoffram to the opposite wall.

"What is it?" He looked to where a single thin strip had suddenly come to life near the base of the wall, blazing with an angry yellow pulse that seemed almost audible in the narrow hallway.

"An alarm," Ai said as the throbbing rose in intensity. "God-lord, can you feel that? They're using subsonics. It must be all over the ship."

"What does it mean? What's happening?"

"I'm not sure. I've only seen it once before." She turned and stared at him. "In the holo Beautife showed me. It's the alarm that went off while March was in the Dark that last time."

"Lords. Can we call someone, can we find out—" A new thought struck him, and he paled. "Senwy! She's alone in the room. We've got to get to her."

"Here—this way."

Ai raced down the corridor with Geoffram puffing close behind her till they reached the shortway door design she had remembered passing minutes before. The entrance faded at the touch of her hand, and they hopped through. There was a shuttle tube connection halfway down the shortway where they found a shuntcar that brought them to the level of their sleeproom in less than sixty seconds.

They were approaching the door when they felt it.

Like waves rushing through the corridor, the fear and agony swept over them with an almost tangible force. Ai collapsed with a grunt against the wall while Geoffram lurched to the door, tears streaming down his cheeks, and slapped his palm frantically at the sensing plate.

They dragged themselves inside.

"It's empty." Geoffram appeared from the middle bed-bay, his face haggard. He wiped his eyes. "The subsonics must've broken through the wards somehow." He looked to the hallway. "It's like a maze out there. She could be anywhere."

Ai swayed as the room seemed to tilt, the very air churning before her eyes. "We've got to get to her!"

They made their way back into the corridor. They could hear a low roaring noise above the subsonic hum that seemed to be coming from the direction of the main concourse. Ai identified it after a few moments: the screams of a terrified crowd.

Pure panic filled the air around them.

"God-lord, she'll hurt herself, she'll destroy the ship. They don't know what's happening. The Crew at their stations . . ."

Ai sank to her knees while the corridor bucked and swam around her. There were few choices left. She began her breathing exercises, trying to blot out the terror that throbbed with every beat of her heart.

"What are you doing?" Geoffram knelt beside her and put his arm around her shoulder.

No distractions. She pushed him away.

"I have to try to farsee," she said hoarsely. "I have to find her."

"Ai, no! You know you can't farsee while we're still in the Dark. It'll swallow your mind! And there're people running everywhere—it's chaos. You told me yourself that Pathfinders never use the farsight unless they're in the tank, at the precise heart of the ship. It's too dangerous."

"I've got to try!" she cried. "No time, no other way—now leave me alone, *please*."

There was silence for a few moments, and she felt Geoffram leave her side. Then he was back.

"All right. Here. Look—" She blinked an eye open. In his trembling palm was a small sposable containing an ampule of clear purple liquid. He pushed it into a pocket of her vest. "If you find her, just press this against her skin."

The ragged noise from the concourse grew as the waves of fear increased in intensity once again, and Geoffram fell back shaking against the wall. From blurred eyes he watched as Ai staggered to her feet, her eyes shut and her face pinched tight in concentration. She lurched off down the corridor.

It wasn't quite as bad as she'd expected. The quaking terror actually receded a bit when she concentrated on farseeing. She moved along the concourse slowly, stumbling over inert limbs and writhing bodies that lay too near her to be observed as she tried desperately to locate Senwy among the mad torrent of images rushing into her mind.

She cautiously allowed the field of her farsight to expand as she began simultaneously to search the levels immediately above and below the one through which she walked. She found passengers and Crew everywhere, in various stages of frenzy or collapse. The Flight Deck was still several levels above her, at the ship's center; she prayed that Senwy's influence had a spatial limit that might prevent the Crew up there from being as affected by the mindless terror as those on the lower levels.

Each new face that swam into her ken had to be examined, each crumpled body inspected.

No Senwy.

She marveled at the speed with which the girl had managed to lose herself in the giant vessel.

Above, beneath, ahead, behind. Face after contorted face was located, scanned, and rejected. She expanded the sphere of awareness once more.

There—

She glimpsed a familiar brown jacket huddled behind a cluster of stately mourning palms. Straining with the effort, she rotated the scene three hundred and sixty degrees in her mind and looked down on the rigid mask of Senwy's face from the other side of the trees.

The palms were two levels below the one she was on, near a restaurant at the end of a short promenade. She absorbed the details quickly, banished the farsight for an instant, then held her breath and opened her eyes. She looked up and down the concourse till she spotted a dropshaft, her stomach heaving with nausea as the different kinds of sight met and clashed in her mind. Palms clammy with chill sweat, she crept into the tube, felt the floor drop away, and waited for the hiss of the opening door.

Crawling from the tube, she reached carefully outward with farsight again, trying with excruciating control to limit the scope of her vision to the immediate vicinity of the dropshaft. Corridors raced and turned; bodies spasmed here and there on the floor.

With a sob of gratitude she recognized the grouping of tall plants and pushed herself erect. She was half running, half stumbling, propelling herself forward by pushing with her hand on the nearest wall, when—

Blazing colors, jeweled darkness, great slow shapes drifting all around her amid pulsing ribbons of green and golden fire . . .

She woke up face down on the cool floor. Blood tasted flat in her throat, dripped steadily from both nostirls.

"Where . . ." She heaved herself to her knees and then to her feet and started out again, one hand on the wall, the other rubbing fiercely at her eyes.

"God-lord, not now, not now," she crooned. She could see nothing but darkness, though her eyes were open wide. She squeezed them shut and concentrated.

Nothing. Both true sight and farsight had deserted her.

Days seemed to go by as she pulled herself down the corridor. When her feet encountered something solid but yielding, and long papery fronds brushed her cheeks, she stopped, puzzled. She stood there, swaying, then gave a small cry and sank down next to the tightly huddled figure. Senwy clutched at her, pulling her closer and raving softly as Ai tried to smooth her damp hair.

Searching in her pockets, Ai finally found the ampule, split the sposable carefully, and pressed the capsule against a trembling cheek.

The waves of panic subsided gradually as the girl relaxed. Senwy murmured drowsily, and Ai hugged her close.

"Hush, it's all right now, Senwy, it's all over. Only I can't see, so we're going to have to wait here for someone to find us."

Her fingers brushed the girl's face, then recoiled suddenly as the farsight returned unbidden, carrying her perception through the entire ship and beyond its outer boundaries in a single terrible instant. She waited for the devouring Dark to leap at her, her body tensed and doubled forward over Senwy's thin frame.

Then colors blossomed in her mind, wild and glorious as an explosion of wanderlights. She remembered: *Blazing colors and jeweled darkness—it wasn't a dream!*

She watched, completely entranced, as the great shapes rose and fell with infinite grace about her. *O beautiful*, she thought, mesmerized by the twining golden currents and the ribbons of pulsing green.

Death, danger, away, away, away—

At first she thought there had been words, but Senwy moaned incoherently at her side, and her own lips were pressed tightly shut.

Then she saw the wild darkness approaching on the far side of the ship, a roiling hungry void that seemed to devour the light and color between them as they drifted slowly toward it.

Death, away, away—

"I know," she muttered. "I see it now. We're headed right into it, it's going to get us." Shapes darted and flashed in agitation through the shimmering colors, racing along the pulsing threads of gold and green.

Like chaos incarnate, the swirling darkness lay before them.

"Ai?" The voice wavered childishly. "Where are we? I don't like it."

"Senwy! Oh, Senwy—" Warm tears brimmed her eyes and fell on her hands where they clasped the unseen face. "We've got to turn around. We've got to make the Pathfinder move the ship."

"The Path—"

"At the center of the ship, above us—search with your mind. She'll be alone, one woman, away from all the other Crew. Oh hurry, Senwy."

"Floating alone, all alone, all alone. Pilots—oh, Pilots, I see you . . . Hello, Pathfinder."

"Did you find her, Senwy?"

"I found her. I'm in her mind. She's upset. She needs to be calmed."

"No." Ai's hands tightened. "Don't calm her!"

"Don't? *Ow*, you're—"

"Upset her some more, hurt her, frighten her till she moves the ship. Make her turn to get away from you."

The ship was almost touching the curve of deadly darkness, the hunger.

"She's trying to get away. She doesn't like this."

"I know, Senwy. Good girl. More—quickly!"

Was she imagining it or had the void receded almost imperceptibly? She waited, unable to breathe. The gap grew suddenly wider, paused, began to narrow slowly again.

"That's it—no, *back*! Make her go back like she was a second ago. Yes! That's it! Make her go that way, Senwy, oh, make her feel good when she goes in that direction. Oh, yes, yes . . ."

The mad darkness receded until it lurked only at the very edge of Ai's perception. There was color streaming everywhere in veils of cool fire, and gentle shapes moved beside them, filled with beauty.

Senwy sighed contentedly, slipping gradually into sleep, while Ai drifted in a glory of jeweled light.

Joy now, said the wordless voice in her mind, *calm now, safe* . . .

CHAPTER 11

Dorothy began to fear they were getting a good way from the farm-house, since here everything was strange to her; but it would do no good at all to go back where the other roads all met, because the next one they chose might lead her just as far from home.

FROM THE ROAD TO OZ,
BY L. FRANK BAUM

1

The room was hot. The air was dry.

She sneezed once, and her head ached. She murmured to the room in brev, then waited for the cool breeze to bathe her face.

When nothing happened, she opened one eye.

The ceiling was made of rough gray stone. She opened the other eye and saw walls of stone, hot sunlight slanting in through parallel window slits, a shadow at the far end of the room.

"Ai?"

The shadow split in two, one half moving forward into the light. She rubbed her eyes.

"Ai, are you awake? How do you feel?" Geoffram stood beside the low sleeping platform, his face creased with concern.

"Pre—" She coughed, tried again. "Pretty awful. How do I look?"

"Pretty awful." He gave her a sad smile. "You've got a big bandage on your nose, and one eye's all purple." He took her hand and held it gently. "They say you're going to be fine."

"*Mirabile*," she groaned. "Now convince my head."

Geoffram turned and spoke softly to the other end of the room. Ai blinked as Senwy came into the light, a small vial of liquid in her hand.

"Here," Geoffram said. "This should lessen the pain."

"Thanks." Ai took the tiny flask and tilted her head to read the scrap of waxy paper which had been pasted lengthwise to the glass. The words DRINK ME had been printed on the paper in careful block letters.

"Senwy made the label," Geoffram said with a shrug of his dark brows. "She wanted to make sure everything was clear."

"I see. *Eheu*—didn't go overboard on the flavor, did they?"

"I'm afraid the pleasures of the low senses aren't of primary concern to most people here," Geoffram said, his smile steadier.

"I knew it. I've died and gone to hell." She leaned back on the thin pallet and closed her eyes. "Either that or we made it to Maribon after all."

"We are on Maribon." Senwy's voice was little more than a whisper. "You came after me, through great danger. You found me."

Ai looked up at the thin, solemn face, which was pale as porcelain in the white light from the windows. "Hello, Senwy. Looks like you came out of it better than I did— at least your nose is still showing."

"My fault." The dark eyes were hopeless. "Your injuries came because of me."

Ai snorted. "Look, if your idea of being helpful is to stand here and try to blame everything on yourself, you might as well leave the room. I'm not in the mood for it. Besides: as I remember, you did exactly what I asked you to at the end there—" She broke off, puzzled.

"What's the matter?" Geoffram hovered near. "Pain worse?"

"I... No, I was trying to remember exactly what went on there at the end."

"Well, you found Senwy, and the drug calmed her. The panic went away. Then we came out into normal space and found you. We were going to have to meet the space-boat at Tan-to-Da, so I had them put you in a *bain-sense* and slow down your body. That's why you haven't healed yet—unfortunately, there's no such thing as a medipal on Maribon." He spread his hands. "You've lost about three weeks of travel time on the *Dolly Dorcas*, but other than that you should be all caught up."

"Uh-uh..." She shook her head, winced. The room was beginning to blur, and she felt drowsy. "There was something else, on the *Imca Limbra*, in the Dark." She swallowed a yawn. "Senwy, do you remember anything?"

"I remember." The young communicant gave the barest nod. "You saved my life."

"Terminate connection."

Emrys turned from the wall as the sound of static gradually died away and the blue flicker faded on the Screen. He rose from the table and motioned to the communicant who stood near the door.

"You can have your seat back now. Thank you, ah..." He watched as the young woman resumed her place at the table and bent her cap of dark curls gracefully over the simple control panel.

"Still no name, I suppose..." He shook his head as he walked from the Screen Room. "We'll have to see about that."

He caught up with Geoffram in the outside corridor.

"Congratulate me—I finally got through. I've just spoken to Cil. She's leaving Earth on the next ship for Sipril. Jefany wasn't there. She's offworld visiting one of the children—hers or theirs, I don't know which—but Cil will get in touch with her as soon as possible and arrange for them to meet at Tan-to-Da. With Jack and Marysu arriving here any time now, that's the last of us. How strange to have the Group together again . . . What's the matter? Why are we walking so fast?"

"I can't find Ai," Geoffram said. "When I left her earlier this afternoon, she was sound asleep. I just went to wake her, but she's not there."

They crossed the courtyard diagonally and headed up a small ramp that opened on a long hallway.

Raille was waiting for them when they entered the vaulted chamber, seated at a desk by the wall with her hands folded before her.

"Ai's gone," Geoffram said. "Her room was empty."

"I know," Raille said.

"You know? She shouldn't have gotten out of bed so soon." Geoffram paced in front of the great basalt desk. "Do you have any idea where she's run off to?"

Raille turned to the narrow window at her side and gazed out over the empty courtyard. "Can't you guess?" she said softly.

It had taken her almost an hour to reach the bondsmen's village. She had gotten a ride with several gray-clad communicants on a drilling vehicle. They had brought her as far as the new well site that lay a few miles beyond the city gates. Then she had walked the rest of the way by herself, following the dusty roadway in the scorching heat until the sprawl of low-roofed buildings appeared abruptly over a small rise.

An old man directed her to the construction shacks on the outskirts of the village, where she walked past half-completed foundations and rows of newly measured building plots.

She came around the side of a roofless two-story structure made of mudbricks and gray stone and found herself looking down a line of perhaps thirty men and women standing on either side of several low, narrow tables that had been set end to end and covered with variously shaped pieces of dull metalmock. They were assembling something—tools, machine parts? Ai squinted at the line. Clothed in motley, tattered coveralls, the silent workers moved in unison with a precise and mechanical efficiency: stoop, lift, attach, pass to the one behind. The last person in line deposited the completed items in one of several numbered bins.

As Ai watched, the man at the bin looked at his wrist and shouted hoarsely to the others through cupped hands. At once the rhythm of the line dissolved into chaos as the workers stretched and shook their heads. There was movement and noise everywhere: boisterous laughter, conversation, snatches of lively song. They wandered to a nearby drum filled with water where another, less organized line was forming.

Ai approached the bin-man, who frowned when she greeted him in Inter. He shrugged broadly at her questions, running a scarred, three-fingered hand through the matted blond hair beneath his cowl, and replied with a few puzzled words in another language. She used gestures to communicate her request, and he finally nodded and pointed her toward a small lean-to at the edge of the construction area.

Ai peered into the darkness beneath the slanting roof of the lean-to. Someone was working intently on something that sparkled with dozens of tiny lights along its twisted length. She glimpsed dark hands with lighter palms; a dark profile. She started to withdraw, then squinted and ducked her head back into the shadows. "Beautife?"

The face that came around to stare at her was dark brown beneath the streaks of dusty sweat. Pale eyes widened. "Ai?"

The other woman emerged slowly from the darkness and stood blinking in the harsh sunlight.

"It *is* you!" Ai looked in amazement at the tall figure. Beautife wore a pair of patched blue shorts and a strip of ragged green cloth around her unkempt hair. Face, arms, legs, and torso gleamed the color of polished mahogany. "I didn't expect—"

"Oh, right." The Dancer followed Ai's gaze. "The skin decoration. It died about a month ago. Something in the food here." She shrugged with a faint smile. "How are you, Ai? I didn't know you'd arrived. There's not much news out here. What happened to your nose?"

"It's a long, strange story. Beautife, what are you doing

here? I thought you'd be in Delphys. I had to ask and ask before someone could tell me where to find you." She looked behind her to where the ragtag assembly gang lounged, cowls thrown back, in the shade of an unfinished building. "Who are these people? They sure don't look like communicants."

"They're the bondsmen. What's left of the original unmutated human strain on Maribon." Beautife untied the strip of cloth and combed long brown fingers through her tangled dark hair. "This village is called Quindeeja Salt." She looked around her. "See how these people live? This is paradise compared to what it was like a generation ago. Huts, disease, ignorance." She walked to a nearby water drum, lifted the cover, and bent to drink deeply from a rust-spotted dipper. "The empaths used to use them as . . . gauges, I guess you'd say. Choose the ones they wanted and take them into the city for a year or two. The young novices would be put into rapport with them, bonded one-to-one so they could learn intimately about touch-man emotions and how to properly manipulate them. When they were finished, it was back to the village. Oh, and they also interbred with them from time to time to keep their gene pool from stagnating, returning periodically to cull the communicant offspring from among the other children. Then things changed, and Raille arrived. Now, after centuries of partial symbiosis, the communicants have begun to look elsewhere, and the bondsmen are completely on their own. I spoke to her about it. She helps as much as she can with gifts of food and medication, but her hands are full with the communicants. I don't blame her—she's only one person. In the meantime they still live like this, in little villages scattered all over the habitable land. No electricity, no communication, not even indoor plumbing." She took another swig of warm brownish water, then dropped the dipper back into the drum. "I've been patterning them to the Dance, helping their bodies work while I try to teach their minds. It's been done before. This way they can accomplish things that they need to do without waiting to learn how. I've got a few books here, along with some materials that I had them bring me from Sipril, but there's much better information out on the Maren."

She glanced up at the sun and scratched her dark cheek. "They'll be coming for the new templates soon. I've made up a rough power-masonry pattern that I think will work. The Dance they're on now is to make the tools for it." She shaded her eyes in the direction of the work site, wiped her hands on her shorts, and started to turn back to the lean-to. "I'd better get—"

"Beautife!" Ai found that she was shaking. Her head had begun to ache again as she stood in the glare of the sun and listened to the talk of patterning and masonry. "Beautife, what about March?"

The tall woman stood still for a minute, staring at the ground. "Oh," she said. "Didn't anyone tell you? It didn't work." She began to wind the strip of cloth about her hair again, her eyes still averted. "Poor Emrys. He came running to tell me as soon as they finished that deepdelve business—he thought she'd found something, you see. 'She says there's *life* in there!' he cried, and the two of us were wild with joy until Raille herself showed up, all tired and sober-faced. She explained to us that the words Emrys had heard were March's own, like an echo left behind in his brain, his own last thoughts before—" She wiped her lips with the back of her hand, then continued more softly. "Just before his mind was lost in the Dark." She looked up, avoiding the stricken look on Ai's face. "They're coming now. I really have to get back to work."

Raille lifted her eyes from the book and extinguished one of the small yellow candles. She sat back in her chair and waited in the dim circle of light that remained in the room.

After several minutes the sound of sandals slapping on stone became audible. The footsteps approached steadily down the long, torchlit hall, suddenly faltered as they neared the open doorway to her sleeproom.

"Come in," she said softly.

A young girl with bright pink skin beneath a tousled shock of auburn hair a shade darker than Raille's entered the room. Squinting in the dimness, she walked to Raille's chair and stood glowering at the older woman with her hands on her thin hips.

"I'm Ai." The defiant chin quivered.

"Good evening. I'm Raille."

"You're that Her, aren't you? The one they're always talking about. The one I left home to come see, it seems like so long ago. I wanted you to help me."

"Yes. I've been waiting to meet you. Would you like to sit down?"

"No, I want to know what you're going to do about Beautife. I've been to see her. She needs help so bad. She told me about March, about what you found." Tears appeared suddenly on the burnt pink cheeks. "I'm sorry, I . . . look—you can handle emotions, you're supposed to be so good at that. Why don't you help her?" The small figure began to sway slightly on the rough floor.

"Come with me." Raille rose to her feet and led the girl into the cool shadows at the back of the room. She disappeared into an alcove. There was the brief sound of water splashing, and she returned carrying a small basin. "Here, lie down."

Ai lowered herself reluctantly to the sleeping platform and winced at the touch of the linen coverlet.

"You'd better lie still. That sunburn is going to be painful for a while." Raille lifted a cool cloth from the basin, wrung it out carefully, and laid it across Ai's hot brow. "I thought you were the one who needed my help, Ai."

"I did, I do, but—God-lord, that feels good. Thank you. My problems can wait. They're nothing compared to hers." She shook her head. "I don't understand why you didn't fix up her mind. How could you just let her go off like that—live out there with those poor people?"

"She's helping them. They need that help," Raille said, seating herself gingerly on the edge of the sleeping platform. "She's teaching them how to build, using her skill to work their bodies while their minds struggle with the learning. Before she left Delphys she spent her days in a room like this one, sitting at the side of an unopened box and staring at the wall. Now she works hard every day, falls exhausted into her sleeproll, and wakes to find things a tiny bit better in the village than they were the day before. It was I who suggested that she leave the city."

Ai was silent for a long time. Finally she spoke. "What about the body? Have they already—"

Raille gestured to the narrow windows where tiny stars were beginning to prick through the pall of darkening night. "The *Dolly Dorcas* will be here before morning with two more of March's old friends on board. Emrys wants us all to be together when we decide what's to be done." She rose from the pallet. "I have work that needs doing, and you look as if you could use some sleep." She removed the damp cloth from Ai's forehead, then replaced it for a moment with her own work-roughened hand. "Stay here. We'll talk more tomorrow." She crossed the room and cupped her hand behind the remaining candle.

Ai stared into the darkness after the other woman had left the room.

Decide what's to be done, she repeated to herself drowsily. *Does that mean there's more than one choice?*

She woke in the night to a sound like muffled thunder. Blue light flashed in the small room, and she stumbled over to peer through a narrow window slit. Outside, the squat spaceboat settled slowly onto the landing field.

She made her way to the alcove and splashed cold water on her face. Ignoring the sting of her sunburnt limbs, she left the room and hurried past wavering torches down the hall.

2

Geoffram stood with Raille and Emrys just inside the great stone gates. In the distance he could hear the harsh whine of the duster's engines as the vehicle approached the city under a moonless sky. He was straining his eyes to pick out movement in the darkness when he felt Raille's fingers lightly on his arm.

"We have company," she said softly.

"What?" He followed her gaze and saw the thin figure standing to one side of the open gate, arms crossed over her worn vest. He crossed quickly to her side.

"Ai, what are you doing here? Are you all right?"

"I'm sorry I took off this afternoon, Geoff." The thin face was mournful. "I had to go see Beautife."

"I know. Raille told me. Here, do you want to share my cloak? It's chilly out here."

"No thanks. My skin's a little sensitive."

He nodded sympathetically. "Mizar-the-Sun can't tell the visitors from the natives, I'm afraid. No one goes out uncovered during the day here." He cocked his head to one side. "At least your nose didn't get burned."

"Right. Of course, I can never take this bandage off now." She squinted toward the rocky plain beyond the gates. A dark shape defined by a double row of pale lights was approaching through the shrieking whine, growing larger as it bobbed on its cushion of whirling dust and pebbles. "Is that what everybody's waiting for?"

"Yes. Come on." He ushered her back from the entryway as the grating whine finally began to lessen and the bulky vehicle coasted through the gates and past the two of them to touch ground with a jolt in the center of the floodlit courtyard.

Dark-cloaked men and women began to emerge from the oval port as Geoffram and Ai joined the others. Pale faces bowed in silent acknowledgment of Raille's presence, and the line of communicants filed stiffly past them and into the nearest building.

Then there was a flash of startling color at the port as a final figure stepped forth into the light.

"God-lord—what a ride! That thing's worse than your toy spaceship." The woman flung back the hood of her golden travel cloak and shook her head forward to free long black hair that shimmered under the floodlights like a waterfall of night. "*Whoof*—and here you all are!"

Her face was dark, the color of burnished bronze, with sardonic, ice-chip blue eyes above an expressive mouth. She lifted slender arms heavy with bracelets and came toward them, eyes glittering like sapphires as she flicked her gaze from one face to the next.

"Emrys, you haven't changed a bit, but I know you're the oldest, so I'll hug you first in case you have to sit down. Raille, you *have* changed. *Bravissima!* I always thought your face could use some character lines. I'm glad to see you've finally gotten them. Ah, it's good to see you—give me a hug. I'm afraid I won't bow to you yet like your whey-faced disciples, but give me time . . . Sink me, is that Choddy with that grin on his face? God-lord, it is! So this is what you had hidden under that beard on Belthannis. What a shame. And who is—"

The brilliant eyes widened as she released Geoffram and stared at the face in the shadows behind him.

"This is Ai," Geoffram said as he stepped to one side. "She's gotten a touch of sunburn. Ai was on the ship with Beautife. She's a Pathfinder, from Dunbar's World, and she's become our friend." He turned with a smile. "Ai, I'd like to present Marysu, one of the top Panlinguists in the entire Community."

"One of?" Marysu narrowed her eyes momentarily at Geoffram, stepped forward, and touched Ai's trembling hand. She drew the girl slowly into the light. "Very happy to meet you—Ai, was it?" A smile curved the expressive lips. "From Dunbar's World?" She peered at the thin face intently, nodded, and murmured a rapid string of words in a language unfamiliar to Geoffram.

"Yes." Ai answered her in Inter, her face a rigid mask. "Nice to meet you, Marysu."

"And now—" The dark-skinned woman turned back to the others, her long hair swirling against the golden cloak. "If someone will help me with my luggage, I'd love to be shown to my suite long enough to wash some of the dust from my face. *Bozhe moi*—it's good to see you all again, *mes amis!*"

Geoffram looked at Ai as the others started off. "What was that all about? Did you understand what she said to you?"

"Yes." She watched as the woman strode up the wide ramp to the main building between Raille and Emrys, her slender arms weaving dramatically in the air as she spoke. "She was speaking Lido, the language of the Endless Beach. It was . . . a greeting." She shivered and clutched her thin shoulders as she turned back to Geoffram. "Can we go inside now? I think I'm getting a chill."

"I had to leave Jack on Sipril. He was kind enough to volunteer to stay behind. My work on Marik is at a very delicate stage, and I can't afford to alienate the matriarchs, so someone had to be near a Screen. Lords know we couldn't trust yours." Marysu stood nude in the center of a puddle of dampness, toweling the water from her long black hair as she spoke. Raille sat in a chair at her side, and Emrys stood near the sleeping platform. "I can't stay here forever, either. Jack does quite well with the language—you'd be proud of him—but they'll only deal with a male for so long. Ah! Now I know it's really you, Choddy—who else would blush like that?" She smiled at the dark-haired man who stood in the doorway. "Or should I be calling you Geoffram these days?"

"Choddy—Choss, at any rate, will be fine, Marysu." He walked to Emrys' side and sat on the edge of the low sleeping platform. "I took Ai back to her sleeproom."

"Mm," Marysu said, smoothing her hair back over her shoulders so that it fell past her waist. "A wise decision. Your little friend looked like she needed a place to lie down. I thought that nose ornament was an interesting touch." She shook out the towel and wrapped it loosely around her hips. "So." She lifted an eyebrow at Emrys. "I've gotten the first layer of dust off. What now? Can I see him?"

"If you'd rather get some rest, Marysu—"

"I slept on the ship, believe it or not. I'm wide awake. This is not a task I want to put off."

"Very well, then," Emrys said. "Whenever you're ready."

Marysu dropped the towel and reached into the large carrysack she had unfolded at one end of the sleeping platform. "I suppose we don't want to upset the natives," she remarked, drawing forth a brief leaf-colored wraparound. She slipped into the translucent garment and secured it with a golden sash. "I'm ready."

The linguist stood nearest the gleaming casket, her head bowed and her back to the rest of the group as the echoes died in the empty room and the silver head moved stiffly back to rest.

The room remained silent until Emrys moved to Marysu's side and cleared his throat. "Beautife told us it means—" he began.

"I speak Felashwa," she snapped, her voice clotted with emotion. "I know what it means."

"Of course. I'm sorry . . ."

"You were right, you know," Marysu said over her shoulder. "He's not in there anymore, not where we could find him. I know speaking, I know voices. His is gone." She wiped moisture from a bronze cheek as she turned from the still figure. "I was hoping you were wrong, but you weren't. It's just a body now. What are we going to do with it?" She straightened and turned her bright gaze on Raille. "Do you bury your dead here?"

"I have something to propose, Marysu," Emrys said softly in the silence that followed. "But I have to present it to the whole Group. March would have approved of that, I think. He knew I never went ahead with any plan without full support from you all."

"You have a plan?" Marysu watched him, a strange half smile beginning to curve her lips. "I know that shouldn't make me feel hopeful, Jon Emerson, but it does. This is almost beginning to sound like old times."

3

"Leaving?" Ai set her eating tong back on the tray and stared at Geoffram. "What for? I thought—"

"There's a time factor involved." He looked down the rows of silent white faces bending and rising above their bowls of gruel and compared the scene to the busy refectory back at Alembic House on Stone's Throw, with Jurian at one end of the table and Pennifar at the other, questioning the young ones on the day's events and speculating on tomorrow's weather. "Marysu has to return to Marik soon," he said, turning back to her with a sigh. "And three members of our Group aren't here. Two of them haven't even gotten to Sipril yet. Emrys received another message this morning. Something's delayed them."

"So what're you planning to do?" Ai watched him warily. "Meet them there?"

"It seems like the only way. If we leave by tomorrow, we should all arrive at Tan-to-Da within a few days of each other. Then Emrys can have his Group meeting, Marysu and Jack can go back to the catpeople, and the rest of us..." He let the sentence die with a vague gesture.

"Tomorrow." Ai scratched her cheek, still peeling from its recent sunburn, and took a thoughtful bite of nettle-cake. The rest of her face had begun to tan, and freckles sprinkled her cheeks and right forearm.

"I know it's sudden," Geoffram said. "And I know you've been doing a lot of work out at the village, but you've been with us from the start, and I figured—"

"Of course I want to go! Beautife's coming, too, isn't she? You've got to let her in on this."

"I hope she'll agree to come, Ai. Would you like to ask her for us?"

Ai nodded, chewing slowly. Abruptly she pushed back from the table and got to her feet.

"I'd better go make sure I don't miss my ride to the village. I told Senwy to meet me just before noon. Thanks, Geoff." She moved toward the doorway, halted, and came back to the table.

"You know, these things really aren't half bad," she said, emptying the nearest plateful of nettlecakes into her carrysack.

CHAPTER 12

I have stretched ropes from steeple to steeple;
garlands from window to window; golden chains
from star to star, and I dance.

ARTHUR RIMBAUD

1

A hundred subtle shades of brown and gray mottled randomly with spots of black oil, nugget mountains, and pebble cities, the dusty orb of Maribon dwindled behind them in the viewing ports.

After the all-clear was sounded, Ai roamed the narrow corridors of the *Dolly Dorcas* with one brow raised in open skepticism.

"I'm glad I made my first trip asleep," she remarked to Geoffram as they stood in the cramped control room. "This is not the kind of experience you want to have with your eyes open. See those two over there?" She nodded to a pair of silent communicants staring face to face over a cluster of complex instrumentation. "Those are our trusty navigators, from the looks of the machinery, and they've been gesturing and twitching at each other ever since we walked in. I think they're having an argument about how to find Sipril from here."

"I think I don't want to know that," Geoffram said with a wince and a smile. "I suggest we go back to the main salon with the others before you get the urge to crawl into one of the washbasins and try to farsee."

"Farsee? In this little puzzlebox?" she said incredulously as he ushered her down the twisting corridor. "Not a chance."

When they reached the salon, Geoffram joined Raille, Emrys, and Marysu at the small S-shaped table at one end of the room, while Ai went to the low cushions beneath the viewing ports, where Beautife sat staring at a dog-eared book.

"Are you really reading that, or can I sit down?"

"You can sit down." Beautife raised her head slightly and touched the cushion next to her with mahogany fingers. "I don't even know what the book is about. I just didn't want them to feel that they had to come talk to me." She glanced at the group by the curving table.

"Would you rather I didn't talk to you, either?" Ai stood poised above the cushion.

"No, Ai, sit down. Please." The Dancer's smile was unhappy. "I know that they want to be careful around me, I know that they're trying to include me. I just..." She leaned back and closed her eyes. "I came because I have to see the end of it. I have to know that it's over. They don't owe me anything beyond that."

"They're your friends, Beautife. Friends share."

The other woman said nothing, remaining with her head against the padded wall and her eyes shut until Ai believed her to be asleep. But she opened her pale eyes after a while and looked at Ai. "The work's not halfway finished at Quindeeja Salt. The headman told me there's a dry season coming soon. A dry season! Can you imagine what that must be like? I was discussing with Raille the possibility of hooking the village in to the communicants' new well site. The problem will be getting them to accept anything from the empaths now. Having Senwy there these past weeks has been a good start, but deep inside they're still afraid things are going to change back someday to the way they were before, and the communicants are going to need them again." She sighed, closed her eyes again. "Who will negotiate for them, bring them the skills and equipment they need from the Maren?"

A young communicant entered the salon and began serving mugs of steaming chetto from an awkwardly balanced tray to those who sat at the table.

"I don't know, Beautife. If someone cares enough, it'll get done. Raille's only one person, as you told me yourself. You can't—" Ai paused, stared across the room. "Hey!" She sat up straight. "What are *you* doing here?"

"Hello, Ai. Are you having a pleasurable trip?" Senwy crossed the room to the viewing area, tilting the tray forward as liquid sloshed from the remaining mugs. "Would you like to drink something with a hot flavor?"

"Senwy—"

"No? Beautife? No?" The thin face turned back to Ai. "I requested to come on this trip. They always need someone to take care of food." Her dark eyes were serious above the tray of cheerfully painted mugs. "I thought maybe you would not be coming back to Maribon, Ai. It's been very satisfying for me to work at the village with you and Beautife. I have learned more in a few weeks in Quindeeja Salt than in months on Stone's Throw and years before that in my own city of Delphys."

"God-lord, I've never heard you say so much in one breath," Ai said. "Why didn't you tell me you wanted to come? I could've asked them for you."

"I asked them for myself, and they looked into me and said that I had stabilized sufficiently to make the trip. A person must do some things for herself, Ai. You saved my life for me. I can manage the small details."

"Senwy, I don't think I really—"

A series of sharp clicks sounded behind them, and Ai turned to see the deadlights sliding into place over the viewing ports.

"First jump coming up," Beautife said.

"It'll be a short one, I think. You better put that tray down and sit somewhere," Ai said. "They told me in the control room there's a lurch when the jumpdrive comes on because the ship is so small."

Senwy turned obediently and headed across the floor

toward the curving table. When she was halfway there the room began to quake, and she stood with legs splayed to the sides, holding the tray out in front of her with an expression of determination on her pale face.

The tremor passed, and she turned to Ai.

"I did it," she said in quiet triumph. Then her eyes rolled back beneath her lids, and she pitched forward with a strangled shriek of terror.

The tray clattered on the floor, spraying hot chetto and fragments of pottery. Ai leaped up and started for the fallen girl, her teeth biting deep into her lower lip as the air in the room began to churn and the familiar wave of agony exploded in her mind—

And vanished.

"Senwy." Raille rose slowly from the table, her eyes like wells of comfort as she moved slowly toward the stricken girl. The air between them boiled and stormed, but Ai felt nothing but wave after wave of enfolding calm as she knelt by the young communicant.

Senwy's head lay against the floor, and her body was rigid, drawn up in a tight fetal position.

"It's the same as before," Ai said, looking up as Raille approached. "We thought it was the alarm that triggered it, but it must have something to do with the jump itself. Poor Senwy." She put her hand on the girl's shoulder and reached down to gently turn her face from the floor.

The room went suddenly black.

"No!" She fell back, banging her elbow painfully on the floor.

"Ai, what's wrong?" Beautife asked from behind her. Other voices cried out from across the room. She felt someone's arms clasp her shoulders and pushed them away.

"I'm all right!" She took a deep breath to calm herself and felt anger erupt in her mind. *I don't want this to be happening now*, she told herself furiously, *I want to see—*

Colors blazed, shimmering in currents through a gentle darkness hung with jewels. Great shapes moved beneath her, descending gracefully until they, too, were jewels . . .

It wasn't a dream, she thought with wonder. *I remember—it was real!*

There were voices all around her, but muted and far away as if heard through a thick wall of glass. Hands seemed to touch her, to hold her, but she felt as though her whole body had become numb, swathed in layers of nothingness that lay between the sensation and her skin.

O beautiful, I remember . . .

"Ai?" It was Senwy's voice, just as it had been the other time. "My nose hurts."

"I wish you could see this Senwy," she murmured. "I wish I could share . . ."

"Do you want to play the game again, Ai?" Senwy's words reached her from a great distance. "Do you want me to make someone move?"

Move. Death, danger, away, away—

Memories cascaded into her mind, and she stiffened with remembered fear. Frantically she searched the light-ribboned currents, probing the veils of shifting colors.

"What is it, Ai? What are you looking for?" A different voice this time, stronger, a voice that gently compelled her to answer. She groped for words.

"The wild darkness," she said. "The bad, the devouring, like before, like the other time."

"What happened the other time? Tell us about the darkness." Waves of quiet peace flowed through her, calming the dreadful fear.

"I can't—it's hard to—" Words slipped from her grasp to be replaced by glory as she bathed again in the ribbons of gold and emerald and the great jewel-colored shapes that surrounded her. "I want to watch," she said finally. "Just let me watch . . ."

She felt a deep sadness envelope her when at last the colors began to fade. But the peace remained about her like a cloak, and the sorrow was a thing of the far distance, like the voices and the hands. The bright darkness became true darkness, and she clenched her eyes tight, desperately willing the wonder back into her sight.

She blinked, and the light of the real world flashed painfully.

She squinted up at the circle of faces. The closest one

belonged to Raille, and she realized that her head was resting on the older woman's lap.

"You can see us now, can't you?" Raille asked, smoothing Ai's damp hair with a gentle hand.

"Yes." Ai managed a weak nod. "But all the beauty's gone away."

2

"We should never have brought her along." Geoffram's hand shook as he searched through the racks of tiny ampules in the old-fashioned medical storage unit. "We should have gone to Sipril alone, the four of us, if Emrys insisted on having his Group meeting. We had no right to expose her to this, not after that first incident on the *Imca Limbra* . . . Which did she say, blue or green?" His fingers probed uncertainly, scattering the ampules.

"She said both." Marysu reached past him, bracelets clashing quietly, and plucked a handful of each from the drawer. "There was absolutely no way of knowing that either Ai or Senwy would have any problems on this trip. Stop beating yourself. You're not their keeper, *grâce à Dieu*."

"But there was no need." Geoffram pushed the drawer into the wall and pounded on it when it jammed in the slot. "There were four of us—five, counting March, and it was his wish that Emrys make the decision, anyway. Only three Group members were absent."

"Three absent? I can see your arithmetic hasn't improved over the years, Choddy. I hope you're doing better at history. God-lord, let me do it. 'Her Hand' seems to be a bit shaky." Marysu pulled the drawer from his grasp and slid it smoothly into the wall.

"My arithmetic?" Geoffram stared at her in bewilderment. "What are you talking about? Aren't you counting Jack?"

"Hush," she said. "It's time to go tend to the wounded."

3

"If only I could describe it more clearly." Ai sat cross-legged on the floor next to the cushions as Raille pressed first one ampule and then another against Senwy's wrist.

"Green for pain," she said to the young communicant. "Blue for trauma." She nodded to Ai. "I think she's going to need a bandage like the one you had."

"I should have saved it," Ai said.

"I don't understand how you can all be so cheerful," Geoffram said. The rest of them had pulled chairs and loungers from other parts of the room into a semicircle around the cushioned viewing area where Senwy lay.

"I feel all right," the patient said, rubbing her nose with a cautious finger. "It was better than the last time, even if I have to have a bandage."

"It was incredible, Geoff. I didn't want to come back."

"But where were you?" He looked around at the others helplessly. "What were you seeing?"

"The same as before, on the *Imca Limbra* with you and Senwy. Only I didn't remember it until it happened again."

"*Bain-sense* effect," Emrys said thoughtfully. "Memories are sometimes misplaced when there's been severe mental trauma." He glanced at Raille.

She nodded. "It's not common, but it happens. Ai, was that the first time you'd ever experienced those colors and shapes: on board the *Imca Limbra*?"

"Uh-huh. Well, the first time for the . . . vision part. I've had the blindness for a while now."

"What blindness?" Geoffram asked. "You've never said anything about blindness."

"That's why I wanted to find you in the first place," Ai said to Raille. "I'd been having spells of blindness for the past year and a half."

"I thought it was March you came looking for, not Raille," Beautife said.

"Because I didn't know where to find Raille, and I knew March could tell me." Ai's tone was apologetic.

"March?" Geoffram looked from Ai to Beautife with a puzzled frown. "I thought she was *your* friend." He came back to Ai. "You knew March before the *Imca Limbra*?"

"Curiouser and curiouser, isn't it, Choddy?" Marysu said with a quiet smile. "Tell us about the blindness, child."

"Well—" Ai looked doubtfully from face to face, settled on Raille's. "Ever since about a year and a half ago, I've been having these ... spells where suddenly I couldn't see anything. Regular medical tests didn't find anything wrong with me. But I'm a Pathfinder, and what it means when a Pathfinder has spontaneous sensory loss is one of two things: Either you've been farseeing too long and it's time to retire—three centuries seems to be the maximum anyone can use the skill ..." She toyed with a fragment of blue pottery on the floor by her knee. "Or you're causing the blindness yourself, because you're so badly messed up emotionally that you're trying to punish yourself." She shrugged. "I'm only fifteen."

"So after your diagnosis you decided I'd be able to help you with your emotional problems, and you came looking for me." Raille watched as a flush of pink spread across the freckled cheeks. "Ai, can you recall how many of these attacks you've had and when they happened?"

"There've only been five—six counting just now. They've been lasting for a shorter time but coming closer together." She counted slowly on her fingers. "First was a year and a half ago—no, it's been more than two true-years by now." She blinked. "I'm going to be sixteen in three weeks, I just realized ... I was at the Port the first time—I thought the scrub crew was *hoking* me. That one lasted for about half an hour. The second time was shorter, about a year later. I almost drowned with that one. Then, oh, seven, eight months ago, in bed one morning. The next one was about a week before I left home and signed on board the *Imca Limbra*. Then again on the *Imca Limbra* with Senwy." She tapped the thumb of her hand. "You all saw the last one."

Raille turned her gaze to the tall figure standing next to Emrys. "You told me that March had experienced strange sensations in the Dark a few times, a sort of presence . . ."

The brown-skinned Dancer raised her head and frowned. "Three times," she said. "Why?"

"When did it happen? For how long?" Emrys asked. He nodded to Raille. "I begin to see."

"Oh, Lords, the first one was shortly after the beginning of the project, over two years ago now. Those first Dives were the longest ones. We stayed in nearly half an hour." Her eyes widened. "The next time I remember because I felt it, too—ten months later, maybe? I don't know about the third time."

"What about the last Dive, the day his mind was lost," Emrys prompted. "What day was that?"

"The fifteenth, no the sixteenth . . . I'm not—"

Emrys gestured impatiently. "Was it shortly before Ai came on board? About a week, say?"

"Yes." Beautife nodded in thoughtful confirmation.

"I saw the holo," Ai said in a hushed voice. "I remember. They were only out for a short time. Five, ten minutes? The same as my last spell of blindness on Dunbar's World." She hugged her arms to her chest and stared at the others. "They've all been the same."

"Yes," said Raille. "I think we've found the true catalyst for your sensory loss. Just now—when you were having the vision—something frightened you. Senwy mentioned a game, and you radiated terror so great I had to damp it for you. When I questioned you, you spoke of a wild darkness that devoured. Do you remember that?"

"Some of it, yes. The fear was left over from before. I think . . ." She leaned forward with her elbows on her thighs, forehead cradled in her palms. "I think that's more of what got lost in the *bain-sense*."

"I can help you find it," Raille said. "The *bain-sense* was originally created by the communicants as a tool for their own use. Its effects are fairly easy to undo." She held Ai's gaze. "Do you want to remember?"

"Yes, it's important. What do I have to do?"

"Nothing," Raille said with a smile. "Just . . . remember."

Fear flowed into the thin face, swelled in the dark eyes.

"Calmly," Raille said softly. "It's a thing of the past and cannot harm you."

Ai swallowed slowly and nodded, mastering the terror with a visible effort. "It was coming at us—or we were drifting toward it. I didn't see it, I didn't understand about the danger at first. I was looking at the colors and the shapes rising and falling like great jewels all around . . ." Her eyes narrowed as if she were looking toward a far horizon. Suddenly her face changed. "There was a warning! Something spoke to me."

"Spoke?" Marysu asked. "How?"

"I don't know." Ai considered the question. "Not with a voice, not with words. But I felt it clearly. I think—" She turned to the young communicant regarding her solemnly from the raised cushions. "I think Senwy told me. Not with words, but it came from her."

"I don't remember, Ai," Senwy said. "I just remember the Pathfinder that we moved."

"That's right—I felt the warning, and I—I told Senwy to find the Pathfinder, to go inside her mind and make her move the ship away from the danger. And it worked!" She stared at the other girl with her mouth wide. "We saved the ship, Senwy—you and I saved the *Imca Limbra* from being eaten in the Dark!"

"But where did this warning come from?" Emrys had risen from his chair and begun to pace slowly back and forth. "Senwy didn't see your vision, so how could she have warned you?"

"No, it wasn't her warning; it didn't feel like her." Ai struggled for the right words. "It only came from her."

"Or *through* her," Raille said. "From something in the Dark that saw the danger. 'There is life in here,'" she quoted softly, looking at Emrys. "March found what they were looking for—or it found him. And perhaps we have a way to speak to it at last."

4

"Each time March sensed a presence in the Dark, it triggered blindness in a girl on a world light-years away. Why?"

Geoffram spoke half to himself, half to the group of silent communicants who watched with him as Beautife and Emrys conferred with the three women sitting propped against the cushions. "Then later, with Senwy." He turned to study the nearest blank face. "But surely other communicants have gone into the Dark and felt things." The young man returned his gaze from expressionless black eyes and said nothing. "So why—"

"It wouldn't matter if they had, without someone like Ai along—if ever there's been someone like Ai before, which I doubt." Marysu came from behind to stand by his side. "Without her there to be catalyzed, it would have been just another Darkdream."

"But if she had to be there with Senwy, physically present on the ship in order to react, why did March's encounters affect her? He wasn't a communicant, and they weren't even in the same solar system when it happened!"

"They're about ready to try again," Marysu said. "We'd better get comfortable."

The main salon had been rearranged: The curving table, now overflowing with a tangle of interconnected instrumentation, had been moved to face the cushioned viewing area. Ai reclined in the center of the cushions, her back raised and her head supported. Flanking her were Raille and Senwy, and rows of slender, twinkling wires ran from the three of them to the table. Beautife turned and climbed to her feet as Marysu and Geoffram took their seats to one side of the strange tableau.

"It's not proper usage of a patterning frame," she said with a grimace, "but Raille says it'll help share the sensory information." She stood back, surveyed the scene with hands on hips. "I guess that's it."

Raille lifted a spangled arm and smiled at Geoffram.

"Would you tell the captain to begin, please? Everyone seems to be ready for another try."

Geoffram signaled to the tall woman with short black hair who stood by the door of the salon. "We're ready for the next jump, Domi. Five minutes, like the last time: in and out."

"Five minutes." The woman nodded and disappeared into the corridor.

Geoffram examined Ai's tanned face for signs of nervousness and found only anticipation. He started as the deadlights snapped over the viewing ports for the third time in as many hours.

"Hey, Geoff!" Ai winked at him from the cushions. "Watch out for flying chetto."

He had time to return her smile; then the ship lurched, and her eyes turned from him sightlessly.

It was easier each time.

Ai forced herself to breathe calmly, the Pathfinder relaxation mnemonics whispering through her mind like a lullaby as she floated once more in a realm of indescribable beauty.

There had been a sense of control last time that was missing from the earlier attempts. This time she had consciously willed the new perception into being when the blindness closed around her and had been rewarded with an instant response in her mind as the blaze of colors began to stream in through the darkness. *If only I had my tank and my complink*, she thought, *I bet this would start to feel almost natural*. It was similar to the sensation she got from farseeing but not exactly the same: a different focus of the same perception, perhaps. She concentrated, feeling as if she were learning to flex a new muscle in her brain, and the images sharpened and strengthened obediently around her.

As her sense of control grew, she felt the numbing euphoria of the first few experiences beginning to diminish. There was still a blazing glory to be found in each aspect of the shimmering vision-world, a joy in viewing that she found almost inexpressible, but her innate curiosity had begun to assert itself, and she probed the wonderland about her with a conscious purpose.

I could stay here forever, she thought sadly as the colors began to fade once more.

"But you felt nothing?" Emrys peered at Ai intently as he spoke. "No presence, no voices? No danger?"

She shook her head. "No, it was different. The colors and the currents have all looked different the past few times. I didn't notice it before, but I think I'm starting to recognize more individual features. This time it was ... bluer? And darker." She narrowed her eyes as she tried to recreate the splendor in her mind. "And I only saw one of the jewel-shapes, very far off. It was there for a minute, then it disappeared."

"I wonder if we've gone to a new place each time," Emrys mused. "Could there be a correspondence between where we are in realspace when we go in and where we'll turn up inside? If so ..." He raised his eyes to the rest of them, speculation in his tone. "I wonder what might happen if we went back to the place where the *Imca Limbra* jumped on its last Dive with the research team—and went in there ourselves."

"Difficult to pinpoint without access to their log," Marysu murmured.

"I have the coordinates." Beautife's voice was a whisper. Her hands trembled as they clutched the back of a tall white lounger. "On the holodot in my carrysack." Her eyes went to the hallway, but she stood rooted behind the shielding chair.

"Come on," Ai said, clambering to her feet from the pile of cushions. She took the long, dark hand. "I'll go with you."

"Each time when I've thought I knew for sure, I've been wrong. I don't know what to think anymore." Beautife sat on the edge of the sleeping platform, knees drawn up under her chin, brown hands clasped tightly around her long legs.

"I know," Ai said. "It's all been pretty strange, and I think it's going to get stranger." She pulled a tab from a cluttered compartment at one end of the carrysack and held it up to the light. "This is it, isn't it?"

"Ai." Beautife's voice was barely audible. "Suppose whatever took his mind is still in there when we go back?"

Ai pocketed the tab and set the carrysack back on its low shelf. She looked at her friend.

"Do you want to stop now?" she asked quietly. "Give up, go home, and never find out?"

"No." The other woman shook her head at last, watched her from azure eyes. "I want to know."

"Soon now?" Emrys came to stand with Raille and one of the gray-clad Crewmembers at the forward viewing ports in the main salon.

Raille nodded. "We're almost there. It's time we woke the others." She looked briefly to the left.

The communicant at her side nodded and strode toward the doorway, exchanging a quick opaque glance with two of his fellows as he exited the room.

"What do they make of all this?" Emrys asked. "Do they understand what we're about to do?"

"They have no problem grasping the what," Raille answered. "Most of them are still groping for the why. There's an old saying about the unpredictability of touch-man behavior that's been getting a lot of use on this ship lately."

Emrys looked out at the star-sprinkled black. "I wonder what we'll find in there," he said.

The rest of the group appeared one by one in the salon over the next hour and a half, sipping at mugs of dark chetto and stretching mightily as they strove to throw off the effects of a month of coldsleep. Emrys held a brief meeting over dinner, and plans were made to go into the Dark at the first hour of the following shipday morning.

Seven Thoughts at Once moved aimlessly among the shrunken fans and withered fiber-knots of the detritus garden, searching for fragments of food amid the spoilage. Two sweeps ago the Change had come and the others had deserted the Oldest Path for the Gathering-join, there to mate and barter information with those from other Paths while they awaited the appearance of the food-rich currents that would lead them to their next habitat among the Paths.

Lowmites had long since decimated the uprotected garden, those few areas that had escaped their voracious appetites falling quickly into ruin and neglect with only Seven Thoughts to tend them. A sour flavor filled the murky currents in this part of the underpath, and Seven Thoughts tightened his skin as he probed among the slurry of decomposing tendrils. His own surface was threaded increasingly with silver filaments, and a dull gray sheen had enveloped most of his broad upper body. Soon there would be nothing left to eat, and the substance of the underpath would begin to knit itself deeper and deeper into his skin, until his swim was ended and nothing remained of Seven Thoughts but a brief mist among the blues.

He had resolved not long ago that before that time arrived he would use his remaining strength to rejoin the dying Oldest Path and plunge through the weakened Edge into the Wild.

He dipped and narrowed to peer between two broken fans, pulled forth a tiny scrap of unspoiled food, and began to slowly absorb it, feeling the spark of heat spread along his length. A lowmite darted toward him suddenly out of the darkness, and he swung ponderously to one side, his underbelly glowing with a network of feeble oranges and pinks as he tried to assume a forbidding posture. The lowmite contracted in momentary fear, then slowly opened up, stalking the morsel of food on Seven Thoughts' surface in

wary indecision before finally vanishing into the purple
murk.

He finished the scrap and drifted upward on an under-
current, eyes forming slowly on his back as he scanned
the Oldest Path above him. Dissolution was beginning;
the twining currents moved sluggishly as the end of the
Path approached. He watched listlessly as a tiny shadow
moved high among the uppermost levels, almost beyond
his weakened vision. A late traveler from another Path,
perhaps, on her way to the Gathering-join, or a detached
portion of the wall itself, sloughed off during the Change
to dissolve slowly in the thickening currents. The shadow
grew slowly in size and color against the bright overpath,
and Seven Thoughts halted his lazy ascent as his outer
skin began to vibrate in disbelief.

How long ago she had met the Visitor to the Oldest
Path and started the little-Change that swept through her
life like a tongue of the Wild, cleaving her from the others
of her race, he could not say. Since its touch he had been
barren of purpose, and the long sweeps had passed in a
haze of doubt and apathy.

Now the Visitor hung again in the Oldest Path, and
the Path was dying.

There was a narrow spur not far above him. Gathering
his waning energies for a final climb, he rose like a tar-
nished jewel through the highest blues and began the long
ascent to the Oldest Path.

6

"Nothing?"

The voice reached Ai faintly through the ears of that part
of her which lay curled on her side on the piled cushions.

"No. It's like the others." She spoke with quiet disappointment from the other part, which drifted through
the ragged veils of light and color. "Empty." There was
a dullness to the vision-world, a slow blurring that seemed
to be increasing with each attempt. Was it her new ability

that was fading? She concentrated for a few seconds, saw no change in the lackluster currents.

"Do you want to come out?" the faraway voice asked again, tinged with its own discouragement. Three jumps had been made within the small radius of coordinates given them by Beautife, each yielding nothing but subtle variations on the same barren scene.

"In a minute." She lifted her gaze to the source of the light, lowered it to the purple darkness below. "Just one more minute..."

Something caught her attention, and she focused on it. A mere dab of pale color, it hung below and to the far left of her, so near the dark bottom of her vision that she had almost missed it.

"I see something," she said. "One of the jewel-shapes, I think, far below us. Is it drifting upward or just hanging there? Hard to tell..." She tried to clear her vision, but the colors themselves seemed clouded and the tiny spot was obscured by drifting currents of nearly opaque particles. "I want to try something," she said.

"Yes?" The answer was faint.

"I want to move the ship...down, it feels like—but you'll have to start and let me see if it's right."

Hours seemed to pass before she saw the slight sideward motion of the drifting haze of color.

"How is that? Right way?"

"No, that's not it at all," she murmured. "It may be down for me, but it's clearly something else for you. No, I want to go *this* way—" She squirmed in frustration as her practiced movements brought no automatic response from the tiny ship around her. "If only there were a complink, some way for me to move the ship..."

"Ai, it's Raille. We have an idea. Wait." There was another interminable pause. "We're going to link up the communicants and try to give you more control. From you to me to Senwy and on down the line. We'll try to pass your message to the navigators and the captain— like a sort of living complink. It's not easy, and it may not work—the information is subtle, and our Crewmembers are of different reaches. Do you want to try?"

"Yes, tell me when." She waited, watching the distant spot and feeling a whispering touch grow like hundreds of small wings at the edge of her mind.

"Now," came the faraway voice, and she focused intently on the small patch of color almost lost in the murk below.

At once the tiny spot began to grow as she felt them drift slowly downward and to the left.

"It works!" she cried. "More!"

They descended slowly into the deepening darkness. Suddenly the tiny shape vanished.

"It's gone," she groaned. "I think we scared—no, wait! There it is! It's huge—it's right alongside us!"

"Stop kicking, Ai, and tell us what it looks like." The faint excited voice belonged to Emrys. "You almost hit Senwy's nose."

"I'm sorry, I'm sorry," she sang, grinning as she stared at the massive ovoid. "It looks like—well, actually it looks like a piece of jelly candy more than anything else, but it's huge and beautiful."

"Ai, this is Marysu. We want to try to talk to it."

"Yes, all right." She felt a small tug of disappointment. "I wish I could do more than just see it. Tell me what you say, and if it answers you . . ."

"Ai, you mooncalf, this is your Dive. Do you think we'd keep you out of it? Raille's going to mesh us all with her mind and try to communicate by tapping my panlinguistic abilities. Do you have a suggestion for our greeting? First Contact is a very important time."

"I don't know what to say. God-lord, don't let it know I think it looks like a piece of candy. Wait, wait—'greetings from the *Dolly Dorcas* to the jewel that hangs before our eye.'"

"Very nice. Here we go—"

Ai felt Raille's mind all around her, joining her to the others and holding them, keeping them together in a single smooth flowing in which she could discern hints and flashes of familiar personalities. Then she heard Marysu's voice repeating her words, and simultaneously she "felt" the same words—or was it the feelings behind the words?—go out from the ship, shaped by the silent voices of a score of minds into a form of communication she had never experienced.

There was a long pause while the ovoid hung motionless in front of her, colors shimmering like pale fire across its surface.

"I don't think it understood us," she said mournfully. "Maybe it's not sentient, after all. It just keeps popping little bubbles out onto its skin at this end."

Greetings from Seven Thoughts at Once of the Oldest Path . . . to the Visitor . . .

"Yah!" she shouted. "We did it!" With a thousand questions racing through her mind, Ai stared at the massive shape, stunned by an excitement too great for words. "Say something, somebody—"

Yes . . . so many things to ask . . . came the great slow voice that was not a voice but an indefinable pulsing of meaning in her mind. *Are you real and not a false-dream?*

"We are real, a different kind of life." Ai recognized Emrys, both in the far-off voice and in the flavor of his personality in the multiple sending that came from all around her. "From another world outside of this one. Until this moment, we never knew your world held life. We saw this place as a void, filled only with danger."

Not a void . . . Stay on the Path and there is no danger . . .

"We understand that now. In another place we were warned."

Exultants . . . the Exultants have tried for many Visits . . . many Visitors . . . Why did you go into the Wild before? Was that you . . . or another . . .

"Many others. We used your world to cross our own. We are much faster in your world, and the distance is lessened."

The Rushing Path is faster . . . This Path is dying . . . the Change has come . . . You must not stay . . . See the death of the Oldest Path . . .

"Until this time none of us has ever seen the Paths or the Wilds of your world. Now there is one among us who can see."

You are more than one ... joined to share inside this skin ...

"Yes, many of us are here inside the ship, all different. But only one can see you."

If they want to see ... they must use an eye ... You will show them where to look ...

"Yes." Ai added her own small voice to the sending, felt it go out richly changed by the mind-mingling. "I'll try." She felt the warm clasp of Raille's presence about them all, and through her the emotions of some of the others aboard the ship. "Listen," she said suddenly. "You must tell us. There were others here once, trying to perceive your world: many small ships from a very large one."

The great shape turned ponderously, streaks of silver flashing like agitated lightning along its length.

The child was yours ...

"A man, yes, one of us. One who was lost in the Dark, his mind taken from him." Emotions flickered through the linkage into Ai: hope, sorrow, disbelief. "We came here seeking knowledge of our friend, whose body we still possess. If you know something you can share with us, you must tell us, please."

Too near the Wild ... I tried to save the child ... Joined ... All the thoughts and dark colors into me ...

"You tried to save him, and his mind—it went into you?" Excitement surged through the minds aboard the ship.

Not the mind ... an image ... through the eyes of the skin into the cells ...

"Then there is nothing there—nothing left of him?"

A moment ... a small fragment of child-life that does not leave ... It makes the little-Change in me, and death will come ... I could not save the child ... but I have kept the memory ...

Ai searched through the tides of mingled emotions, through sorrow and acceptance, to one who waited, still uncertain. She asked a silent question and was answered.

"One among us wishes to share the memory you keep. One who loved him. If this thing is possible, will you do it for us?"

*To share this memory with others... is to share death
...Is it different among your people? You will not die...
to take the memory of death from me...*

"No, we are a different kind of life. Not knowing a
thing may bring death to us, but knowledge—though
painful—will not. Can you do it? Will you share the memory with the one while the rest of us withdraw?"

Yes...please...

There was a moment of dizziness, and Ai felt herself
drifting naked in the world again as Raille slowly released
all but one from the mind-link. Just before contact faded
completely she thought she caught a "voice" from the great
jewel-shape, in a tone that was somehow different from
before:

Beautife?

Then the link was broken, and when they joined again
several moments later, the Dancer's presence was not
among them.

"She has gone from us," Raille said. "To be alone with
her thoughts."

*You have given me back... my life... undone the little-
Change within me.* New color suffused the massive shape
that hung before them. *Now all must go... to another
place... Soon the Edge of the Path is gone... and the
Wild devours what is here...*

"We can return to our own world, but where will you
go?"

*Now to the Gathering-join... if my body will live... I
am free of the death of the child inside...*

"We must leave, then, back to our own world. We have
a great distance still to travel before us."

Seven Thoughts at Once rotated slowly before them
then began to move flowward along the Path.

*Come with me to the Gathering-join... so I may share
your wonder... with my people... Then I will show you
the Rushing Path... where no Visitor has yet swum...
and you will travel your distance... more swiftly than
thought...*

The massive ovoid paused as the little ship caught up
to its side.

But first, Seven Thoughts said, *I need food* . . .

"I don't believe it." Ai grinned as the *Dolly Dorcas* turned and began to follow the great jewel-shape downward along a twisting helix of green and gold. "It's hungry, too. Now I *know* this is all a dream!"

CHAPTER 13

*He who calls what has vanished back again into
being, enjoys a bliss like that of creating.*

BARTHOLD NEIBUHR

1

When the small ship slid into orbit around the green-dark
globe of Sipril and began preparations for its descent to
Tan-to-Da approximately four truedays earlier than originally expected—having traversed in sixty-four hours by
means of the Rushing Path a span of light-years that an
ordinary Darkjumper would have accomplished in just
over a month—then even Ai had to concede that Seven
Thoughts at Once was part of no dream.

"Three-quarters of that time was spent recalibrating
our instruments so the navigator twins could figure out
which way to point us when we jumped the Dark onto
the Path. If we'd had a tank aboard this little marvel, I
could have brought us the whole way in no time. God-
lord—" She turned to Geoffram with a look of delight
and dawning amazement. "This is going to be *important*!"

"It's incredible." He watched her with a wistful admiration. "They're going to need a whole new set of words
for what you've done."

"Yes, and I'm already working on them." Marysu came
to stand at their sides in the cramped control room. "In

the meantime, Emrys suggests we convene in the main salon. We've been given clearance to land."

They found the others seated around the curving table, now bare of instrumentation and back in its original place. Ai glanced at the jumble of cushions beneath the viewing ports, shook her head. "I still say it was all a dream," she muttered as she crossed the room and took her seat next to Raille. "Beautife?"

"She's still in her cabin," the older woman said.

"We had a talk last night," Ai said. "I don't mean to go stepping into your territory, but I think she's going to be all right."

Raille nodded slowly. "I agree with your prognosis," she said with a smile.

"Jack will be waiting for us, I imagine," Emrys said from across the table. "I sent a message down ahead to notify him, as we've managed to turn up somewhat ahead of schedule—" he tilted his head toward Ai, who grinned in return "—despite our small side trip."

It was night on Sipril. The *Dolly Dorcas* touched ground in a small luminous circle that was all but lost in the overlapping shadows of two gargantuan Darkjumpers.

"We've gone somewhere you've never been!" Ai crowed to the nearest ship through the viewing ports as she waited for the signal to disembark.

"Domi and the others will stay with the ship," Raille said. "Our belongings will be safe with them until they're needed."

There was a silent glide like a ribbon of amber film connecting the vast landing stage to the administrative and passenger service buildings several terraces above. Ai skipped past it to the footpath of crushed tourmaline that zigzagged up the slope, its length sparkling under the pale radiance of a score of attentive wanderlights.

"We all need the exercise," she announced when the others had caught up to her. She turned without waiting for an answer and started up the gentle incline.

The laughing, curly-haired man met the group before they had gone halfway, near a bend in the path where clear water poured endlessly from a golden ring set atop a faceted shaft of aquamarine. "I'd just arrived when I saw you land from the waiting room," he said, catching his breath in gasps as he pushed a tumble of dark curls back from his forehead. "Lords, that's a little ship—but you made good time. Did you have a good voyage?"

"Oh," Emrys said. "You must hear about our voyage!"

"Well, you're all looking splendid—I don't know what you're laughing about, but it's wonderful to see you!" Pale green eyes shone with enthusiasm in his handsome, ruddy face.

"You'd never know it from your greeting," Marysu said. "Remember me?"

"You?" He pretended perplexity for an instant, then picked her up and whirled her off the ground in his arms. "You're a—" He buried his laughing face in her slender throat and murmured a long string of hissing syllables.

"I told you he did quite well with that language," Marysu said, lightly caressing his face from temple to chin as he lowered her to the ground.

Jack exchanged warm embraces with Geoffram, Raille, and Emrys, then returned to Marysu's side to be presented to the remaining three members of the party.

"Senwy of Maribon," she said, drawing Jack forward by the hand. "Allow me to present my Diamond-Jack."

"A very great pleasure, Senwy of Maribon." He bowed low before the solemnly blinking girl. "I like the nose decoration."

"Thank you."

Marysu turned next to the tall Dancer. "Beautife of Street of Dreams."

"Beautife." He took the long hand in both of his, the carefree eyes darkening for a moment. "My friend's friend."

"March spoke to me of the cheer your bright smile brought him," Beautife said, bending to lay her dark cheek against his ruddy one. "And also of the beauty you created with your art."

Marysu watched with a small, expectant smile as she made her final introduction. "And this is Ai, late of Dun-

bar's World, an unexpected and most extraordinary addi-
tion to our company."

"Ai ..." He took her hand, eyes widening slightly as
he looked closely at her features beneath the tousled
auburn hair. "I—"

"Come along, then," Marysu said with a nod of satisfaction. "We'll be reaching the top of this mountain by
morning's light if you insist on dawdling."

Jack smiled, glancing between his lover and the thin
Pathfinder. "I feel as if I've known you for years," he
said softly to Ai, and released her hand.

"I've taken a small house for us outside the city," he
said over his shoulder as he led them up the twisting path.
"It wasn't easy to find something large enough in the
middle of the season, but I used to live here, and I still
have a little influence left. Well, actually—" He tossed
back a cheerful gin. "I mentioned the name of the Sessept
Emrys, and they suddenly came up with something."

The villa was constructed in typical Sipril fashion, as
a rambling collection of squarish boxes on different levels
interconnected by ramps and ladderways, the whole intricate structure set high above the ground on massive poles
of sturdy new-bamboo.

Jack set his palm against the cab's sensor plate and
sent the yellow saucer shape lofting back to Sipril-city.
The seven travelers followed him single file through the
dark to the lift which, upon their arrival, had descended
silently from the underside of the main quarters. Below
the house stretched a wide vista of dark green, where tiny
dim figures moved in a stooping, shuffling rhythm beneath
clusters of shepherding wanderlights.

"Harvest time," he said. "All day, all night, all year."
He sighed, pressed a hand to the base of his spine as the
lift floated upward. "Forty years ago that was me out
there. I still can't stand the taste of *mulel* ..."

When Geoffram entered the wide open-air dining court
on the morning after their arrival, he found the others
already gathered.

"Jack's gone after Cil in the skipper," Marysu said, pushing out a seat for him next to hers at a great *oke* table. "We're expecting them back any time. Hungry?" She leaned back to reveal a small, recessed keyboard hidden just under the rim of the table. "I'm playing host. Anything you want."

"Just a piece of local melon and some tea, thank you." He stroked the polished surface of the table and bent to inspect the keyboard with curiosity.

"Dull, Choddy, dull." Slender fingers danced on the keys.

Geoffram nodded to himself as a hidden slot opened in front of him moments later and a plate of sliced purple fruit rose beside a shallow ceramic bowl with a fluted finger handle. "I thought so. This is like the table we had in the Hearth Room of the Hut," he said, leaning forward to watch as the bowl filled miraculously from the bottom with steaming golden liquid. "I've never seen another one like it in all these years."

"There may not be another like it," she said. "Jack's little surprise. He's been to this house before. The owners don't know where the table was purchased. Since none of us was foresighted enough to carve her initials in it, we'll probably never know for sure if it's the original."

"Ah." Geoffram looked across the room to where Emrys sat with Raille and Ai. "If only we could bring back the past, Marysu."

"Or at least a small part of it now and then, *n'est-ce pas?*"

She tapped absently at the keys, and a tall glass of dark blue rose before her. "I've already had my breakfast, hours ago," she explained to Geoffram, and took a long sip of the cobalt-colored wine.

When Geoffram had finished his melon, he left the table and wandered over to the other side of the dining court. Beautife had engaged Senwy in a quiet game of Golden Ring at the edge of a lush white carpet, leaning forward above her crossed legs as she patiently instructed the young communicant in the proper way to roll the various dice.

Ai was curled up in a cavernous chair between Emrys

and Raille, her small hands punctuating her animated conversation as they darted ceaselessly through the air.

"What I'm thinking now is that maybe it's something
other Pathfinders will be able to do—once someone's
shown them how. Maybe the communicants can help me
with that. Morning, Geoff." She scratched her left shoulder just above the gauntlet. "I mean, suppose it's *not*
inevitable that the farsight's used up with age, like we
always thought. Suppose it just means they're getting ready
for the next step, and the blindness is a way of preparing
for the Darksight." She smiled self-conciously at the new
word. "A sort of built-in sendep tank. I had to be on a
ship in the middle of a jump before I could actually use
the talent—but maybe the potential to See in the Dark
was there right from the first attack of sensory loss—
back when March was starting to explore the Paths. Then,
on the *Imca Limbra*—with Senwy's panic as catalyst—
it all just flowed together."

She leaned back and chewed a knuckle, gazing at the
clear sky above the scalloped rim of her chair. "If more
Pathfinders learn to do this and we can access the quicker
Paths through Seven Thoughts and the others like we did
on the *Dolly Dorcas*, it could change the whole way we
travel. We can go faster than ever, with nothing more to
fear from the Wild now that we can See that it's there
and avoid it." She smiled and winked at Geoffram. "What
do you think—will they make me the first ambassador to
the Path People?"

Marysu snorted and shook her head across the room.
"The child's becoming insufferable," she grumbled in mock
disgust.

"You know, I still don't understand one thing." Geoffram leaned his shoulder against the wall and frowned at
the complacently grinning adolescent before him. "Why
in the world were *you* affected by what March was experiencing, so far away in the Dark?"

"Mm." Ai scratched her shoulder again, looked once
at Raille, and turned away with a shrug. Somewhere a
bird or a plant began a high monotonous trilling.

"Look," Geoffram said stubbornly, "If someone doesn't—"

"Remember that conversation we had over blue at my house a while ago?" Emrys asked quietly. "We were right. The bonds that were established on Belthannis among the members of our Group have proved to be strong bonds indeed."

"On Belthannis?" Geoffram looked blankly from one silent face to another in the sunlit court. Ai was staring at the floor, one bare foot wagging nervously over the edge of the chair. "That was a quarter of a century ago. Are you talking about Ai?"

"We've all been experiencing something out of the ordinary lately," Emrys said. "Dreams, nostalgia, preoccupation with the past and with each other. I think the onset of it was linked somehow to March's forays into the Dark— some kind of signal drawing us together again, pointing us along the right path. I remember once on Belthannis I had a daydream in the presence of the empath: I was traveling somewhere in my mind, through levels of jeweled darkness and colored light, while great creatures moved gracefully at my side, guiding me ... At the time I thought it no more than a dream-fancy sparked by Chassman's presence, but now I'm inclined to think otherwise. Was a true connection to the Dark established back there on the Autumnworld, a link that none of us could fully sense or utilize—and does it mean those unseen Others whom I believe orchestrated our stay on Belthannis are still reaching out to us with their influence? I don't know. But I do know that Ai here was born possessing the Pathfinder's gift, a very rare talent. Perhaps this link was waiting to manifest itself in her as it couldn't in the rest of us."

"Emrys, Ai wasn't even *alive* a quarter century ago! She's never been to Belthannis—nor have any humans since our own Group left and the Emperor declared the world a closed protectorate." Geoffram scowled in confusion at the older man, then turned to the girl. "Ai, what is he talking about? What do the two of you understand that I can't seem to fathom?"

She raised her eyes, defiance competing uncertainly with apology in her gaze. "I've never—actually—lied about anything, Geoff. I just didn't get around to bringing it up. I wanted to do things on my own, as myself. I mean, if you'd ever come out and *asked* me before . . ." Her eyes sought the haven of Raille's calm features, and Geoffram's followed them.

"Raille?" he asked. "Do you know what's going on as well? Does everyone here but me?"

"Oh, tell him," Ai said beseechingly. "God-lord, somebody please tell him. I don't care. He'll know soon enough, anyway." She leaned back in the chair and stared at a blue-tufted branch waving above the open court, her thin face scarlet.

"Raille," Geoffram said again. "For—"

"She is our child."

Geoffram's mouth fell open. He stared at Raille with an expression of comical bewilderment. "She's *what*?"

"Listen to me," Raille said gently. "Twenty-five years ago our human bodies moved where they pleased on a planet where all other living things were deeply enmeshed in and controlled by a pattern of incredible complexity. Twenty-five years ago our minds flowed together for a brief time in the Hearth Room of the Hut, united by the communicant called Chassman to merge with one another and with the world Belthannis itself. Forces we still cannot fully comprehend were at work during that experience—indeed, during our entire stay on that world—and changes were effected in all of us, deep and permanent changes, it seems. Ai is a child of the bond forged by that merging. The child of the flesh of Jefany and Cil, but *our* child nonetheless, linked to us all."

"The flesh of . . ." Geoffram felt electricity tingle in his limbs as he recalled the day sixteen years ago when news of the birth had reached them on Maribon. At that time he had been pleased for his friends' good fortune but curious as to its nature and only dimly aware of the unique process that had been employed to achieve it.

The product of a relatively sheltered upbringing in a taciturn family environment on a conservative world,

Geoffram had experienced too much strangeness in his own later life to be skeptical when the method of the child's genesis was explained to him. Still, as he stood and watched the tiny auburn-haired infant stretch and yawn on the flickering Screen, the concept had remained a foreign one, an intriguing possibility to be found in the "thought variant" tales he had devoured as a youth rather than an example of proven reality.

On his homeworld of Hinderland, as on the majority of Community Worlds at that time, procreation was still largely restricted by custom or law to those methods regarded as traditional, if not sacred. But Geoffram knew somewhere in the back of his mind that it had been possible for centuries to recreate a living organism from a single one of its cells, to bring forth after a time an infant that was genetically identical to the donor of that cell. And he had even heard that there were some places in the Community, Dunbar's World among them, where a cell from one individual and a cell from another could be *united* to produce a child of the geneshift that was not a re-creation of either parent but a true fusion of the two.

He turned and regarded the thin, defiant figure. ". . . Jefany and Cil."

"There now, he's got his arithmetic straight at last," Marysu said.

"It's true," Ai said. "Jefany for Cil, Cil for Jefany. Ai for no one."

"Is that what you think?" said a new voice from the other side of the room.

The woman who stood next to Jack in the doorway was small and fine-boned, her tired face exquisitely beautiful beneath short white-gold hair. Pale green clothed her from collarbone to ankle in an iridescent garment that shone like a butterfly's wing in the morning sunlight and stirred delicately as she moved into the court.

Ai stiffened and got to her feet, stepping forward a pace to face the newcomer.

"Afwen," the woman said. "We didn't know where—"

"Why did you want me?" The words emerged as a whisper of despair and accusation.

The woman stopped in the center of the room. "Why does anyone want a child?"

"I wasn't a child. I was a piece of you and a piece of her!"

"And that is a child: union, with love."

"But you didn't want *me*. You didn't want somebody new. You just wanted more of her, and she wanted more of you. That's why you did it, but it didn't work! I'm not you, I'm not Jefany." She looked around in anguish at the others. "I'm not any of you. It didn't work!"

"Why haven't you told us before about these feelings?" Dark eyes like her own watched her with puzzled compassion from the delicate face. "I never—"

"Because I didn't want you to be disappointed in me, and I didn't want to hurt you. I never wanted to do that to either of you!"

The woman shook her head, a flashing of white-gold in the lambent sunbeams. "Oh, child, of course you're not me—or Jefany—or any of us!" Cil came slowly across the court to stand before Ai, pale green stirring above sandaled feet. "You're what we gave you and what your own life has made of that. You've been our joy, Afwen, but what began you is not what you are. Jefany and I have no power over that, nor would we wish it otherwise."

Raille stirred in her chair at the edge of the room. "Nothing is the same in life, Ai," she said softly. "Remember that. Nothing is ever meant to be the same. The chief glory of being alive lies in its endless possibilities."

"But I thought . . ." Ai chewed her lower lip, fell silent.

"Listen, little kettlehead." Cil reached out and set her ivory hands on the thin shoulders before her. "A child is an adventure for her parents. A singularity. An uncertainty." She gave a rueful smile. "And sometimes more excitement than one had expected. But, Afwen, I have had such wonder in my life from watching you grow and change and become the person that you are—such wonder to see your own path lengthen before you, sometimes near to mine or to Jefany's, sometimes far apart, and to know that we two set your feet on that path long ago." She shook her head again. "Without you there surely would have been far less richness in my life, far less wonder, and surely—" she arched a delicate eyebrow and smiled, drawing the girl to her "—far, far fewer surprises."

Ai stood unmoving, a small frown on her face, for the space of several heartbeats; then she raised her arms and clasped the other woman through the robe of pale butterfly-green.

"Um, Raille?" she said, sniffling as she wiped her eyes awkwardly on the back of one hand. "I sort of made most of this up, didn't I—my 'emotional problem'? I thought I had a conflict about something, so I started to give myself one, right?"

"You managed to build a fine fire from bits and sparks of doubt," Raille said. "It's not uncommon, Ai. We've all done the same thing at one time or another."

"Even so." Ai pushed Cil gently to arm's length, made a wry face of apology, and drew her mother close again. "Yeesh, kettlehead is right. I wonder if they'll still want me for ambassador . . ."

On the other side of the room Geoffram turned to Marysu, who stood watching with her braceleted arms folded in front of her. "You knew who she was all along, didn't you?" he said with a frown.

"Of course. I helped name her when she was brought home to Earth shortly after her birth. And I seldom forget the people I name." She smiled in satisfaction. "It's from the ancient Siuan tongue of World Melkior. Ai *sen* Velu *sen* Afwen: *Of a Harmony of Darkness and of Light . . .*"

The following day, when Ai had returned in the skipper with a passenger from Tan-to-Da, she brought the tall red-haired woman into the study and led her directly to Geoffram.

"Geoff, I'm glad you're here! I want you to—*oh . . .*" She stopped, blinked once. "God-lord, I keep forgetting—you two already know each other."

Jefany smiled warmly and embraced the dark-haired man. "Well, Choss," she said to Geoffram, an arm about each of them and pride in her clear gray eyes. "What do you think of my daughter?"

2

Jack looked around the great *oke* table with quiet approval, cupped his hand beside his mouth, and leaned over to Marysu.

"I don't care what you say about arithmetic," he told her in a low voice. "*Now* the Group is complete again."

"After so many years one of our Group has been lost to us. One of our Group ... Words are inadequate, but in the language of my birthworld, Green Asylum, we say *dwynnand*, 'great friend.'"

Emrys stood between the massive table where the others sat and the gleaming coffin of pearl-gray that had been brought into the center of the dining court. At one end of the sealed *bain-sense* was a small carrysack, and next to that stood a strange cylindrical object made of shiny black metalmock. It was early evening, and wanderlights were beginning to gather at the room's four corners, just above the high walls, to shed their pale beams on the scene below.

"Now we've come together here to remember our greatfriend as we loved him, but also to make a decision, as he desired, about the disposition of his body, the living shell he has left behind." He paused, looked around the table at the nine grave faces. "I think an explanation is necessary before we try to make that decision. Our March was not one prone to idle words. You all know that he was spare in his speech, concise in his utterances." His gaze rested on Beautife, who sat in the center of the semicircle. "When March asked you to bring his body to me on University, he never intended for us to destroy or discard it. Could you tell us his words again as exactly as you can translate them?"

"Bring this body to Emrys on University," the tall Dancer recited softly, watching the High Scholar as she spoke with a wary, puzzled look in her azure eyes. "He was my friend and may have a use for it."

"A use for it." Emrys nodded. "Thank you, Beautife. The last time I spoke with March in the flesh was about eight years ago. He was midtrip, on his way back to the Maren from somewhere, but he altered his plans to allow a stopover at Lekkole. He stayed at my house for a week, and we talked about everything old friends could think of. He told me about the teaching he was doing out on the Maren worlds, and of the research: the work on Dance refinements he had undertaken, with his own body as hand and instrument. I remember him saying as he looked down at himself one time: 'I've put so many Dances into this flesh and bone, I could die tomorrow and no one would notice for a month!' I laughed, and he laughed, and we went on to talk of other matters. But later, when I brought him to the College and took him down to Low-level to let him see my own work, he mentioned death to me again." Emrys' face grew somber. He crossed the floor and bent, half turned away from them, to inspect the objects lying by the closed casket.

"Nine came to Belthannis twenty-five years ago, and nine left a year later, though one—the communicant Chassman—remained behind. A riddle?" He searched out Jefany's gray-eyed calm among the signs of confusion at the table and gave a trembling laugh. "It has the sound of a riddle, but to those of us who were there it was the truth." He knelt by the sense-bath and began to release the locks on the black cylinder.

"Nine came," Jefany said in a husky whisper, "but then another joined us there and left before we left by a different route."

"I thought a riddle was supposed to elicit laughter," Senwy said quietly to Ai, her dark eyes scanning the table. "Like a joke or a kiss."

Emrys reached out with both hands and carefully drew the top half of the cylinder into the air. What remained in the bottom half was beyond the view of those at the table.

"There was a wonderful dwelling place that had been

provided by University for the Evaluators' use while they presumed to judge the Autumnworld." Emrys opened the carrysack, drew forth a tangled handful of limp straps and fastenings as he spoke. "A fabulous machine with a mind at its heart to see to their needs and comfort their hurts."

"The Hut," Ai said to Senwy. "The Habitable University Terminal, a semivolitional machine intelligence with almost unlimited potential for expansion." She looked at Cil and Jefany, her face forlorn. "I remember now. I always cried at this part of the story when I was little. *'When the plan had failed,'*" she quoted softly, "*'and the ship was in the sky above them, then the mind of the Hut fled the shell of its dwelling rather than betray those who had become its friends, fled to—'*"

She stopped, her eyes wide.

"*'To University,'*" Geoffram finished from across the table. "*'There to be dispersed in the great Well and so lost forever.'*"

"Ah, well, there's an exaggeration in that part, as in all good stories." Emrys made a final adjustment at one wrist and flexed his oddly gloved hands. Leaning over the base of the black cylinder, he drew his hands with deliberate slowness up past its sides and over the top, lifting between his empty palms a flickering column of pure, unbound light that flashed beneath the darkening sky above the court with a hundred fiery colors. "For if a person could search through the great datapool, sift the contents of the Well itself for long enough—"

"But how?" Beautife leaned forward, pale eyes wide in disbelief. "For a *mind*? A mind is a thing without substance or form!"

"No, there is a form to the mind." Raille spoke for the first time, the strange lights from the glowing column glinting in her eyes. "A different form than that which outward eyes might see, but a form and a substance nonetheless."

"Yes," Senwy said, staring raptly at the cylinder, her elbows on the tabletop and her narrow chin cradled in her palms. "Beautiful . . ."

"I asked questions," Emrys said simply to Beautife, holding the column without touching it between the wieldings. "For twenty-five years I questioned the great Well about matters that only the mind of our Hut would know, information that could not otherwise have entered the datapool. And slowly, week after week, month by month, I drew forth in this analog the minute particles that my questions attracted."

"Twenty-five years..." Beautife looked at the face above the flickering column.

"I did it because I could do it," Emrys said softly. "And because the Hut was also my friend, my *dwynnand*. Beautife, I would have searched the Dark from end to end if I thought it would bring March back."

"I know," Beautife said. "I believe that you would."

"Not all of my searching was done in the Well, however." Emrys began to lower the shimmering column slowly back into the base of the cylinder. "Half of what had constituted the mind of our friend I was able to obtain in this form—the knowledge, some of the memories, perhaps even the feelings. For the other part I had to travel far from University, for it had become the property of the Community overgovernment and been put to other uses. I located it at last, forgotten in a tiny outpost on an abandoned planet. But that part was the original matrix of the mind itself, the core of hard intelligence." He moved his hands apart, flexing his fingers as the last of the light disappeared into the half cylinder.

Jefany ran slender fingers through her restless, fiery hair. "Where is the second portion, Jon?" she asked him. "Where is the matrix of the mind?"

Emrys smiled. "Very near to you, in fact. Ai?"

"Me?" She jumped, staring at him in wonder, then sat up straight as understanding came to her face. "God-lord, I'd almost forgotten!" She raised her left arm and stared down at the small oval of polished malachite set into her gauntlet. "No wonder I was having so much trouble getting it to function as a journal."

Emrys approached the table, his face weary.

"So many years I searched and gathered. But when I showed my work to March, he asked me right away exactly what I planned to do when the task was completed. I stared at him, unable to see that far, and mumbled, I suppose, something about host-machines or other Huts. 'It seems a pity to lock it up in another box,' he said. 'You know you'll never find a piece of instrumentation half as complex as the original had become.' Then he shrugged and talked about other things—or so I thought— the intricacies of the Dance and the dangers inherent in his own strivings, the chance of an eventual accident . . . After a while he looked me in the eye and touched his own chest, saying: 'If something should happen, I'll have to trust you to find a good use for this shell . . .' He said that knowing that I would come to the rest of you for counsel in the matter and that any decision would have to be the decision of all of us."

There was a long silence.

"Oh, Jon, can such a thing be done?" Cil asked finally.

Emrys looked to Raille, and the other woman nodded, one hand absently fingering a lock of gray-streaked auburn hair. "What Chassman attempted with the kin on Belthannis, I can do here with this body and this mind."

"The attempt on Belthannis failed," Marysu said.

"Chassman was working with an incomplete knowledge of his own abilities, with a nonhuman subject and a procedure that was unfamiliar to him," Raille said quietly. "I can accomplish the transfer." She looked slowly around the ring of faces, her eyes resting finally on one whose long hands trembled on the polished tabletop before her. "If that is our decision."

"Do it, if you can. Please." Tears gleamed on Beautife's dark cheek.

When the transfer was begun beneath the bright stars later that night, Ai sat next to Senwy in the darkened court and watched as the column of flickering radiance poured out slowly through Emrys' hands and vanished into the air above the still figure that lay in the open *bain-sense*.

Senwy gasped as the fiery colors faded from the room, leaving only the quiet silhouettes of Raille and Emrys kneeling beside the casket.

"I know," Ai said. "It was beautiful."

"No, no," Senwy said, leaning forward to stare at the shivering, empty air above the motionless figure. "Now it's *really* something—look there!"

Ai squinted through the darkness between the casket and the young communicant. "I can't see it," she said. "What is it like? What do you see?"

"I can't exactly describe it. Like colors, but different. Like music, but more. Oh, but it's beautiful! I'm sorry, Ai..."

"That's all right." Ai grinned in the shadows, watching the joy reflected in her friend's pale face. "I think maybe we're even now."

The next morning Beautife took the skipper into Sipril-city and remained there until early afternoon. When she came back, Ai was waiting for her at the lift, and they walked for a while at the edge of the dark valley.

"I've been making some arrangements. I'm going back to the Maren for a while," the tall Dancer said. "There are things that I need to collect out there: information, equipment. I'm going to ask Raille if I can bring one or two of the communicants along, if they're interested." She looked down at her friend's thin face. "Do you think Senwy might want to come?" She stooped to pluck a leaf of dark grass from the ground. "I won't be staying long. The bondsmen need help, not good intentions—though I might take the time to pick up another virus." She stretched out a long brown arm. "One that's resistant to nettlecakes and gruel."

"I'm glad, Beautife. I'll come visit when I can. I'm thinking of working with the communicants, too, to try to find a way to teach other Pathfinders to See in the Dark."

They walked silently for several minutes. Beautife stood looking out over the lush vegetation of the valley below, her back to Ai.

"Will you do me a favor, Ai, before you leave here? Will you make sure they don't go on calling him March?"

"Of course."

"Thank you. Because it really isn't . . ." She shrugged as Ai laid a small hand on her trembling arm. "And as for that 'Whilom' business—" She shook her head. "Well."

That night at dinner Ai suggested a new name for the silver-skinned man who sat unspeaking in a corner of the room, staring in solemn wonder at the sky above the walls.

"I think we should call him Manse," she said, and Marysu seconded the name after a moment's silence.

"Perfect. Manse: no longer a Hut, with part of March and more of Man." Sapphire eyes turned to the corner, measured the quiet figure. "Fit dwelling for a noble spirit. I couldn't have done better myself . . ."

3

Jefany sat with Ai and watched as her daughter worked with glittering microtools on the blue-green stone set near the top of her gauntlet.

"When are they going to need the expansion node?"

"Oh, not for another day or so. I just thought I'd remove it while I had the time." Ai looked up with a grin. "Things are going to get busy again soon. We have to find Ki-mo-li-Set before we leave Sipril so we can tell her what we found in the Dark. It seems only fair to let her in on this— March was a member of her team, after all. Besides, maybe she'll be willing to help cut through the bureaucracy when we make the announcement and see the information goes where it'll do the most good. Emrys is going back to the Well—has he told you that? He says he has a bit more of the Hut to collect before he can let himself rest. Only thing is—" She chirruped to the gauntlet, and tiny lights winked along its length. "He doesn't think he should bring the . . . bring Manse with him. Not till the transfer's stabilized and there've been some definite signs of reemerging sentience. So he needs some people he can trust to take care of him for a while—a few months at least, maybe a year."

"And did you by any chance have a suggestion for him?" Gray eyes watched her fondly.

"Well . . . I did tell him that I knew two people who were pretty good at making human beings out of raw material when they put their minds to it. I didn't name any names, but I think he'll figure it out." She grinned at her mother. "So, what do you think?"

"Let me discuss it with Cil and we'll see."

"Discuss what with me?" Cil appeared in the doorway to the study, a small green carrysack in one hand.

"Hey, is that for me?" Ai asked.

"Ah." Her mother brushed a wisp of white-gold hair back from her brow, regarded the young Pathfinder fondly with dark-brown eyes. "And what makes you think that?"

"Well, I did have a birthday almost two weeks ago, and so far nobody's said anything about it."

"Mm. The child has a streak of genius in her from somewhere."

Cil handed the carrysack to Jefany, who opened it cautiously and peered inside.

"I'd originally planned to give you this when I saw you on Dunbar's World," she said, "but when Gillerie told me you'd gone off to learn your trade on a Darkjumper, I was afraid we'd be stuck with it for a while."

She pulled a brown oblong from the sack, showed it to Ai. "What do you think?"

"Oh, no!" Ai snatched the little volume, cradled it in her palms, and opened it reverently. "*The Twisty Path*, by Norton Erb—a first edition—I can't believe you found it!" Her eyes sparkled. "God-lord, it's wonderful!"

"There's something else, Afwen, something you seem to have forgotten." Cil leaned over and put her own hand into the carrysack. "If I can find it . . ."

"I think we should give it to her only if she agrees to stop saying 'God-lord' every other word," Jefany observed. "I knew that summer on Babel with Marysu was a mistake."

"Ah, here," Cil said. "Now maybe you'll stop fiddling

with that piece of malachite and just take the whole thing off. It's time you had some sun on that arm." She drew forth a diminutive golden flask. "With our love," she said, and handed it to Ai.

"I had forgotten," the girl said softly, setting the book carefully aside to accept the flask with both hands. She held it up to the light and watched the play of fiery colors in the swirling liquid. "Ember," she breathed. "There's enough in here for two, isn't there?"

Geoffram entered the room noiselessly, stood watching as Raille packed the last of her things and sealed the carrysack.

"What would you think of another Mission so soon after Stone's Throw?" she asked without looking up.

"Wherever I'm needed," he said.

"With me," she said. "The two of us to Weldon."

"Weldon?" His eyes widened.

"It's time I made peace with the other half of my life. I can't ignore something just because I'm not happy about the way I've handled it in the past." She smoothed her right palm along the back of the other hand and watched the fingers passing over one another. "It'll be difficult at first. I don't know if they'll accept me . . . but I want to try. And I'd like you to come with me, if you will."

"All right. Of course." He stood by the door. "Raille. I wanted to say something."

She turned and sat down on the edge of the fluffy bed.

"Before—when everyone else seemed to know what was going on with Ai, and only I was blind—" He faltered, took a breath. "I think I know why I couldn't see her for who she was, despite the bond." He raised his eyes. "Do you?"

She nodded. "You had someone else in your mind when you looked at Ai, someone you wanted to see so much that you half convinced yourself she was really there. I know because I saw her there, too, from time to time."

"What I wanted to say . . ." His dark eyes watched her earnestly. "Was that it doesn't matter to me. For a while there I was seeing the past in front of my eyes and you

... as you were ... and it seemed almost magical, like a second chance was being offered to us if only I did it right this time. I know we've never spoken of it before, but your decision years ago back on Maribon ... well, it was yours and only yours to make and my selfishness shouldn't—"

"Geoffram—ch, Choss, don't say it." She turned her face away from him, her hands clenching the soft bed coverlet at her sides.

"What's wrong? Raille, if—"

But when she turned back to him, it was joy that shone in her eyes.

"I had a visit this morning from that younger self," she said. "She brought with her a flask of golden liquid and two small cups. First she delivered a very solemn and well-rehearsed speech to me about life's endless possibilities and the truly enormous amount of work that's left to be done by all of us—" She laughed and wiped at her eye with a shaky finger. "Then she asked me if I would share her birthday gift with her." Raille shook her head at the naked wonder in his face and opened her arms to him. "I said yes this time."

"They'll take good care of him." Ai stood watching with Emrys as her parents guided the hesitant steps of the silver man from the lift to the skipper.

"We're going to stop on Dunbar's for a while. I have some people to see. Gil—my mother's friend I've been staying with the past couple of years while I did my Pathfinder training—and my friend Shin, to loan him some more books and make sure he's been keeping his hands clean while he reads them. Oh, and someone named Miguel de la Sa who's going to fall over backward when I introduce him to Jefany and Cil." She grinned at the prospect. "Hey, I was showing my first editions to Raille this morning, and she asked if she could borrow *The Twisty Path*." She shrugged. "I hated to part with it after just getting it, but of course I couldn't pass up the opportunity to gain the Monkey Pod Boy another convert. She said she'd give it back within the year."

He smiled. "I'd like to read them again someday, too. Perhaps you'll be making your way back to University before too long."

"That's a promise." She watched as trembling silver legs took their last steps up the ramp to the low ship. "I have the feeling we're all going to be seeing a lot more of each other in the time to come."

4

She found him sitting on a wrought iron bench facing the window that faced the planet. On the great disk that hung before them Sene Continent was just coming into view, a cloud-streaked curve of brown flecked with the blue sparkle of thousands of placid lakes.

He smiled without taking his eyes from the great curve of battleglass as she seated herself next to him on the faded blue cushion.

"A bit sooner than I thought," he said with a nod by way of greeting. "But I did manage to guess the respective destinations: you going down, me coming up." His chest rose and fell in a sigh. "You'll forgive me if I keep my eyes on the world. It'll be another ten-year before I can sit here again, most likely."

"I understand."

He nodded. "I thought you would." He allowed himself a quick appraising glance from the corner of one dark eye. "Taken the drug, haven't you?"

Raille's face became warm. "How could you—"

"I don't know, I really don't." He lifted both hands in the air as if to prove they were empty. "Something changes, that's all. Especially in one of us. I can always tell."

"I decided—with the help of some people who care about me—that there are a good many things left to do in this life that I haven't gotten around to yet. Efforts already begun that will need watching for a long time to come. And some new things, barely out of the planning stage. Part of it is here. We're going down to search for some others like myself that I have reason to believe we'll find." She shook her head, her own eyes on the great disk. "I should have come sooner, I should have done this long ago. I know what it's like to be different and not understand why."

"You're here now."

"Yes—if they let us do what we want to. We're trying to be candid about our purpose here, but there's only so much you can explain without starting to frighten people." She turned on the bench, looking behind them to where a slender, dark-haired man was bent in earnest discussion over a sheaf of papers at the Customs counter. "My friend is good at fitting stories together so the sense shines through. With luck, we'll be allowed to purchase our Tourist Passes."

"Tourist Passes!" He grimaced in surprise. "You told them about the Ember, then?"

"Oh, I couldn't lie to them." She lowered her face, clasped her fingers around the small carrysack she held cradled in her lap. "It's not the sort of beginning we should have here."

"Well, good luck to you," the man mused. "Honesty can be a fearful liability in any undertaking. Though in the right hands, I've heard it's an instrument of remarkable power." He spared her another sidelong glance, quirked his lips. "You know, it's a good three hours before my ship leaves, and they won't dare send up their shuttle from Gammelstad for you till our corrupting influence has safely cleared the system. Will you tell me about your work now—or must I wait another ten-year to satisfy my curiosity? I have at least a thousand questions ready, so you don't have to worry about organizing your thoughts."

Raille smiled assent.

"I'll gladly answer your thousand questions," she said. "But first I have to ask a single favor of you."

"You need only name it!" He performed a mock bow in her direction. "My lands, my wealth, my reputation— all yours for the asking and all worth slightly less than the coat on my back."

She opened the carrysack and drew forth first a writing stylus and then a small brown oblong.

"All I ask is a few seconds of your time away from the window and the use of one of your names. I've a close friend who's recently completed her collection of first editions by a certain writer whose work she holds very dear." She turned the volume around so he could see the cover. "She told me that the other four have been signed by the author."

"I suppose we'll have to oblige her, then." He took the book from her, held it for a moment unopened. "*The Twisty Path*," he said with a smile. "My favorite."

CODA: DUNBAR'S WORLD

How can anything end in a circle?

What lies between the sand and the water, the journey and the Path, the hand and the instrument?

He moved slowly along the empty stretch of sand, the wind in his hair. The other part of the beach had been darker, filled with people. Hawkers sold globes of ink-colored wine by day, and at night there was a luminous band to mark the surf.

Here the sand was lighter, he noted, and smaller in average particle size. He knelt to pour the pink-white granules carefully from palm to palm, measured their weight precisely in some fashion, and stored the information without knowing why he did so. The ocean was a dark reflection of the sky's high steel, deserted here except for the two far-off fishing boats bobbing their way back to shore beneath the great yellow sun.

He noticed a small object in the sand and examined it with interest, knowing at once its name, function, and origin but handling it anyway: turning it over and over in his fingers and marveling in the feel of its rough surface; the scent of it, unique among the thousand scents offered by this day; the delicate colors turning, turning under his fingers. He held it to his eye and peered at the chambered, spiraling complexity within, noting the spaces left by that which had departed.

A sound tugged at his attention, and he turned slowly in a semicircle to capture it, his eyes coming to rest on the distant figures moving toward him on the beach. The two women walked slowly, their clasped hands parting from time to time to include the slender girl who danced between them and ahead of them, now listening to one as she laughed at the other and talking ceaselessly to both of them.

All the previous day he had practiced the difficult coordination of mouth and throat, tongue, teeth, and lips, polishing and refining the words until they lost the thread of sense and he had to turn to other matters for a while.

As they neared him, he got to his feet, still shaky, and extended his gauntleted arm to the laughing, dancing girl who approached with her eyes now closed and now open, breaking ahead of the others to turn and walk backward for a few seconds before rejoining them. A part of him wanted to laugh with her, and a part of him wanted to weep. Still another part felt nothing but crouched deep within the shell and waited.

She paused for a moment, grinning at him. Then she was at his side, her small hand slipping into his own, and he opened his mouth to speak.

ABOUT THE AUTHOR

Geary Gravel has been a nationally certified Inter-
preter for the Deaf since 1978. He lives and works in
Amherst, Massachusetts.

His faithful dog, Bell, continues to be a remarkable
example of the potentials of canine evolution.

Introducing...

The Science Fiction Collection

Del Rey has gathered the forces of four of its greatest authors into a thrilling, mind-boggling series that no Science Fiction fan will want to do without!!